When his mouth opened and his tongue stroked the soft inner tissue of her lower lip, a thousand summer suns burnished her insides. His tongue thrust deeper, as if it would impale her. She heard her own rapid breathing; smelled the musky heat of his body; felt her veins engorged by the sudden rush of blood; tasted the deliciously salty flavor of his wet mouth.

Never had she been so acutely alive . . .

Fawcett Columbine Books
by Parris Afton Bonds:

DEEP PURPLE
LAVENDER BLUE

Mood Indigo

PARRIS AFTON BONDS

Fawcett Columbine • New York

A Fawcett Columbine Book
Published by Ballantine Books
Copyright © 1984 by Parris Afton Bonds

Library of Congress Catalog Card Number: 84-90834
ISBN 0-449-90134-3

Manufactured in the United States of America
First Ballantine Books Edition: August 1984

10 9 8 7 6 5 4 3 2 1

FOR OLETA NORTH . . .
Thank you, friend.

Mood Indigo

Chapter 1

The old Hindu, his cadaverous body wrapped in the loose white *dhoti*, sat with his legs entwined before him, his back against the cart's high, wooden wheel. He held the chipped and cracked porcelain cup between brown, gnarled hands. Beneath the glare of England's bright August sun, his hooded eyes studied with detachment the mystical arrangement of tea leaves, the dregs that were left in Lady Jane Lennox's cup.

Captain Terence MacKenzie of Her Majesty's Royal Dragoons watched the uncommonly tall young woman arch a skeptical brow—a raven's wing, as black as her high-piled cluster of curls. Her beauty was more subtle than breathtaking and she was the personification of unbending pride.

Quite different, he thought, from the awkward little girl who at one time had run to hide her ungainly height from visitors. Now Jane carried her regal frame with a magnificent sense of the old noblesse, God damn them to hell.

Terence shook his tawny head at her, counseling patience, and her too-wide mouth formed a piquant *moue* of feigned long-suffering.

The swami at last spoke, almost reluctantly it seemed. His Tamil dialect was but strange mutterings to Lady Jane. The officer, however, was quite familiar with it. Not yet thirty-two, he had absorbed the Hindustani language during three years of distinguished military service in India for His Majesty King George III.

The boisterous jetsam of humanity that crowded Wychwood's green for St. Bartholomew's Fair made listening difficult. At the nearby puppet show Punch and Judy clobbered each other with shrill yells, and at the wagon's far side two men sparred in the boxing match, championed by shouts of encouragement from the spectators. The officer propped an immaculately shined Hessian boot on the colorful cart's tailgate and leaned closer to hear the old Hindu.

"*Puphiyawar, nwengel santhikkavendum oru adayala manitharai,*" the swami murmured in what seemed a resigned tone.

When he paused between breaths, Terence translated. "The stranger you are to meet is a marked man."

Lady Jane rapped the epaulettes of the officer's scarlet coat with her ivory fan. "Faith, Terence, that diddle the gypsies can do better."

"But not as authentically." The East had taught him well the existence of that supernatural outer realm. Yet he did not fear that realm as others did. Perhaps that was why the wagon, off from the welter of gaily decorated booths, had drawn him. He nodded at the Hindu. "Go on, old man."

Once again the swami spoke, and the lean, sun-browned officer translated. "He says, Jane, that like the stranger, you, too, shall be marked."

The young woman, the salon set's favorite, laughed, a delightful trill that for the past three years the courtiers of the Queen's Buckingham House had enjoyed—though not as much as they had suffered under her sharp tongue. "And, pray, Terence, what of you?"

He was a little above average height; still, his deep-set, long-lashed eyes were on a level with those of the young woman he had known since she was six and he sixteen. After his twenty-first year, he had served duty in England's various foreign colonies; but those five years he had had with Jane, before the thin, hulking girl matured into the magnetic young woman before him—yes, those years had wrought his dreams. He saw in her blue-violet eyes that she was irrevocably in love with him.

He returned his gaze to the swami and fired off a rapid sentence in Tamil, then translated the answer. "The old man says that I, my dear Jane, wait for you at the end of a long road."

"You're making that up!" she accused, laughing again. Her mouth lost that little-girl vulnerability to form a delightfully appealing curve at the corners of her lips. The lips were asymmetrical, with the top too narrow and the bottom much fuller and wider. But no one ever noticed, for it was her exceptionally beautiful eyes in the fair face that enchanted.

He flipped the swami a shilling and guided her back into the stream of revelers heading for the bowling green. "I'm not making it up at all. I don't have to, for it is indeed the truth. I shall yet have you."

With a flick of her wrist, Jane splayed the fan's ribs and waved it against the English countryside's muggy heat and stench of unwashed people. "Do you seriously think you will?" she challenged.

Her face was animated with a lively intelligence that, apart from her eyes' extraordinary color, had been her only redeeming quality as a homely, love-starved child; for her hair had been a dull, lifeless black without the glorious luster its cascade of ringlets now possessed.

"Do not doubt me, Jane."

The breathless excitement eased from her lips, and she looked away, her eyes as bleak as a channel fog. "My father will never consent to marriage with a—a natural son."

Terence's smile was frank—and relentless. "And the fact that I am Lady MacKenzie's bastard, will that stop you?"

She halted in the midst of the jostling villagers, unaware of the sudden awkward curtseys and doffing hats made by the few who recognized Lord Wychwood's daughter, and faced him. "No less than it shall stop you, Terence."

He drew his fingertips in a line along both sides of her jaw and kissed her, there before everyone—including lackeys and hirelings who would carry the story back to her father. He felt her hungry response, restrained only by the curious eyes. "With your love," he murmured into her mouth, "nothing shall stop me, Jane. Nothing."

Chapter 2

Lady Jane Lennox felt as if she were in the Haymarket or Drury Lane Theatre, watching—but not a part of the revelry that went on about her. It was one of those private dinners where the cabinet ministers met hastily after the meal to discuss the kingdom's problems.

This time the problem was twofold: budgeting the troops for the protection of the American colonies without further taxation, and controlling the few rabble-rousers stirring up trouble, mostly in Massachusetts and Virginia, the latter being the oldest, largest, and wealthiest of Great Britain's colonies. The empire that ranged from the dusty plains of India to the green islands of the Carribbean to the ramparts of Quebec had long since outgrown the British Isles.

This time the private dinner was at the crenellated, Tudor-style Bedford House with its forty-two indoor and outdoor servants. These did not include the page boys and blackamoors who hovered discreetly in the shadows of the marbled pilasters where the prismed candlelight of four giant crystal chandeliers did not quite reach. Chamber music drifted down from the gallery to provide entertaining sonatas for the guests.

In her honorary position as part of Queen Charlotte's retinue, Lady Jane Lennox stood in attendance beside the royal couple, towering over both of them. George III, a young man with straight, thick lips and vapid blue eyes, wore his jeweled crown of state with a notable lack of regal bearing, unlike the French and Spanish Bourbon kings.

Few apart from Jane and the queen, the king's valet, and the royal doctors ever suspected from George III's robust appearance that the stuffy monarch was periodically bled, cupped, and fed asses' milk. For a recurring mental aberration, so the word went. Whatever the problem, it did not hinder his determination to keep the reins of government from his ministers. More than once Jane had overheard that George III was buying up boroughs to stack the House of Commons in his favor.

At his side Queen Charlotte was gowned in white satin edged with royal purple ermine. The king and his thin German queen, whose dark-skinned features gave her a pleasant appearance, watched with staid countenances the procession of peacocks.

Gallants, known as macaronis for their grand tours of Italy, pranced by in red heels, gold brocade coats, lavishly curled perukes, hose-padded calves, and flagrant codpieces to enhance that certain private part of their anatomies.

The women were no less flamboyant. Mouse-skin strips covered shaven eyebrows and often slipped with the heat; enormous paniered skirts distorted the body's natural shape;

multitiered wigs of artificial and natural hair, pomade, and powder towered a yard high. One dame's coif actually resembled a frigate under full sail.

Jane was accustomed to these extravagant displays at soirées, fêtes, banquets, and grand balls. She was also utterly bored. Here among the fops, she longed for Terence—for the sight of his superb soldier's physique, for his directness that blunted the mincing conversation of the dandies at court, for his shrewd mind that challenged hers. He had held a fascination for her beginning with that first rose he had plucked from her mother's garden and handed her.

At first, as the lonely, sole child of Wychwood Estates, she desperately wished and pretended he was her brother; then gradually during those many splendid hours he had spent with her and her mother—or the best times, with only herself—she became glad he was not.

She knew Terence, as a bastard, would not be invited to such a distinguished gathering of MP's, barristers, baronets, and earls; nor would he be invited to the Lennox country estate at Wychwood. Her father would never countenance that. As a Member of Parliament, he was most assuredly aware that Terence's regiment had recently been called back from India for a more pressing assignment. Yet she doubted whether her father knew that the week before she had spent St. Bartholomew's Day with Terence. Her father was too busy, had always been too busy with politics and position to think of his daughter.

Perhaps if her mother had not taken her life that year Jane was seven . . . But then she would not have had Terence all to herself to enjoy those next five years. She had waited for him all this time. There would be no other for her.

Her gaze sought out her father's exceptionally tall figure. He was deep in conversation with the fiftyish, Roman-nosed Lord Sandwich. As the scandalous First Lord of the

Admiralty, Lord Sandwich was a member of the Hell's Fire Club, a secret society whose members, so gossiped the wags, held orgies in the abandoned Medmenham Abbey with young women dressed as nuns. With the two men was the new Secretary for the Colonies, the supercilious Lord George Germain, said by London's Fleet Street to be a homosexual.

The exchange between her father and his coterie of peers was interrupted by the arrival of the London agent for the Massachusetts Assembly, a balding, bespectacled man whose droll wit was quite the delight of London society, Benjamin Franklin. Jane saw her opportunity to speak with her father and, begging her leave of the royal couple, made her way through the press of noblemen and titled ladies.

Here and there came fragments of conversation—the king's review of the fleet off Portsmouth . . . the recent duel at Hyde Park . . . American violence and smuggling. And a peripheral area of her mind responded, as it often did, with indignation. The Boston Massacre, as the American colonists termed that tragic fracas, had been provoked by themselves.

Lord Wychwood eyed his daughter's approach with his usual austere countenance. His only child had inherited his extraordinary height, quick mind, and, some thought, his haughty pride.

"I would talk with you, Father," she said when he removed himself from the growing number of people crowding about the provincial agent for the Massachusetts colony.

He ignored the pleading in the eyes that were neither violet nor blue. "We will discuss it tomorrow, Jane."

She held the sandalwood fan tightly between her palms. "You know, don't you? You know about Terence."

"Do you seriously think you two could romp through Wychwood Green and no report filter back to me?" he muttered through clenched teeth.

"We did not—romp. We were scarcely together three hours."

"And that shall be the last three hours Lady Mac-Kenzie's bastard shall spend with you."

"Why—why do you hate him so? You took Manor House from his mother—"

"And I shall keep you from him."

"Do you think to stop me?" she asked in a voice that betrayed none of the old fear she felt before her father's cold wrath. A few of the guests near Jane and her father paused in the midst of trivial conversation, drawn by the almost tangible friction that issued between the two. But she continued. "I am past the age of consent. I no longer need your consent nor approval to marry Terence."

For the first time her father smiled, displaying the Briton's poor teeth, a trait his daughter had not inherited. Instead her French Huguenot mother had bequeathed to her shell-like, albeit slightly uneven teeth. "This week I was closeted at Whitehall for more than an hour with Barrington. The Secretary of War assured me that your MacKenzie would find duty in the Canadian provinces, enough to occupy an ambitious man of his likes."

"Terence has left?" she breathed.

He snapped open the opal-inlaid lid of his snuff box. "Sailed three days ago."

Her shoulders straightened. "You can't stop me from joining him, Father."

Her father lifted a heavy brow. "With what funds?"

Her hand went to the topaz necklace inset with rose diamonds that graced the long column of her throat, and he chuckled as he sniffed a pinch of snuff up one nostril. "I took the precaution of warning every ship's captain between here and Bristol against giving you passage. Do you think any would dare flaunt Lord North's command?"

"You went to the Prime Minister?"

"I'll go to King George himself if I have to." He pocketed the snuff box. "'Tis time you made an advantageous marriage, Jane."

"With whom?" she sneered, gesturing with her fan toward Lord Sandwich. "The Mad Monk of Medmenham?"

If someone could be both pampered and neglected, Lord Wychwood reflected, his daughter most definitely was. At times, when he thought about it, he regretted his ineptitude as a father. "You could do worse than Lord Sandwich," he tempered. "Jane, for all that you are of the female sex, you have inherited my stubbornness. An unfortunate and abominable trait in a woman. Do not try my hand this time." With that pronouncement, he left her to join a group of tittering ladies with flashing fans.

Pleading an early-morning stag hunt at Windsor Park, the stolid George III and his wife chose to retire early, as usual, before dinner was served, which would not be until near midnight. During those intervening hours, Jane's mind whirled, sorting out all possible recourse to her dilemma. And none presented itself. Should she manage to sell her jewelry, there were few vessels, other than army transports, bound for the American colonies and Canada, and none whose captains would dare defy an edict from the Prime Minister.

The dinner table, brightened by hundreds of candles burning in the crystal-prismed candelabra overhead, groaned with roast duck and veal pies and gooseberry sauce; with plum puddings, fruit tarts, and syllabubs; with brandy, Madeira, and Bordeaux. Liveried servants faded tactfully into the background. Jane was relieved to find herself seated at the far end of the table from her father. Mr. Franklin, peering through his spectacles, held sway over the guests at that end of the table, where French, the court language, could be heard.

Tales of the colonial agent ran rampant. It was whispered that he played chess with a high-born French lady— she in her bathtub; it was rumored that he salubriously left his windows open at night and rose for half an hour each morning to sit stark naked in the boarding house's chilly room, which he rented from the Widow Stevenson.

Jane was seated to the left of an MP, a country squire who proved to possess a dependable lack of imagination and a passion for meticulous gardening. On her left sat a massively built man whose sober clothing was only spared total drabness by his deep red hair, tied in a queue and unpowdered.

"One of those American provincials," whispered the squire maliciously.

A little later when the squire paused in his monologue on the value of the boxwood hedge in maze gardens, she escaped his droning by turning her attention to the colonist and the Duchess of Marborough across from him. The American's profile was devilishly handsome in an unpolished sort of way; as if God had reached the seventh day and left his chiseling unfinished. The sharply squared jaw jutted, the prominent cheekbone angled almost defiantly, and the nose, from Jane's view, appeared slightly crooked.

The big man so far had remained silent before the voluble speech of the duchess. Obviously of no social brilliance, he watched and listened and sometimes smiled.

"And you, sir," Jane asked perfunctorily when the duchess paused. "How do you find England?" She only wished the evening would end.

For the first time the big man looked her full in the face. The left hollow of his cheek was marred by a bad burn. She smothered her gasp with a quick sip of the Bordeaux, but above the crystal rim of her glass she caught the amused glimmer in his black-flecked eyes and knew he had noted her start.

He had a big man's lack of assurance, and his words came clumsily. "Pardon me, mistress—what did milady say?"

She set down the long-stemmed glass and said gently, "I asked how you find your mother country."

"I find her quite"—he paused and she heard the beginnings of amusement in his voice, a curious mixture of Irish brogue and colonial dialect that was difficult to understand—"quite revealing."

She saw the way his gaze offhandedly assessed her blue-powdered hair, her beauty patch placed strategically on her cheekbone, her naked shoulders above the peach satin gown. All empathy with the man dissolved. "Are you enjoying your tour of her, sir?" she snapped.

He grinned, his irregular teeth white against his weather-tanned skin, and for a moment she forgot the disfiguring burn. "That would be difficult to say, milady, until I have seen everything of her."

The insolence of the man! She flashed an artificial smile. "Do I sense a tone of disrespect to the mother country?"

The rise of his thick, dark-auburn brows acknowledged her thrust. "That I did not say, Mistress—?"

"Lady," she said frostily. "Lady Jane Lennox. And you are Lord—?"

"Mister," he drawled with an impertinent and humorous tone. The bumpkin was quite obviously enjoying himself. "Mr. Ethan Gordon."

"And I suppose you are here with Mr. Franklin to protest the closing of the Boston port? No, don't tell me," she interrupted with a disparaging smile. "You, no doubt, are one of those colonial oafs who threw East India's tea chests into the Boston Harbor last December."

He held his large palms up in a gesture of mock defense. "Please, Lady Jane. I don't believe in violence—nor disloyalty to the mother country. I am a member of the Society of Friends."

A Quaker as a dinner partner! Her father's doing,

doubtless. No wonder she had sensed contempt in the curl of the provincial's cleanly defined lips. "You don't look like a Quaker," she murmured, and at his wry grimace that somehow passed for a smile, she hastily added, "The red hair—and all."

"And pray tell, what do I look like, Lady Jane?"

She chewed on a bite of the roast duck, while her face took on a pensive air. With the sun-and-wind pleats about his mouth and the squint lines fanning eyes that were somewhere between brown and black, she judged the big man to be in his late twenties or maybe Terence's age, though Terence eclipsed him in every other way. "Oh, perhaps a pirate."

"Thy jest misses the mark."

Mark! She felt as if she had suddenly ridden to the brink of a precipice that yawned before her. *The stranger shall be marked.* The fine hairs at the back of her neck prickled.

Her gaze swerved to the shriveled patch of burned skin. No, she refused to believe in the sham and chicanery of gypsies' cards and swamis' tea leaves. But the colonist *was* a marked man. Faith, but she was not a marked woman. So much for the old Hindu's hoax.

"Since you are neither a pirate nor a rebel Yankee, what does bring you to London, Mr. Gordon—other than the grand tour?"

"I am but a simple planter come to purchase supplies and indentured servants, milady."

This time she almost choked on the veal pie. "Indentured servants?"

"Of course," he said casually. "Quakers don't hold to slavery, Lady Jane."

Jane barely managed to control her excitement. "And where does one go in the city of London to purchase indentures, Mr. Gordon?"

*   *   *

A heavy swinging sign suspended from an ornamental bracket portrayed a silvered half circle, which announced the address of the Half Moon Coffee House near Ratliff Crossing. Inside, Jane sat at a tiny table, dawdling over a cup of tea. That morning, with her maid in tow, she had made the perfunctory calls. Afterward, she visited Charing Cross and the Strand to browse among the shops, which was becoming a national pastime. People journeyed from as far as France and Germany to visit London, the City of Shopkeepers.

After a drapier patiently unfolded a hundred bolts of material, regaled her with a glass of wine, and bowed and scraped as he handed her into her coach, she deemed it safe enough to set out on her primary mission.

In the Half Moon Coffee House she and her personal maid, who sat stiffly opposite her, were the only women customers. The men exchanged stocks and shares and discussed politics, philosophy, the "American" problem, and life's vicissitudes in general.

Female customers were not unknown at the Half Moon, though few came dressed as elegantly as she. True, she wore her singularly black hair not powdered but covered by a large, concealing Lunardi hat that dipped charmingly over her classical brow. And true, her satins were decorously hidden by a summer pelisse of the finest broadcloth. Yet the quality of the lady was clearly evident. Then again, it was impossible not to notice her, if only because of her unusual height.

Ignoring the rowdy conversations of the gentlemen at the rear of the coffeehouse, she slowly sipped the tea in her Wedgwood cup. Through the leaded casement window she watched the people enter and leave the establishment diagonally opposite the coffeehouse, the guildhall.

"Ma'am, are 'oo certain that 'oor father would be approving 'oo being 'ere."

Jane drew her gaze away from the guildhall to fasten on

Meg O'Reilly. The Irishwoman shifted uncomfortably, unaccustomed to sitting at the same board as her mistress. The reddish brown hair that peeked out from her high starched mob cap reminded Jane of the Quaker and her purpose for being at Ratliff Crossing. "Of course, I'm certain, Meg." She set down the cup with a resolute motion. "Now wait for me, and I shall return shortly."

Oblivious to her maid's protests, she gathered up her parasol, her reticule, and her long gloves with the fashionable open fingers. She left the coffeehouse to wend her way through the maze of post chaises and chariots to the far side of the narrow, littered street. Here at the guildhall, people desperate for employment after the Panic of '72 were lined up to indenture themselves before the Board of Trade's magistrate.

Others who came to indenture themselves were husbands who had forsaken their wives, wives who wished to abandon their husbands, children who were running away from parents, and, quite often, criminals escaping from prosecution. In addition, there were the maids who despaired of ever having husbands in England and sought to indenture themselves to employers in the New World where members of the female sex were at a premium.

Indenturing herself was Jane's one hope. The mighty political arm of her father reached far. Even if she could sell her jewelry and persuade some unsuspecting captain to give her passage to the American continent, her father could still track her down before she found Terence.

But, she hoped, her father would never think to look for her disguised as an indentured servant.

Still, she couldn't bring herself to enter the open doors of the guildhall. Studying the people over her cup of tea, she had seen the misery, the poverty, the hunger etched on each of their faces. But was she that desperate—to sign away anywhere from two to seven years of her life, merely in exchange for passage to the American continent—and to Terence?

And then, high above the stream of people coming and going like ants, she saw the deep red hair of the Quaker. "Mr. Gordon," she called out impulsively. He stopped and looked at her with a puzzled frown, and she hastened to identify herself, feeling suddenly quite foolish. "Lady Jane Lennox—your dinner partner at Buckingham House last night."

He crossed to her, and she noted then that he had not the honed, lean length of Terence but rather was more solidly built and measured a full six inches taller than she. With him, certainly, she need never resort to that old childish ploy of hunching her shoulders to minimize her height. She drew herself up tall and said calmly, "I am hoping that you can perhaps help me."

"Ahh, yes . . . mother country." His big hand engulfed hers as he made a deep, mocking bow, and she could feel the calluses on his blunt farmer's hands. "I am at your service, Lady Jane."

She ignored his barb. "No." She put out a restraining gloved hand. "That's just it, Mr. Gordon. I wish to be at your service."

His black eyes quizzed hers politely, but she could see him curb the impatience at the corners of his mouth. "How so, Lady Jane?"

She nodded toward the doors of the guildhall. "I wish to indenture myself to you."

Amidst the cacophony of the city, an abrupt strained silence held between the two people. Jane knew full well what she meant to do. She was securing passage to the American continent in order to join Terence. And after her three years of international intrigue at St. James's Court she felt she was a good enough judge of character.

This Yankee planter seemed of a kindly nature, if his

membership in the Quaker sect was any indication. But for the most part, she was counting on her sophistry and charm to handle the plodding colonial. Surely, after but a few months of dutiful servitude, she could convince him to release her from her bondage.

And as for the provincial's reaction, she could see flickering behind the dark eyes first surprise and then doubt, which was followed once more by mild impatience. His marred countenance was an easy one to read. "I don't have time to waste with bored, spoiled noblewomen who indulge in pranks, Lady Jane. Tell thy companions, whomever they are, that thee has lost thy wager."

"Spoiled!" she sputtered. The strain of the past few days broke her cool reserve. She had lowered herself to petition this simpleton for help, and he had castigated her! She glared up at him, hands on hips. "And a yokel such as you deem yourself capable of judging character? You insensitive swine, you haven't the slightest knowledge of me or what forces me to come—"

The fine weather lines about his black-flecked eyes gathered to narrow the deep, thick-lashed lids, and the brows lowered over a nose that most certainly had been broken. "Thee needs to be humbled, mistress, and I would take great delight in the task, had I the time."

He pivoted from her. "Follow me, Betsy—Jonah," he said to the slight, shabbily dressed woman and rail-thin boy whom Jane had failed to notice standing next to him. Only then did Jane spy the indenture papers the Quaker held rolled in his hamhock hands. He strolled off with the middle-aged woman and child dutifully trailing him.

Jane, her spirits drooping, watched the crowd swallow up the three. She had let her pride get the best of her. She turned back to the guildhall's open doorway. Before a board the people who could read pressed to study the public notices posted.

"A Pennsylvanian colonist desires a tutor," someone near the front called out.

Jane's eyes swept over the list:

> Men: tanners, coopers, shipwrights, sawyers, ropemakers, carpenters, wigmakers, millers, ironworkers, bricklayers, ship chandlers, binders, bookkeepers, cardswainers.
>
> Women: seamstresses, cooks, domestics.

The paucity of occupations on the women's list explained why so many men were gathered at the guildhall. Apparently few in the colonies wanted maids. They wanted craftsmen to build the New World.

"You be needing help," a haggle-toothed woman said to Jane.

"No—no, I don't," she murmured, backing away from the men and women who suddenly encircled her with hope-filled faces. She hurried away to the comparative safety of the coffee shop.

Yet the dawn of the next day found her slipping through London's fog-shrouded streets. No one would have recognized Lady Jane Lennox as the frowzy wench who took her place in the line that formed before the guildhall's as yet unopened doors.

Her heart pounded erratically against her rib cage. What ever was she about? She could still change her mind. Yet when the double doors were thrown open and business began, she willed her feet to cross to the caged counter along with the other men, women, and even children—most of them looking as if they had recently come from the countryside in the hope of finding employment in the already overcrowded metropolis. The burgeoning malt shops and gin joints that flourished in the slums and now jostled for elbow room in the middle-class districts testified to the hopelessness of gaining employment in London.

When she neared her turn at the cage, the freckle-faced boy ahead of her hunched himself down, much as she used to do as a young girl, and piped, "Ye got chimney sweep work here in the city?"

"Nothing," the old clerk muttered, not even bothering to look up from the paper he wrote on. "Only in the colonies. Ship sailing next week. Mark an X on the line, boy. Then take the paper over to the magistrate in the next room and swear you have not been coerced into signing."

Parliament had passed a law requiring the signature before a magistrate the year after the Earl of Anglesey's son had mistakenly been kidnaped for indentured service in the Barbados. But men were still gang-pressed into service; women abducted, never to see their families again; children and infants often indentured to serve until their twenty-first year.

Jane took the boy's place, and the clerk, busy again writing, asked without looking up, "Well—what qualifications?"

She hesitated. With her education, she could tutor. But that was a man's job. And her father's wealth had made it unnecessary to learn a vocation like cooking or sewing. Maids had done everything for her. She naturally knew needlepoint, but how many positions were open for that fine craft? "I am afraid I have none," she finally got out.

The clerk's head snapped up, and she knew her refined voice had given her away. Now what? The man's wrinkled lids narrowed. "It's employment in the colonies you be wanting?" he asked dubiously.

Canada would be better, but beggars could not be choosers. Virginia was the nearest she could manage. "Aye."

After a moment his head bobbed, as if he had been suddenly enlightened. One thin eyelid closed in a sly wink. "Ran afoul of the law, did you? All right. Just sign your name. You know 'ow to do that, don't you?"

She nodded, unable to speak.

"Let's see . . ." His ink-stained finger jabbed at a name on another list. "Your ship—the *Cornwall*—is bound for Virginia." He passed her the paper. "Your indentured papers, they are. They will be auctioned off in the colonies. Take them along now to the magistrate."

Jane stared blindly at the parchment for several moments before the words came into focus.

> *THIS INDENTURE made the twelfth day of August in the Year of our Lord one thousand, seven hundred and seventy-four between   on the one part and   of the other part do hereby promise to serve in such employment as is the custom of the country for a period of years, of which the said   shall pay the passage and allow meat, drink, apparel, and lodging during the said term; and at the end of the said term to pay the usual allowance according to the custom of the country. IN WITNESS whereof the parties abovementioned to these Indentures have interchangeably put their Hands and Seals. Signed, Sealed, and Delivered in the Presence of:*

Below was the one sentence: *I hereby acknowledge that I have not been coerced into service.* Jane took up the quill, dipped it in the inkwell and beneath the sentence wrote the name Meg O'Reilly.

Chapter 3

Ethan lit the pewter lamp on the escritoire and set to writing. Penmanship came laboriously to the backwoodsman, but his quill scratched hastily over the parchment, for his ship was due to sail with the tide.

> *My dear Franklin,*
> *I learned today that our illustrious King George, as Prince of Hesse-Kassel and Hanau, has called for the troops of that German ministate to relieve those English soldiers stationed in the Mediterranean—so that the royal troops can reinforce those already stationed in the Massachusetts Bay Colony. Also discovered that a certain member of the*

cabinet has put forth the idea of appealing to
Catherine of Russia for troops to conquer those
"rebellious Boston provincials." This from my
voluble dinner partner, the Duchess.

He paused, the quill twirling absently between fingers the size of piano keys. His other dinner partner . . . aloof, distant, witty, sparkling. In a way she reminded him of Susan. But Susan warmed and soothed like wine and did not go to the head like champagne. The Lady Jane—brilliant and brittle.

Chapter 4

The lean, bronzed body slipped lower past the woman's flesh-padded rib cage. The Canadian cabinet member's wife gasped, "*Mon Dieu!*" as the tawny head buried itself between her ample thighs. The British officer was doing something her husband had never attempted to. "*Mon Dieu!*" the Frenchwoman cried out again, and clutched the sun-streaked head to her.

Afterward, she lay spent on the rumpled sheets, her soft, voluptuous body exposed. The officer, supporting himself on one elbow, plucked with teasing fingers at the thick tufts of hair beneath her outstretched arm. Yet she sensed with some disquiet that he was no more aware of her now than he had been during the hours he had made love to her. She knew the officer no better now than she had three weeks earlier. Assigned to the governor's retinue, he had been in her husband's office with Governor Carleton one afternoon when she called upon her husband.

She could not honestly say the officer seduced her. He had offered no flowery blandishments, as did the other British soldiers garrisoned in the Province of Quebec. At another chance meeting in the Château Frontenac he had simply told her he wanted her.

She had been shocked, angered, shamed—and intrigued by those pale-blue eyes whose depths were openly candid yet as distant and unreachable as the night's stars. She watched as he uncoiled his long body and rose to pull on his knee breeches. "Terence?" she called softly.

But either he did not hear her or he ignored her. Bare-chested, his skin baked by the hot sun of India, he crossed to the French doors and threw them open to the pale September sunlight. Out on the balcony he braced his hands on the black wrought-iron grillwork and looked out upon the walled citadel. As the English General Wolf had breached that citadel, claiming the French province as England's own, so would Terence breach London society to claim again the Manor House as his own—but not from a backwoods province like Quebec.

Once more Robert Lennox of Wychwood had bested him. But Terence knew his own assets. His patience—and shrewdness—would bring about that for which he had been striving since he was sixteen. He was in no hurry.

His transfer to Quebec that Lennox had effected—he might make it work for him, under the right circumstances. He considered the chaos erupting in the American colonies. Were he there, the opportunity could present itself for the object he sought—the total devastation of the House of Lennox.

The Frenchwoman murmured his name again, and a patient, unruffled smile creased lines at either side of his mouth. He was already weary of her avaricious hands, yet she, too, would serve his purpose.

Chapter 5

An early-winter gale chased the brig on its voyage across the Atlantic, so the hatches were battened down most of the journey. Mercifully, Jane was too ill to recall fully the five-week nightmare: the narrow slats that slept two or three people; the paltry food, if food it could be called; the lack of ventilation; and always, the vomiting. Every indentured servant had been ill with the bloody flux and ague, and some—like the five-year-old in the cramped bunk across from hers—had died.

For Jane, who had been served tea and crumpets in bed every morning of her life, who had Meg to light the fire each morning before she arose, the cold and aching in her bones was a new and almost unbearable hardship. Yet the captain had been humane. He provided the passengers with lemon juice against the scurvy and periodically ordered the ship scoured with vinegar.

As the brig put into Chesapeake Bay, the indentured servants were brought on deck to wash up and restore their clothing. The captain, who was to be paid for transporting the servants according to the price each was auctioned for, desired the haggled lot to look their best. A clean list was made of the names and accomplishments of the surviving passengers. Jane noticed that sometimes a little fraud was practiced—adorning convicts with wigs to increase their respectability and crediting fictitious abilities to some of the men.

As for her own appearance, it was much altered from that of the tall, lovely Lady Jane Lennox. She had brutally shorn her ebony, hip-length hair with a butcher's knife from the Lennox kitchen. The cropped hair now capped her head in oil-matted locks that had been hastily and spottily hennaed by her inexpert hand.

Her brown cotton dress, buttoned to the neck, had sweat rings beneath her armpits. Five weeks at sea had left her creamy complexion a pasty yellow, and her seasickness had sunken her cheeks. Her father would find it difficult to trace his daughter if he described her as she had once been. Despite the unappealing woman she now appeared, there was still a certain sensualness in the set of the mobile lips, a husky quality in the assumed brogue of the voice. And the shapeless dress could not conceal the high, rounded breasts that taunted the thin cotton. And, of course, there was her unconscious queenly carriage that betrayed her station in life.

When she stepped through the hatch, the early-morning sunlight blinded her. Dazed, she held her forearm across her eyes. Around her the other servants, like flowers' petals unfurling, slowly stretched, lifting their hands to the sun, celebrating the miracle of life. Yet overhead the wind droned in the rigging like a mournful bagpipe, and she repressed a shiver at the uncertain fate that awaited her.

It was one of the few times the men and women had been allowed to mingle. But Jane, as before, turned a frosty, shrewish glare at any swain who had the courage to seek her out. So did Polly, a stout country maid with butternut curls and street-wise Dresden-blue eyes. The buxom young woman had indentured herself in hopes of finding a land-owning husband. Over the five weeks she had recounted to Jane all that she had learned of the New World before making the decision to indenture herself.

Sailors in red knitted caps brought out buckets of water, and everyone fell to washing their faces and hands for the first time in weeks. Jane, however, studied the verdant coastline of Virginia. Somewhere in that vast continent was Terence. She had sailed almost three thousand miles to find him. She was that much nearer her goal.

She turned back to the large staved buckets and knelt by the least crowded one to cleanse herself of the accumulated sweat and filth and stench. Here she could not expect French perfumed soap to wash the grit from her face, neck, hands, and arms. Afterward she rose and straightened her soiled and rumpled dress and long linen apron.

These, along with two other gowns, a black duffel mantle and a frayed gray woolen shawl, she had pilfered from Meg's room the evening she had stolen out of the Lennox London town house. Robert Lennox could easily afford to replace the maid's meager clothing and metal trunk. Unfortunately the hems of Meg's dresses were far too short for Jane's height, and her cotton-stockinged ankles were shockingly displayed.

"Don't be looking too swell, dearie," a woman's peppery voice said behind her, "if ye get my meaning."

Jane turned to find the short, scrappy woman who slept

in a hammock not far from her own. It was this woman who had lost the five-year-old. Lizzie, whose age was difficult for Jane to discern, did not shed a tear the night the little girl stopped breathing.

"One less to suffer through this journey 'e 'ath set us on," Lizzie had muttered briskly and closed her daughter's lids.

"Why shouldn't I try to make myself presentable?" Jane asked the middle-aged woman. It only made sense to her that the fresher she looked the better chance she would have of her indenture papers being bought by someone who kept a clean, reputable house.

Lizzie ran toil-worn fingers through her dingy, wind-blown brown hair and nodded toward the shore. "Those that write back say that the brigs sometimes put in first to one of the coastal towns, where soul drivers come aboard."

"Soul drivers?"

"They buy off the papers of a dozen or so of the servants. 'Erd the servants like sheep across the mountains to the western frontier, they do, where they peddle them as goods to Indian and 'eathen alike."

"Why are you telling me this?"

Lizzie shrugged her narrow shoulders, and Jane wondered if the woman had a husband somewhere to embrace those brittle yet strong shoulders. "Mayhap cause you gave me wee one yer share of water the night wot she took sick."

Jane could not forget that night. It was the first time she had ever seen someone die. "It was little enough to do," she managed to say, feeling verbally inadequate for once.

The woman's nut-brown eyes squinched quizzically. "You be educated, hain't you now."

Jane bit back a smile. She had read Plato in the original when she was thirteen, and the following year had translated the *Mirror of the Sinful Soul*, the famous work by Margaret of France.

Until her arrival at St. James, her isolation at Wychwood had left her little escape from the tedium of needlework but books. Unless she counted the few times her father returned from London with his political cronies. From them she had absorbed a profound knowledge of politics. She now understood statesmanship and rigid protocol of court better than most men. But, like other intelligent women, she was restricted because politics was believed to be too difficult for the fair sex.

"I can cipher to the rule of three or more and write a legible hand," she told Liz, who accepted the statement at face value.

Polly joined Jane and Liz at the railing to wait, along with the other three hundred-odd passengers, for the brig to reach shore. At the port city of Hampton Roads, which looked little more than a scattering of one-story wooden and brick homes, no soul sellers came aboard, and the three women breathed a little easier.

"I 'ope I get meself a 'andsome cove," Polly said.

"'Tis a God-fearing master I 'ope to 'ave," Lizzie muttered.

Jane thought of the Quaker, Ethan Gordon. God-fearing, probably. But handsome, no. Not unless one considered the rusticity and savagery about him appealing, She thought that savagery was quite in keeping with the wild, forbidding forests of the New World. The vine-roped and moss-draped trees encroached on the small, insignificant port of Hampton Roads as if they would strangle that representative of civilization.

The indentured servants were not allowed to disembark while the *Cornwall* discharged its cargo of salt and took on lumber hewed from the abundant forests and hogsheads of the precious weed tobacco.

During all this, Jane stood at the railing, the salt wind playing with the frazzled ends of her chopped hair as she impatiently watched and waited. Her fingers gripped the sun-heated bulwark's edge, so strong was the need to set foot on land again. After the period of virtual imprisonment below deck, the fresh scent of the loblolly pines and cypresses that lined the shore, almost obscuring the view of the wharves, tantalized her more than any feast cooked by His Majesty's royal chef. She was tired of the briny taste of food and water and the salty smell of the sea that pervaded her damp bunk, her moldy clothing, even her hair.

Overhead the enervating Southern sun rose higher, until at last the brig weighed anchor. Up the James River the *Cornwall* sailed to an inlet that stretched blue fingers into the lush walls of green foliage, Virginia's soil-rich Tidewater area. Here, at high noon, the brig, with lines slung ashore from her bows and stern, was eased gently alongside the crowded quay. With drums rolling and bosun's pipes shrilling, the indentured servants descended the gangplank amidst the turnout of curious children, barefoot black slaves, and carriages of well-to-do planters.

Fear, uncertainty, belated regret, and excitement were painted across the pale faces of the indentured servants as they were loaded into the rear ends of creaking wagons to be carted over a gently undulating forest floor to a destination seven miles distant.

For the first time since signing her indenture papers Jane's hopes soared. The wagons occasionally passed immense cleared fields dominated by great mansions with their collections of stables, dairies, shops, kitchens, and slave quarters spread like small self-contained towns at the foot of expansive fields of tobacco. These great homes, glistening with whitewashed brick and adorned with tall Doric pillars, reminded Jane of her family's country estate at Wychwood— if she could ignore the slaves who worked naked in the fields, their black skin glistening with sweat and their genitals swaying with their bodies' motions.

A strange world, she thought angrily, where a lady's delicate sensibilities were offended by romantic novels like *Pamela* but not at the sight of a naked man. Polly sat, unaffected by the spectacle before her. "Hits the masters of places like those yew be wanting to buy yewr papers, love," she said, gesturing with her mob-capped head toward one red-brick Georgian mansion that was sheltered by rows of enormous tulip poplars.

"And what of the mistresses?" Jane muttered, and was instantly sorry at the shadow that crossed Polly's rounded blue eyes. She laid a hand on the girl's rounded arm. "Yew'll find yewr young man 'ere, yew will," she said, mimicking the Cockney accent the best she could.

But would she find the man she sought?

Straggling one-room log cabins with apple orchards and fields set round with rails shimmered in the violent heat of the hot fall day. The isolated farmsteads—on the outskirts of Williamsburg, the capital of the Virginia colony—greeted the wagonloads of indentured servants. Jane tried to tell herself that life at a colonial household would not be very different from her old life—if she could force herself to play the role of the servant instead of the mistress.

"And wot about yew?" Polly asked Lizzie. "Ye don't want a Tidewater gent fer a husband?"

Lizzie snorted. "The likes of me? Not likely. It's Meg O'Reilly 'ere wot has the chance of makin' such a contact—'er with 'er fine ways."

Jane started. Was her deception so poor? "Wot makes you say that now?"

"Why, hain't none of the Billingsgate fish market about yew, love. Ye were a grand lady's maid, weren't yew now?"

"More or less."

"Hit's content I'll be to settle for one of those Virginia backwoodsmen with 'is own land," Polly said. "Hit's more'n me father 'ad in 'is lifetime."

Williamsburg was much more than Jane could have hoped for. Unlike London, with its houses cramped together on narrow streets darkened by huge signs hanging from brackets, Williamsburg was spacious and clean. Picket fences defined the half-acre lots of each brick or painted frame house. And wild flowers, bright-orange day lilies, mountain laurel, and tall hollyhocks carpeted the town's knolls and adorned the fences. A multitude of red-bricked shops and taverns indicated that it was not the primitive settlement she had feared. Indeed, at the west end of the town a large college, William and Mary, served the students who came from as far away as Virginia's western boundary on the Mississippi River.

A little over a hundred years old, Williamsburg was young, compared to London's millenneum of years. And there were the pungent smells of animal manure, rooting hogs, and backyard privies that were to be found in every rural town, Old World or New.

She could see the Union Jack unfurled high over the H-shaped capitol with its arched Renaissance windows and cupola, and she was mildly surprised by the reassurance she felt. As the caravan of indentured servants neared the spacious Palace Green, more and more of the townsfolk stopped to watch the procession. Saddle and draft horses and two-wheeled chairs were abruptly halted.

The currier put aside his moon knife and pincers to stand at the doorway and the old wigmaker left her shears and curling pins to watch the arrival of the indentured servants. Squawking children flocked after the caravan like wild turkeys flushed from the forest. A burly man whose apron and cleaver proclaimed him a butcher raised his tool in a jolly wave at Polly, who broadly returned the greeting with a flirtatious wink.

To Jane's wonderment, the men and women were as fashionably dressed as Londoners, though even the more elegantly dressed women wore wigs that did not tower so high and the men wore simple brown perukes with sausage curls above their ears. She became aware that, in turn, she and the other indentured servants were being stared at, and she ducked her head and hunched her shoulders.

At the market square the wagons halted before the courthouse where a large marquee tent of red-striped Flanders ticking had been erected. Here, before the servants were herded into the tent, prospective purchasers walked up and down among them, looking them over and conversing with them to discover their degrees of intelligence and docility.

A drooping-jowled purchaser felt the muscles of each male servant and asked, "You skilled with an axe?"

An old painted woman who wore an enormous powdered wig and, incongruously, smoked a pipe talked briskly with a few of the women servants. Not wishing to give herself away, Jane mumbled a few garbled answers about her place of birth, her last place of service, her reason for leaving. She was terribly nervous and only wanted the ordeal to be over with. More than once she wiped her damp palms down the dress where it molded her long thighs.

At last the auction was ready to begin and the servants were ushered inside the tent. The afternoon sun had turned it into an oven. Sweat poured down between her breasts and soaked the kersey petticoat that stuck to the inside of her legs. Horseflies that seemed as big as sparrows swarmed from the nearby stables to fleck the stockinged legs of the men and buzz incessantly about the faces of Jane and the other women. No water was offered by the militiamen on duty during the long afternoon.

"This is outrageous," she muttered. "Englishmen treat their cattle better than this."

Several heads jerked around, stirred from their apathy by her outburst. Liz poked her in the ribs, and one little man who looked like a dormouse demanded, "What did ye expect? Governor Dunmore himself to welcome us?"

Realizing she was acting out of character, Jane said no more but waited with frustrated impatience—until a drum thudded, signaling the auction's beginning. Then a cold fear started to creep along her spine. She was going to be sold, like a cow at market, even though the selling was euphemistically called "setting over." The drum rapped ominously as each servant was taken outside the tent and presented to the townsfolk. Words like "artisan" and "skilled" reached her. Sometimes men's laughter.

Barbarians! But her contempt did not crowd out her panic. It was only a matter of months, she consoled herself. She would find Terence. He could purchase her papers from whomever bought her.

What if she didn't immediately find where Terence was posted, a nagging voice asked. She would run away. And she *would* find him. From the day he had ridden from Manor House to visit, she had known he had been meant for her. No matter that her mother had claimed his time more, Jane had somehow known her day would come to have Terence for her own.

The captain stepped inside the tent, checked off another name, then called out the name of Meg O'Reilly—the first name on the list of females. "God 'elp ye," Liz said as Jane rose unsteadily to her feet.

Polly squeezed her hand. "Git yewrself a good man, love."

Jane straightened her hooded cloak and smoothed down her skirts. The mere actions served to still her shaking hands. What folly had she committed? Her impetuous nature, one rash act on her part, had brought her to this—selling herself as a chattel!

Sunlight blinded her, then a sea of faces came into focus, some with gaping expressions, others smirking. Her mouth felt as dry as tinder. Here and there she saw men gesture at her and make their observations about her worth. "Plain as a pikestaff," she overheard from one man near the front. "But look at those tits."

Defensively she drew the cloak over her, though she sweltered under the sun's glare. The heavy, humid air made drawing a breath nigh impossible.

A brown-skinned old man, his grizzled hair plaited in chest-length braids and his bony body wrapped in a woolen blanket despite the heat, watched her with a detached glimmer in his eyes, and she shivered. Surely she would not be purchased by an Indian.

"We have here one Meg O'Reilly," began the auctioneer, a plump, pink man in a white bag wig who stood with self-importance behind the nearby podium. "No skills other than those of a domestic, but a strong constitution at"—he looked down at the list he carried—"at twenty-two years."

She went rigid as the auctioneer stepped to her side and took her jaw, forcing open her mouth. "Good teeth, as you can see."

"What about the rest of her?" a faceless voice jeered.

"That the buyer will have to ascertain for himself, gentlemen," the auctioneer announced with a lascivious wink. "What do I hear for this country maid?"

Humiliation flagged her cheeks. She ducked her head to hide angry tears.

"Four years—fourteen pounds!" a voice called out.

Her innate pride swept away the shame of her degradation. She was a lady. Lady Jane Lennox! Her head shot up and, after that, she glared scornfully at each man who bid— with the result that the bidding slowed, then stopped. "What?" cried the auctioneer. "A mere seventeen pounds/five shillings? Where's your Englishman's gallantry?"

"Aye, where indeed, my fine gallant gentlemen?" Jane

asked bitingly, her eyes sweeping over the faces of the men crowded on the green.

A small man whose face was narrow and pointed like a fox's called, "Four years—eighteen pounds."

Jane restrained a tremble. Something about him made her skin crawl. Please, she thought, let someone else bid.

"Seven years and thirty pounds," a voice drawled. Her head, like that of every man's there, swiveled to the left of the marquee tent, where a solitary man lounged beneath the shade of a catalpa, waiting.

"Wainwright?" the auctioneer asked the fox-faced man. "Do ye bid higher?"

Jane held her breath. Wainwright's lashless eyes ran over her length. "Thirty-one pounds," he growled.

"Seven years—fifty pounds," countered the man under the heavily bean-podded catalpa.

"Sold!" announced the auctioneer and immediately banged his gavel on the podium, as if he were afraid the man would regret his offer of such an unheard-of sum.

Jane's fingernails dug into her palms. Seven years!

The man stepped out from the catalpa's leafy shadows, and she gasped. The red hair! Only one such man—the marked man!

Chapter 6

Before her eyes flashed the porcelain cup with its mysterious arrangement of tea leaves. The old Hindu had been right. In a strange way the knowledge gave her comfort, for she recalled, too, his other prophecy—Terence would be waiting for her at the end of a long road.

She watched the giant Quaker stroll across the green toward her. Instead of the sober city clothes she had seen him wear in London, he sported an ordinary ozenbrig shirt, the sleeves rolled to the elbows, and a cotton singlet and leather breeches above common wool stockings. His shoes lacked even the simple adornment of buckles. All her hopes were dashed. This was not the Tidewater gentleman on whom she had counted.

When the Quaker stood before her, the auctioneer said, "If you'll just sign Meg O'Reilly's papers now, Mr. Gordon."

But Ethan Gordon reached out and pushed the mantle's hood off her head to reveal her cropped, hennaed hair. Grunts of surprise rose from the crowd at his action. Uncertainty flickered in his eyes, then a dawning smile crimped his lips. He made a leg. "Meg O'Reilly—your ladyship."

Those nearest the podium laughed at his mockery. But Jane cringed. He had recognized her. *Thee needs to be humbled, mistress, and I would take great delight in the task, had I the time.*

She wanted the earth to open up and swallow her. But instead she glared her scorn. Then for the first time in five long weeks she smiled, a grin that dimpled the emaciated hollows beneath her cheekbones. "Mr. Gordon, it would seem that you have bought a pig in the poke, for I know neither how to cook nor sew nor spin."

At the refined and precise speech, a low hum of wonder passed among the bidders, and she could have bitten her tongue at her lapse.

The Quaker merely smiled, and trapped in the beauty of that smile, she quite forgot the fact that he was now her master . . . until he replied with a quiet certainty, "Thee will learn, never doubt that."

He paid for her with a bill of exchange, the currency used since paper money and coins were forbidden by British law, and hefted her metal trunk over his shoulder as easily as an axe. Taking her elbow, gently enough, he steered her past the press of gawking townsfolk. "You're not going to put me in an iron collar and leg irons to keep me from running away?" she asked sarcastically, trying to keep up with his longer stride. Despite his mammoth size, he covered the ground with an almost preternatural grace.

"No place to run," he said laconically as he continued along the broad and dusty Duke of Gloucester Street. "Besides, Virginia's penalty for running away is thirty-nine lashes with a hickory switch." He flicked her a glance with black eyes that sparkled. "Thee wouldn't wish for me to have to administer lashes, would thee?"

She shot him a withering look before jerking her chin up and staring straight ahead. What would become of Polly and Liz and the other women she had come to know over the weeks of the voyage? Suddenly she felt very lonely—and terribly afraid. What if . . . what if this man decided not to honor her maiden's status? But, no, he was a Quaker. She sighed with a bitter sense of relief. She could be much worse off.

When he halted before a large, two-story house, she asked, "This is where you live?" Her eyes ran appreciatively over the fine blue-glazed brick, counted the six front entrances, noted the many chimneys. The Quaker was of more worth than she had judged.

"Hardly," Ethan said drily. "This is an ordinary—the Brick House Tavern. But a physic owns it, and it's him I want thee to see."

Her head whipped around. "Me? I'm not sick."

She had never been sick, much less resorted to having herself bled, as some did in order to achieve the pale, wan complexion that was the fashion of the day. "Why am I to see a physic?" she demanded, shoving the Quaker's hand away when he propelled her up the steps.

"I want Dr. Gilmer to inoculate thee."

"You want wot! Wot for?"

"Forget the Cockney accent, milady," he sneered. His dark eyes brushed over her contemptuously. "Thy hair—thy dress—'tis different. But thy eyes—their inordinate color gave thee away. I'm afraid thy madcap prank will cost thee dearly, mistress."

She shivered at his tone. "I'm worthless to you. Take me back to the auction. I'm sure you can get someone else to purchase my papers."

"Oh, no. I think thee will prove quite entertaining to my more lonely moments."

He opened the door and ushered her in ahead of him. "Tell Dr. Gilmer, Ethan Gordon is here," he told a boy of twelve or thirteen who was busy with a mop and bucket, scrubbing the dark, planked floor.

She stamped her foot, impervious to the startled tavern boy. "I will not be inoculated! It's dangerous, it's unhealthy!"

He ignored her and addressed the boy. "And send this trunk on to the quay, Peter."

"You can't make me do this!" she said, after the boy dropped his mop and hastily disappeared on his errand.

"Thy hair is a crow's nest," he said, and adjusted the mantle's frayed hood over her head while she glared at him. "And as for the inoculation, I *can* make thee, mistress. But it is enough that thee should know one out of every four servants coming to the colonies doesn't survive. Malaria, dry gripes, bloody flux takes them. The two I bought in London—for less than I paid for you alone. They didn't make it, Lady Len—Mistress O'Reilly."

The title was said with a dry smile. That close, the burn on his cheek blotted out all other redeeming features. Or rather, the burn and her righteous anger did. "And so you came here today to purchase new slaves!"

"Slaves, no. A servant—yes. Which, if I remember rightly, was what thee wished of me at the guildhall."

"But I did not wish to be inoculated, and I won't—"

"Dr. George Gilmer," he said, breaking into her diatribe as a dapper little man came into the room with a quick step. Velvet ribbons anchored his breeches about his knees, and lace adorned his stock and cuffs. "I wish to inoculate my maidservant against the smallpox."

"No, I—" Jane began.

"Most certainly, Mr. Gordon. Bring her to the back room. It won't take but a moment."

"Please," she said when Ethan caught her wrist and tugged her along with him. "I don't want to go through with this—this farce. I've changed my mind."

"Has thee now?" he said. He did not bother to look at her as he followed the physic down a hallway lit only by the dust-filtered sunlight streaming through a window at the far end.

"Yes," she whispered, not wishing the physic to overhear her importuning. "And I shall repay you. You know my father is a wealthy man."

"But I haven't changed my mind, mistress. Ah, here we are."

"If you'll just have a seat, dear girl," Dr. Gilmer said as he delved into a glass jar, rattling some small instruments that looked terrifying to Jane. The tiny office was filled with glass and ceramic apothecary jars labeled RED FIT DROPS, FRENCH POX OINTMENT, APOPLEXY PILLS.

Jane thought she would have apoplexy when her gaze settled on the jar of crawling black leeches.

"It's a wise decision to do this," the doctor continued in a reassuring manner. "The stepson of one of our Burgess members—Mr. Washington's—was inoculated only last week with the cowpox. Too bad so many of the Scottish merchants refuse the inoculation. There's little pain or scarring. Lower your bodice, please, mistress."

Jane clutched the mantle more tightly about her. "Sir!"

"This is not a time for maidenly modesty," Ethan said, and forcibly separated her crossed wrists, the strength in his large hands easily overpowering her resistance. With a free hand he shoved the mantle off her shoulders. "Now lower thy bodice—or shall I?"

"Turn around!"

He grinned but did as she ordered. "A meek and docile maidservant I have purchased, have I not, Dr. Gilmer?"

"Merely fear goads her tongue, Mr. Gordon. I find the men swoon as often as the women. She'll suffer a slight fever. Just don't require too much work of her. Might give her a posset cup. And, naturally, keep her abed for a few days."

"To be certain," Ethan said.

She heard the amusement in his voice. She bit her full bottom lip that tempered the sensual bow of her upper one. Would the Quaker—dare the Quaker—require *that* of her?

So preoccupied was she with the trap she had sprung on herself, she failed to notice the physic's approach or the lancet he held. Then the lancet pricked her flesh.

At that point her dignity had suffered all it could sustain, and she burst into tears, burying her face in her hands. The good doctor raised startled brows, but the Quaker turned and, saying nothing, pulled aside her hands. Gently he drew her shabby bodice up over her shoulders, buttoned the myriad buttons with fingers that were deft for their size, and knotted her large black shawl beneath her bosom. "Let's go home, mistress."

Ashamed of her weakness, she wiped the back of her hand across her eyes, refusing to look at the Quaker. Neither did she speak after that. He hired a carriage and in silence they journeyed to the quay, rattling over the long wooden bridges that spanned the unfordable tidal creeks and brackish backwater marshes where flourished ferns and cattails and marshmallow.

Confined in the carriage's small interior with its badly cracked leather, she found it difficult to ignore the darkly handsome Quaker next to her, if only because of his size. Her pride had been shattered, and she could not help but resent this man who had bought her.

The brig was still anchored in the James River, and she knew the ungovernable urge to flee up the gangplank and return to the safety of England. But she would lose all hope of finding Terence. And there was the galling fact that she had no freedom, no rights. She could no longer react on a moment's whim. That part of her impulsive, frivolous nature could not be indulged.

And what of her maidenhood? Was she shortly to find an end to her innocence also? Oh, God, that she could have been so headstrong, so foolish!

The Quaker whistled a sprightly air as he stationed her in the bow of the picturesque gundalow that already contained her trunk. "Mood Hill—my farm—is over forty miles by land from Williamsburg but only twenty-seven by water," he explained cheerfully while he raised the lateen sail. "The journey will not take overly long, mistress."

She turned a deaf ear. Infinitely old red oaks and willows and black locusts arched a brilliant green canopy over clear blue waters that were pleasantly cool to her trailing fingers. A blue heron balanced on one spindly leg in the shallow waters near the shore where a mud turtle and muskrat sunbathed. A thousand birds, it seemed, screamed raucously, as if in a futile effort to harmonize with the Quaker's soft whistling.

Rather than risk a glance at the man, who expertly handled the gundalow's sail, she kept her gaze trained on the occasional small farms that they sailed past. The plots of land were demarcated by the zigzag split-rail worm fences that required no expensive nails or laborious postholes.

"Thee regrets leaving England, its befouled streets and water?" the Quaker asked with a quiet sarcasm.

"I regret everything . . . but would change nothing," she murmured, keeping her haughty profile turned to him. "The mother country is—"

"It's not the mother country," he drawled. "At least not here in the colonies. More people come from the Continent—Germany, France, Sweden, Holland—than England."

She whirled on him. The leafy branches cast dappled shadows on the gundalow and obscured his marred visage.

"England is still the mightiest nation in the world! And you still owe your allegiance—nay, more, your very protection in this savage world—to her!"

"Ah, then you harbor deep Tory sentiments, mistress?"

She shrugged her shoulders, repenting of her outburst. "I care not for the feud between the Crown and her colonies. My allegiance . . . is elsewhere."

After that she saw none of the primitive beauty in the journey by water first up the immensely wide and slow moving James, then the arcadian Chickahominy. Though the trip was only a matter of an hour or so, it seemed to last forever as she felt a tightening in her chest with each league the gundalow carried her from the brig and England. The heavily leafed trees seemed to close in around her, obliterating the bright blue sky.

At last the woods ceded to a clearing on her left. By the time the gundalow drew abreast of the private dock, she was feeling feverish—and keenly disappointed in the farm she viewed by the light of the setting sun. Raw was the only word that came to mind. The Quaker had pushed the forest back to the fields' margins, but the untended edges still grew with the grapevines and wild raspberries that choked the woods. Only the fruit trees, plum and apple, and the smaller fields of corn, beans, and squash were fenced to keep out the roaming cows and other livestock.

On a rise between the fields ringed by a scattering of crude, smaller outbuildings and tall beech and gum, a two-story split-log house shimmered before her eyes. The great stone and clay chimneys at either end and the cypress shingles saved it from being totally primitive.

The Quaker was saying something about raising indigo on the four hundred acres that stretched in a purplish-blue haze beyond the farmhouse as far as the eye could see, but his voice seemed a great distance away. Yet when her knees buckled and the sandy earth wavered before her gaze, he was there, catching her, holding her.

Chapter 7

"Terence . . ."

The word was a litany through that night as Lady Jane Lennox's mind wandered. Ethan smoothed back from the high forehead the lifeless hennaed tendrils that were damp with sweat. Who was Terence? Her fiancé? But why then would she have run away from England? Perhaps her trip was not the prank he had thought. An enigma, this Lady Jane Lennox.

He sat there at the edge of the rope-slung bed that was to be hers, holding her hand when she murmured distractedly. The mother and son he had purchased to see to the domestic chores had died within hours of each other the very day the vessel put into the James River. It happened often enough—from ship fever, if not other maladies. Most people were unused to the hardship of the voyage, unused to the Virginia heat, unused to the sun's brightness that seemed to burn the very eyes.

He had lost other servants who had withstood the voyage but had been unable to survive in the colonial clime, so he had sworn to purchase only those hardy ones already living there. But somehow the spinning and mending and washing had mounted up before he found any to his liking, and he had resorted to purchasing the mother and son. They had seemed strong enough in body and spirit, and certainly eager to come to the New World. But they had not even survived the voyage to have their mettle tested on the virgin shores.

Would he lose this woman also? That night he was indifferent to his own weariness and the various problems that had arisen in his absence—as indifferent as he should be of the tall, taut body who slept in restless delirium before him.

But to be indifferent to Lady Jane Lennox was impossible, as he had known from that first meeting. Brilliant and without substance and most definitely spoiled, he had thought then. His opinion had not changed. But another dimension was added. Stubborn, persevering—and brave, despite the stark fear he had seen in those beguiling eyes. The sharp words that had readily played on her tongue were softened by the strange vulnerability he perceived in the set of her lips.

He leaned forward with elbows braced on knees spread wide, his hands clasped lightly in between. With her deeply asleep now, there was no longer the need to hold back the fingers that unconsciously rubbed at the pasty skin. It would be a shame to mar her face with pox pits, though little was left of the loveliness he had glimpsed in London. Her skin was ravaged, her hair damaged by the henna. Only her refined bone structure saved her from looking truly haggard.

Were Meg O'Reilly and Lady Jane Lennox indeed one and the same woman? And what was he to do with her?

He was a fool to have made the purchase, and he did not doubt that he would rue the day he had done so.

Toward morning her almost inaudible ravings stopped, and he felt it safe to leave for a few hours. Sleep he desperately needed, but the Indian runner, Mattaponi, had entered on silent feet with the message of the clandestine meeting for which he had been waiting. Only a few words were grunted in the Powhatan language—"Committee of Correspondence . . . in the morning . . . the Great Dismal Swamp."

The young woman might awaken while he was absent, might attempt to run away. He sighed, rose, and tucked about her shoulders the quilt she had tossed off. Better for him if she did.

Chapter 8

Under the sullen stares of Boston's unemployed, the British officer made his way among the soldiers' tents pegged out in lines on the Boston Common. That June, the Boston Port Bill had closed the harbor to all commerce until the city paid for the tea the supposed Mohawk Indians had dumped into the water the previous December. Thusly were nearly twenty thousand Bostonians "paying the fiddler" for their tea party, as was predicted by the admiral of one of the British ships in port that fateful December night.

At the British headquarters in the Provincial House the officer was immediately ushered into General Gage's office by the ruddy-faced secretary. The officer entered and saluted Gage, which was becoming the proper form of military greeting now that the high wigs made the wearing and doffing of a hat impossible.

The stout general indicated the Queen Anne armchair in front of the desk he occupied as the new military governor of Massachusetts. Over the pyramid of his fingertips he studied the officer. What he saw augured well. The man stood an inch or so short of six feet, with a trim, sinewy build. The age was more difficult to judge, but he was most likely in his early thirties. The officer wore no powder on his sun-streaked hair, which pleased the general. Against the hair's blond color, the face seemed dark and was faintly lined by the elements. The features might be deemed handsome in an arrogant sort of way. No doubt, Gage thought morosely, his American wife would find the man bloody attractive.

To Gage, the man appeared to be one of those few who maintained a command of himself, of his emotions. But the eyes bothered him. No indication of the man's thoughts could be detected in those pale blue orbs. Gage felt a pinprick of unease. Were there any emotions? Like all soldiers trained by order and policy, he disliked anything that smacked of the unmanageable.

"You come highly recommended from the command at Quebec, MacKenzie." He leaned back against his chair and folded his hands across his paunch.

"Thank you, sir."

Gage shifted in his chair. "Your record indicates that you performed a number of delicate missions against the Punjabi tribes. . . ."

"I went among the Punjabi as one of them."

"Well, yes. And I have a, er, a mission of similar delicacy I would like to discuss with you."

"You want the Boston countryside reconnoitered to locate storehouses of weapons and powder."

Gage managed to control his surprise. "Exactly. You had access to my report?"

"No. I used my eyes and my ears."

Gage did not fail to notice MacKenzie's lack of formality in omitting the respectful "sir" from his reply. He leaned forward, interlocking his fleshy fingers. "Tell me more, MacKenzie."

"In the three weeks I have been stationed in Boston, I have observed that certain of your soldiers are selling uniforms and arms to the colonists. Moreover, despite the curfew you have imposed, pairs of colonists still amble about the waterfront, where your military strength is obviously displayed by the number of British vessels arriving and departing. Talk runs high against the Crown in the ordinaries."

The man paused and shrugged nonchalantly before continuing. "There are other signs. The Massachusetts colonists are riled by this closing of their port, which is an important source of livelihood. They do not intend to accept passively your total British rule."

Silence settled over the oak-paneled room. Then Gage spoke. "MacKenzie, you said 'your' British rule. Not 'our.'"

A lean, feral smile curved the officer's lips. "You are observant. Do not mistake me, General Gage, I am British. But you are motivated by patriotism and idealism, and I—"

"Yes?"

"Another goal motivates me."

Gage had served in the colonies during the French Indian War, more than fifteen years earlier. He was a formidable soldier, and he understood enough about violent men to recognize that the man before him would suit his purpose very well. "Your mission will mean traveling incognito. You will need to go by a code name."

"I expected as much."

"You realize that I cannot command you to accept the mission? If you are caught—without your uniform—well, while we are not officially at war, it could mean a very untidy mess should your identity be discovered."

"I won't be caught."

"No one can be sure of—"

"I can."

The words were spoken with such conviction that Gage blinked in surprise. "Just why are you so certain?"

Terence MacKenzie rested his hands calmly on the chair's arms. He could tell the general he had learned in India everything there was to know about destruction; that he had trained himself to be an expert in fighting with all weapons—the saber, the rifle, the stiletto, the claymore—as well as in unarmed combat; that he had acquired the art of subtle torture as well as silent assassination.

Instead he replied, "Because patriotism can be misplaced under the right persuasion, idealism can sometimes flag under materialistic conditions. I don't profess a nobility of spirit. Should the necessity of killing a man arise, I will do so as automatically as I would step on a cockroach."

Chapter 9

E than Gordon—a commonplace, ordinary, bumptious backwoodsman, she told herself as she dressed for the first time in the week since she had become ill after arriving at Mood Hill.

Her scorn for the indigo farm—for it could not be compared to the grand tobacco plantations she had seen—vied with her reluctant gratitude for the care he had shown her since that night when she became ill with the smallpox. She remembered little of those first few days . . . only the coolness of his hand on her forehead and the gentle drawl of his deep voice. But then the fever, the pustules that scabbed her flesh—and the resulting pox scar at the tip of her chin—had been his fault to begin with!

Her anger was exceeded only by her acute embarrassment at whatever intimate services he had performed for her
during her illness. Her first memory was awakening to find
herself clad in Meg's muslin nightrail, so different from the
brilliantly colored, soft silk banyans to which she was accustomed. Then the horror slowly dawned on her—Ethan
Gordon had seen her nude!

Lacing the bodice strings of her dress, she groaned at
the thought. As it was, whenever he entered her small, win-
dowless room, consuming it with his solid breadth and
height, it was difficult to meet those steady black eyes without flinching with shame.

She had to admit that the soups and porridges he
brought her were tasty. Better than she could do—which
worried her somewhat. How was she to earn her keep? From
the kitchen she could hear Ethan's baritone voice along with
those of the field hands as they left the breakfast table for
work. Soon she would be expected to prepare the meals herself. If she could only stay in bed . . . Yet she chafed to be
about after the week of inactivity.

When the voices faded away, she deemed it safe to venture from her cubicle. The tantalizing smell of fried ham
drew her to the kitchen, which adjoined her maid's quarters.
Wooden tumblers and trenches were scattered over a long,
roughly hewn trestle table. Her gaze swept dismally over the
rest of the rustic kitchen, which was apparently to be her
domain.

Copper and brass sauce pots, looking as if they had
never been used, hung from heavy oaken rafters blackened
by smoke. Three white-washed, limestone walls were less
smudged. Red brick, the same as the floor, spanned the
fourth wall and housed a small oval-shaped oven and an
arched fireplace large enough for a dozen people to sit
within.

Below the table, a raccoon lapped at a plate of left-over

fried tomatoes, morsels of grits, and charred ham fat. Jane dimly recalled the bizarre sight of the raccoon perched on Ethan Gordon's shoulder one of the times she awoke during those first feverish hours. In her delirium she had attributed the furry gray creature to an hallucination.

She crossed to the table and stooped to run her hand along the docile animal's back. The raccoon's sharp little black nose wrinkled. "One of us is going to have to learn how to wash dishes, my fine pet."

"I doubt that it's going to be King George, mistress."

Startled, Jane straightened, only to bump her head on the table's edge. "Damnation!" she muttered.

"Tsk-tsk," a tongue clicked. "Swearing—from such a fine lady."

Ethan leaned through the upper half of the kitchen's Dutch door. The brilliant morning sunlight streaming in behind him, cast his face in shadow. But she could make out the way he eyed the frazzled mop that was her hair. She had forgotten the mobcap. Frustrated, her hands went to her hips, and she deflected his amusement with an imperious glare. "And you think you're a titled gentleman, sir?"

"I think 'tis time thee baked bread before the morning grows any later."

"Bake bread? I don't know how to bake bread!"

He pushed open the door's lower half and strode over to her, walking around her slowly, eyeing her length. She flushed under his penetrating regard, but did not deign to look at him. Rather she stood as haughtily as a princess until he came around to face her again. "'Tis a shame, then, because I don't think thee will fetch a goodly price on the market," he said blandly.

Too quickly she recalled the fox-faced Wainwright, and she knew she could be much worse off. "You wouldn't dare sell me!"

"I would."

The glint in his eye told her he would only be too happy to rid himself of his misbegotten purchase. "Then you'll have to instruct me."

"Done!" Crossing to the flour bin, he pushed up the full, gathered sleeves of his linsey-woolsey shirt. He dug out a gourd of stone-ground brown flour, saying, "I've had to make do with my own cooking, mistress, and for that reason, among others, purchased thee."

Her mind would have questioned what other reasons, but her attention was diverted as she watched in amazement while he adeptly filled a large wooden bowl with flour, honey, salt, and warm water. The sight was so ludicrous—a man of his massive build making bread—that she began to chuckle.

He flicked her a disgusted look. "'Tis thy turn." He shoved the bowl across the table toward her. "Knead the dough."

She smiled sweetly. "I don't know how." The two of them were battling wills, but with a little Machiavellian finesse she would win out over this oaf.

He braced his hands on the table and studied her for a long moment. "Thee needs to be humbled," he said slowly.

Her eyes widened in wariness. "I'll try to knead the dough."

He straightened. "Good."

She wanted to hurl the bowl at his departing back, but when he forgot to duck his head and banged it on the door's lintel, a small smile of satisfaction curled her lips. The smile faded as the morning progressed. The dough was pasted all the way up her forearms, and flour ringed her eyes the same way black fur ringed King George's.

By the time she plopped the sticky globs of dough in the black iron kettle and set it to rise on the hearth next to the ash-covered coals, she resolved that she was not staying a day longer than necessary.

*   *   *

Jane wiped the dust from one cheek with the back of her arm and went back to drawing the hackle's teeth through the flax. It was dirty work, and, despite the early-morning hour of the mild October day, it was stifling in the airless ell of the house's main room, reserved for the hand loom and spinning wheel.

After all the hackling it constantly surprised her to see how little good filament was left from such a large mass of fiber. But then it was equally surprising to see how much linen thread could be made from the small amount of fine flax. Unfortunately, she often had more tow, the short broken residue of the fiber, than the long, fine filaments that would be converted into spinning thread.

From the kitchen Josiah, the scarecrow-thin deaf mute, spied her predicament and crossed the parlor to squat next to her. She thought the field hand's kindly eyes beneath the thatch of straw-colored hair were almost eloquent, as if God had given his eyes the gift of communicating that his tongue lacked. She saw in their hazel depths a wry humor at her inferior product.

He picked up the thick, poorly hackled linen thread she had combed and rolled it between his callused fingers. His head shook in a sad commentary on her work. Holding up a forefinger to catch her attention, he took up the hackle and a handful of damp flax, then deftly drew the fibers through the hackle. Little tow was left, and the resulting thread he passed her was fine and silky to the touch. His eyes caught hers to see if she understood the way he had done it.

She nodded and touched his shoulder in gratitude. "Thank you, Josiah. But I don't think I shall ever make an adequate spinster."

After he left, she rose and stretched, rubbing her hands along the back of her narrow waist. Holding her hands out before her critical eyes, she reflected that not even her maid Meg's were so chapped and red. But then Meg had not washed linen in burning lye soap.

This much deterioration in the space of a fortnight! She alone was doing the tasks Wychwood's numerous servants performed: Betty the cook, Becky the scullion, Jenny the washwoman, Mimia who ironed, Sally the seamstress. Jane's life had been one of unbroken elegance, of rustling silks, of feather boas and belt knots, of tuckers and lace flounces, of French perfumes and rose-scented soap., And now all she knew was drudgery from dawn to long past dusk.

And then there was her complexion. Her hand went to the fresh red scar that pitted her chin. A glimpse in the looking glass Ethan Gordon used for shaving revealed that her hair, tufting from below the mobcap, resembled frizzled, carrot-red flax tow. What would she look like after a year in this God-forsaken land?

Longingly her gaze went to the delicately beautiful harpsicord in the parlor's corner. It, like the elegantly furnished bedroom opposite that of Ethan Gordon's, was so out of keeping with the rest of the rooms, which bore a distinctly sparse, masculine stamp. The back-country house had been constructed from heavy timbers, with thick doors meant to withstand Indian attack.

He had built the house with tall door lintels to accommodate his enormous height; yet both the kitchen and the bedroom across from his had shorter door frames, so that if Jane forgot to stoop, as she often did, she, too, bumped her head. And what of the gleaming new copper sauce pots? Why were they unused?

When Ethan Gordon built the house, he evidently had a wife in mind. Whom?

Her fingers itched to run along the harpsicord's ivory keys rather than rub themselves raw on the spinning wheel. But she had no choice. Ethan had set before her the task that morning—with some impatience at her ineptitude for keeping house. If she failed at this, as she did more often than not at cooking, he might just sell her, as he had threatened.

Ethan Gordon did not yell at her, nor did he whip her. No doubt most masters would have done so immediately upon discovering their maid's lack of domestic skills.

Most important, he made no untoward advances. But then, could she expect a lusty eye from him, or any male, when she presented such a bedraggled spectacle? He seemed totally unaware of her presence, except when she broke a dish or burned the bread or tore his shirt while trying to wash it.

Her lips flattened with frustration at her predicament. She was no nearer joining Terence than the day she signed her indenture papers almost two months before. She began to pace, her feet taking her from the ell into the parlor with its hearth, then back again to stand before the spinning wheel. She had to start laying plans.

Ethan, she knew, was working at the smokehouse, hanging from the rafters the last of the ham he had butchered. She gathered her skirts and hurried up the roughly planed staircase. Her petticoat snagged on a splinter, but she yanked it free and sped on up to his bedroom on the second floor.

Opposite the fireplace was the gigantic bedstead, obviously built specially to accommodate his great frame. But it was the high scrolled desk she sought. Only God knew what he used it for. She had doubted the lout could even read, but evidence to the contrary was found on the shelf above the desk. Her gaze scanned some of the titles—*The Treatise of Agriculture*, *A New Agriculture*, and, of course, a Bible whose edges were charred.

With little time to waste, she pulled out the top drawer and began to rifle through the contents—bills of sale, unsharpened quills, an account ledger. Another drawer produced fresh vellum. After locating an ink bottle, she grabbed up a quill, dipped it in the brown ink, and hastily began to scribble.

Terence—
You last asked if a certain party's
disapproval would stop me. It has not. I
can be found at the indigo plantation of the
Quaker, Ethan Gordon, on the
Chickahominy River below the Piedmont
fall section of Virginia.

Could Terence find her in such a wilderness area with no convenient street address such as those in London to go by? He would. She dashed off her name—Jane Lennox of Wychwood—and with the perforated wooden sander quickly sprinkled fine sand across the page before folding the missive. There was not enough time to search for a wax wafer with which to seal the letter. On the outside she penned Terence's name and regiment and the only address she knew—that of General Carleton in Quebec, though there were many other posts in Canada, most of them mere forts, where he could have been sent.

She could only hope the letter would be forwarded to him. But how to get the letter to the post rider in Williamsburg without alerting the Quaker? Absently she tapped the edge of the folded vellum on the desk top. Somehow she would have to inveigle her way to Williamsburg when the colonial made his next trip. Dear God, that might be another six months!

The opportunity to post the letter came more quickly than Jane could have hoped—that same afternoon—in the form of Susan Fairmont and her husband, Bram, a pleasantly handsome man dressed in nankeen knee breeches and a pea-green frock coat.

Jane had returned to the spinning wheel, its hypnotic hum almost putting her to sleep, when the couple entered with Ethan between them, dwarfing them. His dark eyes were alight as Jane had never seen them. Her foot released the wheel's pedal as she watched Ethan offer his guests seats on the leather-covered bench and take up the maple rocking chair opposite them.

In the shadows of the ell she was able to catch the expressions of the three as they talked. Since none were aware of her presence, she quite clearly was eavesdropping. She was about to clear her throat audibly, when something in Ethan's face stopped her—some undefinable expression. And then she knew. As Susan spoke in a singularly sweet voice, Ethan's eyes held a tenderness that was—why, yes, Ethan was in love with the man's wife!

Jane turned her gaze on Susan, curious as to the type of woman Ethan would love. With eyes gray as a hoary morning mist and brown corkscrew curls that peaked demurely from beneath her calash bonnet, Susan reminded Jane of a lovely china doll with a face as sweet as a madonna's.

The young woman was petite in her flower-sprigged muslin gown and dainty slippers, and Jane thought how drab her scratchy woolen dress, gray and barren of ornamentation, must look in comparison. She recalled those first terrible weeks at St. James Court, when she had towered awkwardly over the other court ladies and desperately wished she could shrink to a delicately feminine stature such as Susan Fairmont's.

Susan, her voice soft, said, "We just returned from Williamsburg and learned that you have a new maidservant, Ethan. All of the women in the county will be anxious to meet her."

"Actually, that is not why we came a-calling, Ethan," Bram interjected, his narrow face wearing an earnest expression. Like Ethan, he kept his long sandy hair unpowdered and tied in a queue. He leaned forward, resting his elbows on his knees. "We just finished the second session of the General Assembly."

Ethan's brow wrinkled thoughtfully. "And—?"

"Don't you know what's in the air, Ethan? Parliament just passed the Quebec Act. The Canadians are not allowed to elect any part of their government. And General Gage has dissolved the Massachusetts Assembly. They no longer can meet as a legal body. Next self-government will be forbidden to all the colonies! It all but has been, since we no longer have the right to decide on local taxes and now are forbidden to settle west of the Alleghenies."

For protection against the Indians, Jane wanted to point out.

"I hardly have time for political rumoring, Bram," Ethan drawled. King George rubbed against his leg for attention, and he reached down to scratch the raccoon's furry neck.

"Ethan, some of Chesterfield's Burgess members have been a-talking, and they want you to go as the county's delegate to a congress of the colonial leaders in Philadelphia."

Ethan's fingers toyed absently with the raccoon's batting paw, indicating a lack of interest in the subject. But Bram persisted. "Something's got to be done to help Massachusetts. Some solution has to be presented to Lord North and the Parliament."

Jane thought the colonials were erring if they attempted to compare their assemblies with the British Parliament. Susan gently waved her fan in a futile effort to conceal her own agitation. "It can only end in more crossfire with England, Bram," she interjected softly. "It means trouble ahead."

"Thou knowest the Society of Friends are pacifist," Ethan said soberly. "We don't hold with armed conflict. I'm afraid I'll have to decline the honor."

The insipid coward! Jane, recalling England's dashing scarlet uniforms, the flashing silver of sabers and bayonets, the golden sparkle of metal epaulets and plumed helmets, almost snorted her contempt. Thank God the Quaker was on the other side or Great Britain would not be the Empire she was. It was men like Terence, who—

"Ethan's right," Susan defended with mild reproof. "If we continue to provoke England, we'll have redcoats quartered in our homes like Boston does now. It frightens me."

"What about the way they provoke us?" Bram demanded. "What about Governor Dunmore dissolving our assembly for voting a day of fasting in sympathy with beleaguered Boston? What about Parliament taxing us to pay for their armies posted here?"

Jane bit back her words of argument. Could these upstart colonials not see that the British Army had been quartered there to protect them from the French and the Indians? Someone had to pay for it.

"What about taxing the tea?" Bram continued in his harangue.

"True, Bram," his wife said, "I dearly miss drinking the tea. But the tax was a small thing compared to refusing to import the tea and drinking odious coffee the rest of our lives."

"What about—"

"What about your new maidservant, Ethan?" Susan diplomatically halted her husband. "The women in Williamsburg tell that you actually removed her hood at the auction for all to behold, and that she is not unpleasant to look upon."

Ethan shrugged his massive shoulders. "Meg O'Reilly's fair enough as servant women go," he said with his customary slow speech. "A little common . . ."

Jane smothered an indignant gasp.

"I would have her serve refreshments, but the lazy wench is no doubt off—"

At that moment King George deserted Ethan's caressing fingers. Scampering across the puncheon floor into the ell, the raccoon playfully entangled its furry body in Jane's skirts. The rustling of the cotton petticoats, combined with her sudden fit of sneezing from the dust stirred up, betrayed her position. All three in the main room turned simultaneously. Guiltily Jane rose from the stool. The embarrassed flush that swept over her only heated her skin that much more.

"This—she is your maidservant?" Susan asked, her bewildered gaze traveling up the long length of Jane's frame.

"I—" Jane remembered to drop a curtsey to Susan and Bram. "I had not meant to listen, but . . ." With a limp gesture her hand indicated the ell room behind her. "I—uh, found myself trapped by your entrance."

"Say no more," Susan said graciously.

Bram grinned. "Now I understand the reason for the gossip. Were your maidservant as old as Methuselah, Ethan, the subject of Meg O'Reilly living under the same roof would go unheralded."

Past Bram, Jane saw the glint in Ethan's eye. He knew all the time she was in the ell! "I'll fetch refreshments, master," she added, delighted at the irritation that immediately darkened his eyes.

To her surprise, Susan offered to help. "There are so few women for neighbors," the young woman chatted amiably as she followed Jane into the kitchen. "I do hope that we will see more of each other."

Jane eyed her from beneath her fringe of weighty lashes as she withdrew the wooden tumblers from the cupboard and set them on the long trestle table. Never did a lady mix sociably with a servant. Yet Susan talked easily while Jane filled the tumblers from the crock of sassafras tea and passed her one.

"My linen is the whitest in Chesterfield County. You'll have to make Ethan let you come over so that I can show you the secret. It's all in the bleaching the flax. I lay the flax on a high rock where the sunlight lingers longer. . . ."

She broke off, choking, and Jane sighed. "I've not much experience in making sassafras tea."

Susan managed a smile. "I'll"—she cleared her throat—"be glad to show you how sometime. But, oh, for a cup of real East India tea."

When they joined the men, Susan pressed Jane to stay. Ethan's stolid expression gave no clue as to his feelings on his maidservant's inclusion with the company. At first the men dominated the conversation with their talk of the renewed threat of Indian warfare in the West and the Cherokees scalping and burning settlers' cabins in South Carolina.

When both women's faces paled, Ethan turned the subject to crops. "Fortunately, England has put a bounty on indigo, so I'm not dependent on the pricing of the London market."

"But you'll admit it's unfair that we have to sell our crops and manufactured products only to English agents and have nothing to say about their prices," Bram decried. "Many of our Tidewater planters are in debt up to their ears to these unscrupulous agents who do them no good!"

"I'm afraid my husband is a rabid Whig at heart," Susan laughingly apologized. "If he and Samuel Adams had their way, we would declare ourselves independent of England, as unthinkable as the idea is."

"It would seem you already have," Jane murmured, catching from the corner of her eye the surprised glance Ethan sliced in her direction.

"Why, yes, I suppose so. But I don't understand politics, much less like to talk about the subject. And if—well, it would never happen, but if a state of war were ever to occur, why, I don't think I could be brave if Bram went off to battle and left me alone, Meg."

Jane started at the mention of the unfamiliar name. She

felt guilty about her deception in the face of Susan's cordial friendship. It was understandable why Ethan was in love with Susan. The young woman was kindhearted and very attractive. Unintellectual and without guile, she was conspicuously devoted to her handsome husband. If she was aware of Ethan's love, Jane sensed that never a word or look would the woman let pass that would divulge that knowledge.

At one point, as the couple prepared to leave, Jane was able to draw Susan away from the two men. It was only a few minutes Jane had to retrieve the letter from her room and press it into Susan's hand. "Please," she quietly implored Susan, "will you deliver the letter to the post rider next time you journey to Williamsburg?"

"A *billet doux*?" Susan's Cupid's bow mouth curved in delight at the prospect of becoming involved in amorous intrigue, but then the corners of her lips dipped. "And all this time today I would have sworn there was something between you and Ethan."

"Ethan?" Jane echoed.

"Half the females in Chesterfield County are waiting for him to make up his mind and marry," Susan teased. "I was engaged to Bram when Ethan claimed his land here four years ago, or I would have married him myself." Despite the teasing, Jane sensed that fidelity to Bram lay like a whalebone corset stay beneath the young woman's gentle humor.

Susan's fan halted, and an uncertain smile settled on her lips. "Bram—I understand Bram exactly, but Ethan . . . I'm never quite sure about him."

Jane was very sure. Ethan Gordon was little more than a rustic yokel whom she would soon work her way with.

Chapter 10

"Thank ye, lass," Icabod Knox said when Jane set the platter of stewed vegetables and brown bread before him and the other two field hands, One-eyed Peter and Josiah. Icabod winked broadly at her. "I bet Josiah two shillings you wouldn't be a-burning the bread this time!"

Icabod, who shared a cabin with Josiah, had been forced to leave a wife and four children in Scotland in order to find work of any kind. He was a little, balding man with a big nose and a big laugh, and his Falstaffian sense of humor usually lightened Jane's loneliness.

"And I," said Peter, with a wink of his one good eye, "wagered my fife you would burn it."

"Your faith is reassuring," she said lightly, though she

was proud of the loaf she had turned out. True, the bread loaf had not risen, but at least this time it was not burned.

Ethan had even set her to making soap. Sometimes she wondered if he was seeing just how far he could push her. She was determined not to show any signs of weakness, though many times that past month tears of weariness and frustration lurked just behind her lids.

She was tired of constantly cooking, cleaning, and waiting on the men, despite the respect and admiration the field hands showed her. The trouble was Ethan Gordon. Her initial pleasure in the kitchen's bright limestone walls, which she had finally found time to scour clean of their smoke smudge, faded when he glanced at her accomplishment that morning, and merely said, "There are the parlor walls, when thee finishes the kitchen."

She could stand it no longer. She was through with her deception. She made up her mind that she would ask him to release her from her bondage. That very day. But for once he did not come to dinner. Usually, he was punctual, washing up at the well with the rest of the men before appearing at three o'clock every day for the main meal.

"Where's Ethan?" she asked of the three field hands.

Peter wolfed down the black-eyed peas in his mouth, and mumbled, "He's in the vat house, mistress . . . steeping the indigo."

Like the other two field hands, Peter's fingers were purple from harvesting the indigo leaves that week. She gathered from the little said during other meals that the steeping required precise timing. It would be best to wait until evening to approach Ethan with her request.

That afternoon she prepared her arguments as she boiled the linen in the large cast-iron kettle. At last her work was finished. She rubbed her sweaty palms down the front of her soiled apron. Still her steps lagged. Instead of going directly to Ethan, she left the kitchen and its smothering heat by the side entrance, remembering to duck her head for the Dutch door's low lintel. Outside, she unbuttoned the top three buttons of her dress, wiping away with her fingertips the perspiration that beaded her neck.

A cool breeze chilled the wilted orange-tipped tendrils clinging damply to her temples. Her hair had grown almost a full inch to curl in unmanageable clusters below her nape. Now only the ends, terribly split by the dye, were that hideous shade of orange. She would soon have to find a way to henna her hair again.

Facing Ethan's unshakable calm was in a way worse than confronting her father's cutting wrath. Postponing the encounter, she held her face up to the cooling evening wind that swept up off the dusky blue waters of the Chickahominy. And she thought of Terence's eyes—sometimes that same smoky blue. At St. James's Court she had seen the wavering eyes of the coward, the dull eyes of the jaded, and the watchful eyes of the politician. But always Terence's eyes had stared back at her, except for the irises—a cool, impenetrable blue. She had been almost eleven before she ever realized that the eyes of her childhood idol had no expression at all. Whatever thoughts did go on behind them, nothing came through.

Whatever his thoughts, she knew she was part of them. There was a bond uniting the two of them; a bond that could not be broken; a bond that she herself could not adequately explain.

A cowbell jingled, startling her out of her reverie. The chill of nightfall crept over the land, and she took reluctant steps toward the front entrance. Already candlelight seeped from beneath the ivy-framed door to fan across the rounded cobblestones laid before it. All her valid reasoning vanished. She could match wits with the liveliest of minds at George III's court; but how did one argue successfully with the simple, unyielding logic of a Quaker yeoman?

She pushed the door ajar to find him sitting on the stool before the hearth, which was cold with a banked fire. He did not look from the long jaeger rifle he cleaned. Next to him the betty lamp suspended from the stand cast flickering shadows and eddied smoke upward to soot the ceiling.

She closed the door behind her but moved no farther into the room. At last Ethan looked up, and the tallow's light flared over the puckered burn on his cheek, lending a frightening appearance to his otherwise pleasing countenance. "You've been out walking?"

"I—" Her hand tightened on the door's hasp behind her. Better to broach her request in the light of day. Not here, alone in the semidark with a man whom she still did not know despite having worked for him a full month. "It was hot . . . and I've finished all my work."

She stepped past him, making for her cubicle. "Stay," he said. She looked over her shoulder to find his dark eyes fastened on her. "Join me, mistress." He flung out a hand, indicating the rocker opposite the hearth from him. "I grow lonely of my company."

Warily she advanced further into the dimly lit room to take a seat in the proffered rush-bottomed chair. Sometimes she sensed that the man actually enjoyed baiting her. Too, she suspected the lout was not as slow-witted as he seemed.

Sitting stiffly, her spine never touching the chair's back, as she had been taught, she folded her roughened hands. Uneasily she searched for something to say.

The Quaker bent his head over the firearm, and he did not seem so formidable now. In fact, that side of his profile was almost handsome. His legs were stretched out before the hearth, his jackboots almost touching her skirts. She watched his hands deftly work the cleaning rod in and out of the flintlock's grooved bore. "I thought you didn't believe in the use of weapons?"

He never lifted his head. "I don't believe in violence.

But there is the necessity of game for food, is there not? And the necessity of protection from the snake that slithers across yonder floor?"

She twisted in the chair in time to see King George bound from a darkened corner to caper about the slender, serpentine form. Unheeding, the snake continued its slow, writhing progress across the plank flooring toward the small chink in the clay-mortared logs.

"A harmless creature, the grass snake," the big man commented and went back to his work.

Her hands gripped the rocker's arms, but she managed to say casually, "You would have me talk. I—"

"I would have thy company."

"I want to buy back my indenture papers," she said baldly.

He looked up, then set the rifle and cleaning rod on the rock hearth. "With what, mistress?"

"I will repay you—within the fortnight. You have my pledge."

"No."

"Why not?"

"Because it would be difficult to replace thee."

She leaned forward, her temper sparking. "A lie! The linen is badly washed, the food more often than not scorched, the spinning a shambles, the candles sputter and die!"

He grinned then. "As I said, it would be difficult to replace thee."

Her fist slammed down on the chair's arm. "You are cruel!"

He rose and stretched, displaying a muscle-roped body that needed no padding as did the courtiers of Buckingham House. "Thou doesn't know the cruelty men are capable of, mistress."

"Lady! Lady Jane! Now release me from my servitude, or—or I shall—"

"Run away?" he asked, reaching for the walnuts in the basket on the side table. "I've warned thee of the penalty—a whipping, which I think thee heartily needs."

Her chin tilted in a characteristically stubborn gesture. "If you can find me."

"If thee can survive the wilderness. Listen—hear the cry of the lynx? His jaws will tear thy soft flesh and crush thy bones as easily as this." The man's powerful knuckles effortlessly cracked a nut's hard shell. "And then there are the Indians. Not all of the tribes are friendly, mistress."

She sprang from her chair. "You do not frighten me!" But she knew he was right. Still, she did not give up. Instead she shifted her tactic, as a general would a military maneuver. Sophistry and charm would yet win the day over this backwoodsman!

Hands clasped demurely before her, she crossed to stand before him. From beneath the tangle of lashes her eyes beseeched his unyielding gaze. "You are in love with your neighbor's wife, yet you cannot have Susan. Do you deny it?"

If black-flecked eyes could darken, his did. "How does thee come by this knowledge?"

"Oh, Ethan," she said softly, "you cannot hide such a strong feeling as love." She could not bring herself to touch that scarred portion of his face and, instead, laid a helpless hand against his cambric shirt. "No more than I can."

One auburn brow arched over the outer corner of his eye. "No more than thee can—what?"

"Why, help loving you, master." Her lids lowered, as surely Susan's must when she was flustered. "It is torture for me to remain here—to see you every day, watch you climb the stairs to your bedroom every night—and yet know you love Susan. That is why I must leave. I am promised to another man, and—"

"And what?"

"And since you love Susan"—her words faltered beneath his dark gaze—"and since there can never be anything between us . . ."

A slow grin crooked his mouth. "My love for Susan is no reason to hold back the desire I and thee may feel for each other."

"But . . . but you're a Quaker. They—"

"I am a man, first, mistress." His fingers caught the tapered hand she laid on his chest, and his lips planted a warm kiss in her callused palm.

She jerked it away. "I am betrothed, sir!"

"Thee is my servant, mistress, and I thy master." He grinned openly now. His gaze perused the hollow of her throat, laid bare by the open collar. "And I wish for thee to warm my bed."

Her hand came up, but his was quicker, halting her intended slap in midarc. "You swine!"

"Careful, or I shall be tempted to use the hickory stick on thy lovely back."

"I will never warm your bed!"

"You will—now."

Something about the eyes, the laughter she saw lurking in their depths, eased her fears. "You would not make me?"

"Nay, mistress." He released her hand. "It is but the warming pan I speak of. The nights grow cold."

Despite her recent anger, dimples creased the unhealthy hollows beneath her cheekbones. "My virtue has been spared," she said wryly, "but I think my pride has been dented."

"Thee has too much pride, mistress."

She turned away from his woodsman's scrutiny. "Not enough. Or else I should not have lowered myself to the status of a servant."

"A servant's position is not without pride."

"How would you know?" she asked bitterly.

The walnut he cracked made the only noise in the room. Then, "Because I was an indentured servant when I came to the colonies."

She heard her bitterness echoed in his voice. She looked over her shoulder. "You jest."

"Scarcely. I came to the colonies on a convict ship."

Her breath whooshed down her throat. She faced him fully. "You were a convict?"

"Aye, mistress." He passed by her. "Now, about warming my bed . . ."

A convict! Dazed, she followed him as he took a candle from the stand and walked to the pitch-black well behind the stairs. No longer did she feel so safe. When he retrieved the long-handled pan and passed it to her, she almost jumped. Above the tallow's light, she saw his sober expression. "I would not harm thee, mistress."

"But you will not let me go, will you?"

"Nay, that I will not."

Chapter 11

The two men shared the same hair color, though the twenty-nine-year-old Ethan's was a deeper, darker red and the other man, at thirty-eight, was graying at the temples. They were both backwoodsmen and former riflemen with the elite Virginia Militia. And they also shared the same political viewpoint. At that moment the raw-boned Patrick Henry sat before Ethan's desk, writing furiously.

Ethan hitched his leg up on the casement of his bedroom window, where he could watch Jane as she hung the freshly washed linen on the hemp stretched between two live oaks. When the delegate for Hanover County had appeared on his doorstep, Ethan introduced him to Jane as a merchant interested in the indigo crop.

Ethan did not fully trust his maidservant. He had no doubt that she was a Tory. But was she also a spy? Her father could have chosen to plant her here as an intelligence mole for the Tory agents in Virginia. But which father would subject his daughter to such hardship? Lord Wychwood, possibly.

Ethan recalled the grains of sand he found on his desk top two days earlier. To whom had she been writing? A Tory agent? A frown furrowed Ethan's broken nose. Would she have reported Bram as a zealous rebel who needed watching? And how would she have smuggled her letter out? With an unsuspecting Susan? A reason, perhaps, for him to ride over and question Susan. No, an excuse to see her, to enjoy the comfort of her quiet laughter and gentle companionship.

His lids narrowed as an afternoon breeze buffeted Jane Lennox's skirts, silhouetting her body's deep indentations and delightful curves. Perhaps he was wrong about the pampered young woman who was now his bondswoman. Perhaps the letter was bound for this Terence she had spoken of during her illness.

"Ethan!"

Ethan looked back at the self-taught lawyer who, though he spoke with a Piedmont twang, was known as the Son of Thunder for his electrifying orations in the House of Burgesses. "I'm sorry—did thee say something, Patrick?"

"Twice now." The delegate laid the quill down. "I've finished. I think everything of import that took place at the Continental Congress is on those pages. Congress has voted to support Massachusetts if Britain tries to use force. It's best you warn the Committees of Correspondence across Virginia to start preparing for war in case of British attack on other Massachusetts towns."

Ethan grunted. "War is already here, Patrick. Last week in Williamsburg a Negro was tarred and feathered for expressing Tory sentiments—some of Uriah Wainwright's vigilante work."

"Fanatics like him only hurt our cause." Henry stretched his lanky arms above his head. Observing his friend's preoccupation, he said gravely, "The Sons of Liberty in Boston report another spy out of Gage's nest, Ethan. Goes by the code name of Ahmad. Your dispatch carriers operating between the Northern and Southern colonies should be made aware of this spy."

Ethan grinned. "I'm beginning to think that serving with the Virginia Militia is easier than this drawing-room diplomacy of yours."

"But not as valuable. What you did in London—learning the names of the Tories entrenched in the colonies' governmental assemblies—proved your worth to the Committee of Correspondence."

Henry rose, clanging on the desk the tip of the scabbard beneath his coat's skirt, and crossed to stand next to Ethan at the window. He laid a companionable hand on the taller man's shoulder. "In Williamsburg, Ethan, there is a welter of skulduggery, rancor, and gossip. Would you think about finding a reason to go to the capital more often?"

Ethan's black eyes turned to the window again, seeking the feminine figure below. Come General Assembly and Public Times, dare he leave her here to create her own political intrigue? Dare he take her with him? Despite her present state of unattractiveness, he could imagine the scandal that would arise in Williamsburg at the idea of a man with so young a maidservant living in the same house. Immorality would be charged from the Wren college building at one end of Duke of Gloucester all the way to the capitol at the other; hardly conducive to his Quaker's image or the low profile he needed to keep.

Jane Lennox was going to be nothing but trouble for him.

"That is the Tory maid you bought?" Henry asked, following the direction of his friend's gaze.

"Aye."

"Can she be trusted, Ethan? There's Dickey Lee and Daniel Franks and the others you are in contact with to think about."

Ethan fixed a sardonical eye on the lawyer. "Should I tar and feather her as the more conservative Whigs would do? Or brand her with a *T*, as the rabid Uriah Wainwrights of the colonies prefer?"

"You could marry her," Patrick said, following Ethan's gaze. "That would solve any problems."

He laughed ruefully. "That would only be the start of my problems, Patrick."

No, his wife would be sweet-tempered like Susan. Small and soft, instead of tall, taut, and slender; obliging instead of distracting and unpredictable; submissive where Jane Lennox challenged. Fragile and loving and gentle. Not a contentious shrew.

Chapter 12

Posing as an ordinary surveyor in brown clothes and a red handkerchief about his neck, the spy Ahmad left Boston on foot. He went by way of Charlestown and passed through Cambridge, a nice town, it seemed, with a college built of brick. The weather was cold but dry for October, and he made good time.

With his surveyor's instruments as a ruse, badly rusted though they were, he made a pretense at charting when he was actually drawing road maps and terrain sketches. And all the while he watched and listened. In the course of five days he counted twenty wagonloads of flour that passed from Marblehead to Worcester. The rebels were laying in supplies of food and munitions. Tools were being made at Menotomy and pickaxes at Mystic. Obviously the skilled American axe-man was a colonial product, not a European import.

Gage wanted roads and distances from town to town, as well as the situation and nature of the country—the streams, woods, hills, defensible places in towns, and local supplies of food, forage, straw, and extra horses.

And most of all, he wanted the mood of the people reported.

Ahmad reached Watertown without being suspected and, before making the last leg of his trip, paused for dinner at the crowded tavern of Jonathan Brewer. The agent quietly took a seat at the board in the taproom and mentally reviewed his report while he waited for the young Negro servantwoman to see to him.

Gage was not going to be happy. Plymouth, Marblehead, Worcester—the towns could easily turn out fifteen thousand minutemen. The rebels already had thirty-eight field guns, most of them at Salem and Concord, along with twelve brass cannon.

The spy's attention was drawn back to the dark-paneled, smoke-congested tavern room. The owner, Brewer, and a dozen or so men, mostly farmers, were gathered about the kegs at the bar, whose rear wall shelved pewter tankards, salt-glazed pitchers, and long-stemmed glassware. The lowered voices, deep in conversation that mixed with laughter, aroused Ahmad's suspicion, for he was quickly learning that innkeepers were often retired militia officers.

The sentence fragment, ". . . adequate supply of tar and feathers laid in for anyone suspected of harboring lobsterbacks," brought a tightening to his lean lips. Whigs. He had walked into a rebel nest.

The neglect of Gage! The general had developed no spy system at all. There should be some way for Tory sympathizers to identify themselves. And there should be a dossier on the location of Tory homes when the need to go underground arose. There was neither a code nor cipher, and no one other than himself who knew how to make them.

When the young Negress, large of hip but with a gazellelike grace, came to his table, he ignored the wide white grin she flashed. "Good cheer to yuh, massa," she purred, eyeing his tawny locks. "What's yo' want?"

He perused the bill of fare. "Planked shad—and grog to drink." No patriot ever ordered tea.

"Yo' shor that's all," she persisted. Here obviously was a man who would know how to handle her . . . who understood the ways of a woman . . . who wouldn't bide by that "unnatural stuff" the white folks' Bible frowned on.

"I'm—" He broke off as he saw the chocolate-brown eyes flare. His gaze followed hers to his set of maps. Most people would expect them to be surveyor's maps. But the uneducated woman, in that atmosphere of general suspicion and with all the talk of spies and tar and feathering, she had jumped to the right conclusion—that he was a spy. He could see it in the way her eyes suddenly narrowed.

"Yassuh, massa, I'll see to yo' order."

Unobtrusively he rose and followed her sashaying hips as she hurried outside to the kitchen in back of the tavern. In the dark his silent footsteps on the marl path gave no warning until he caught up with her. By then it was too late. He gagged her mouth from behind with the red handkerchief. The edge of his left hand chopped the woman's windpipe. He let her slip gently down on all fours. With a gurgled gasp, her hand reached for her throat.

Terence straddled the woman. His left hand he placed against the back of the Negress's head. He gave one short, brutal twist to the neck, backward, upward, and sideways. The crack of the cervical column was barely audible against the muted laughter from within the tavern.

The dead woman's face was twisted to the side, her

tongue protruding slightly between her lips, her lids wide, her eyes staring sightlessly at the youpon holly just beyond the marl path. Brewer, the proprietor, did not find his servantwoman until dawn when the early gray light exposed her awkwardly positioned body within the concealing shrubbery.

Chapter 13

A fire roared in the monstrous brick fireplace that almost girded one wall of the kitchen. The room was a good sixty degrees hotter than the outside temperature on that mildly warm October day. Jane left the roast turning on the spit and went to stand at the Dutch door, using the apron to wipe away the perspiration that trickled down her neck. The brilliant sunlight shimmered the inviting river beyond into a purple haze. Nearer, the cool shade of plum trees ladened with reddish brown leaves beckoned. Beyond the trees and the various outbuildings stretched fields of what looked like prairie grass, though the stalks were purple red—Ethan Gordon's indigo fields.

Her eyes easily picked his form out from among the

three indentured men as they took the last cutting of indigo for the season. It wasn't just his height that betrayed him, for Josiah was tall, but thin. Icabod was, of couse, squat and adorably pudgy. One-eyed Peter was as strapped with muscles as Ethan, but much shorter of stature. And Ethan, who had a good spread to his shoulders, moved with a litheness, swung his sickle with a grace that the others lacked.

King George raced over her shoes and streaked into the kitchen. She sighed and turned back inside. The midday respite the colonists called nooning was past, but there was still the butter to finish churning before she began the late-afternoon meal. She cleared the table while King George sniffed about its legs, his black nose wrinkling. At last he found a few morsels of grits. Burned as usual.

"I cook and I bake, King George, and I get nothing for it!"

"I get indigestion."

Jane spun about. Ethan lounged in the doorway, his deep-red hair illuminated by the fire's light that fortunately shadowed the ravaged cheek. He had a habit of surprising her, walking as silently as the few Indians whom she occasionally spotted from afar cutting across the plantation. Like those nearly naked savages, he possessed an erect, straight-stepping carriage.

"I warned you I couldn't cook."

"So thee did. But then I judged thee would get tired of eating thine own food, mistress."

He straightened and stepped inside. As he drew closer she could see that his coarse homespun shirt was damp with sweat and that his fringed buckskin britches were grass-stained—and tight-fitting. Before she knew what he was about, his forefinger reached out to the small scar that now clefted her square chin. "Thou has been marked as myself, mistress."

She shivered, recalling the old Hindu again. Now both she and Ethan were marked. "And it's your fault—you—"

"Master," he supplied, unruffled. He smiled, an engaging smile that transformed the sun-weathered face. "And now, if thee has water, mistress . . ."

She was hot and sweaty and tired. And she had never worked so hard nor such long hours in her life. She had never worked! "Do not call me mistress. My father was at one time Lord Mayor of London and now is Lord—"

"And my father is Lord knows who," he said with irresistible, good-natured self-mockery.

She swung away and flounced over to sit on the stool before the churn. Furiously she plied the dasher up and down. It had been One-eyed Peter who patiently demonstrated how the churn and dasher were used. The Quaker never offered to help; rather, it seemed he found in her incompetence substantiation of his poor opinion of her.

She slid a glance in his direction as she lifted the churn's lid to peak at her progress. How far could she push this mild-mannered colonial? "There is no water for you. I haven't had time to draw any more."

"Who is Terence?"

The dasher and lid slipped from her hands, sloshing the golden globs of butter that had risen to the top. Plucking the wooden stick from the buttermilk, he restored it to her numbed fingers. He hunched down before her, his black eyes on a level with hers. "Who is Terence, mistress?"

"Why would you know?"

King George took the opportunity to scale Ethan's knee and perch on the man's shoulder, the coon's favorite place. "His name trembled on thine lips when thee was ill with the pox."

She set the churn from her and rose, nervously smoothing her apron over her skirt. "I'll draw your water."

She swished aside her dress, and he obligingly stood to

follow her. As she made her way along the path to the well behind the kitchen, she knew he was behind her though his moccasined feet made not a sound on the pine-needled trail. He was a simple man, she reflected; a man of the earth rather than of the intellect like Walpole, Dr. Johnson, or the American colonist Franklin. And because he was a Quaker, she had no fear of him. Still, as she leaned over the flagstoned well to haul on the pulley, she felt his presence as a powerful force.

"You know, mistress," he said, lazing against the well's cedar post, "Abraham's servant prayed for God to help him find a wife for Isaac."

He paused, stroking the coarse, gray-brown fur of the coon who still clung precariously to his shoulder. "When at the well the maiden Rebecca offered both the thirsty servant and his camel water, he knew that his prayer had been answered. He had found the wife he sought for his master."

The gall of the man! A religious dissenter and a scarred backwoodsman to boot! Pity the poor woman who became his wife. She shoved the oaken bucket at his broad chest. "But I am offering water to neither your camel nor your coon!"

"And I am not seeking a wife," Ethan replied, his dark eyes dancing.

Over the days that followed she pondered the hopeless situation she had contrived for herself. She could run away, but if she were caught without her indenture papers she would be thrown in the stocks at the very least. Even should she find where Ethan had put the papers, she would have to forge his signature to set herself free.

Supposing she decided to risk running away without the papers, she did not even know where to run. To Boston, where more and more British troops were arriving every week, if what Icabod told her was true? And then to

Quebec? And if Terence were not there? Would she return to England?

Her fingers paused in plucking the wild raspberries, and she lifted her head, looking about her for what was really the first time. Overhead a flock of geese winged southward in their *V* formation. About her the scent of the raspberries and pine needles freshened the air. A short distance away the Chickahominy lazily swished its indigo swath of water against the sloping banks. Would she leave this for London's soot and smoke and fog, for an arranged marriage with a man of Lord Sandwich's ilk?

Perhaps she and Terence could start a life here. There was something about the wilderness simplicity that rendered dreams incorruptible.

The beauty of the unseasonably warm October day beckoned her from her task of berry-picking. The sky shimmered a bright blue with a soft autumn haze lingering on the horizon. The leaves of the live oaks and black walnuts and sycamores had already changed to a brilliant red and were beginning to fall.

"'Tis a late Indian summer," Icabod said, startling her. He laid his sickle against a live oak and squatted next to her. "If ye peer through narrowed eyes, lass, the corn shucks will turn into tepees."

She laughed and did as he said.

"And if ye listen, ye can hear the falling leaves rustle as Indians dance about their campfires. 'Tis the Indians' war paint that has rubbed off on the leaves and colored them red," he finished with his hearty laughter.

"Methinks your imagination has become unhinged in this wilderness," she teased.

He rose to go, clapping his hat on his balding head against the sun's glare, and looked down at her with sympathy in his drooping eyes. "The colonies are a good place, lass, if ye give them half a chance. And the master—give him a chance, also."

The master! Up until the night she broached the subject of leaving to Ethan Gordon, she had seen very little of him. He had seldom entered the main house during the day when she swept and dusted and cooked and changed the bed linen at the due times. Only in the early mornings and late afternoons when she served breakfast and dinner did their paths cross.

But now—now that she must return each evening and climb the stairs to his bedroom to place the warming pan, filled with hot coals, between the muslin sheets—her relationship with the man had taken on an intimacy that bothered her. He spoke no untoward words; he spoke rarely. Yet she felt his dark gaze following her up the stairs each evening.

Once, though she had not found him below, she had proceeded to his bedroom with the pan. But as she absently ran the pan over the sheets, concentrating on not scorching them, he appeared in the doorway. Both of them started, surprised at the other's presence. He was bare-chested, his shirt slung over his shoulder, and she stared, fascinated by the springy black hair that etched an inverted triangle across his swarthy chest.

His bare chest had recalled the black slaves' naked bodies, and a sinful thrill had rippled up her spine. The hair that raced across his flesh made the smooth, sleek statues of Greek gods seem effeminate. Collecting herself, she had drawn the warmed sheets over the feather mattress and slipped past him. But that moment the two of them had shared in his bedroom lingered uncomfortably in her mind.

Irritated with her wandering thoughts, Jane returned to berry-picking. Then, as if Icabod's story had rubbed off on her, three dusky Indians—joined by five more—materialized at the far edge of a fallow squash field. The Indians did not walk single file across the land, as she had seen others do a few times in the past; rather they seemed to stalk toward her, keeping to the shadows of the trees that encroached on the field.

Where was Ethan? Of course—he had ridden over to the Fairmonts'. To feast his eyes, no doubt, on soft, sweet Susan. And Peter—Josiah—Icabod? In the far fields, bundling the threshed wheat. Panic-stricken, she dropped the basket of berries and, clutching her long skirts above her ankles, sprinted for the house. She might just make it to the house before the Indians caught up with her.

By the time she reached the front door, her windpipe was sealed like a tomb and her breath was labored. Barely had she plucked Ethan's long rifle from its mount above the mantel when shadows darkened the front doorway. She whirled, the rifle cradled in her arms, the barrel leveled at the half-naked forms that blotted out the sunlight. She didn't even know how to load the bloody weapon. But she hoped the Indians couldn't know of her ignorance.

"Don't." It was all her tongue could manage. The barrel trembled between her sweaty palms.

The Indians, their faces a dark blur in the dim room, looked at each other, gestured at her, and muttered among themselves in what seemed to Jane like threatening grunts. One in the forefront, who wore a lady's plumed hat with a blanket draped about his lower torso, stepped forward. A short knife glittered in his hand.

She jerked the rifle up to her chest and squinched her eyes closed. Her lungs heaved and collapsed like a bellows. She silently prayed that the rifle was primed.

"No!"

Her lids snapped open. Ethan shouldered past the Indians gathered in the doorway. Numb, she watched him advance on her and gently pry the rifle from her hands and set it against the fireplace. "They've come to help bundle the wheat—in exchange for some of it."

He spoke something she did not understand to the one

nearest her, and the Indians faded from the doorway as silently as they had come.

She started to tremble. Belatedly. When her knees sagged, he caught her waist and pressed her against his length in support. "Thee is much thinner, mistress," he drawled, his warm breath stirring the orange-tipped tendrils that lay damply against her neck.

"I hate it here!" she wept. "Danger . . . always danger . . . always work . . . always alone." Hating her weakness, she still cried copiously, uncontrollably. Susan would have known better. She wouldn't have trembled and cried at the sight of the Indians.

Ethan bent and scooped his arms beneath the backs of her legs and cradled her against the breadth of his massive chest. "I know . . . I know," he whispered against her temple as he carried her across the room. "I felt the same way myself once a long time ago."

He settled in the rocking chair with her slanted across his lap. She didn't know which surprised her more—that the rocking chair held the considerable weight of the two of them or that she experienced an inexplicable peace settling over her soul. To be held, comforted—it was a feeling of security, that basic nurturance every child needs, that she could not remember experiencing. Her father preoccupied with politics, her mother—Jane wasn't sure. She suspected a lack of emotional stability in her mother. But then she couldn't remember clearly the time before her mother's death.

"I can't imagine you being afraid of anything," she murmured into the fringe of his leather shirt that emitted earth's sweet-pungent smell.

"I assure thee I was," he said in that curious mixture of Irish brogue and soft colonial drawl. "I came to the colonies as a boy of eight. A skinny, underfed, undersized runt."

"And I can't imagine you ever being underfed or under-sized," she said with a chiming laugh.

"Ah, but I was. In Dublin I had been arrested for thievery—it was the only way orphans could survive those hard times. I faced the gallows at Kilmainham Gaol when a nobleman, a proprietor of a small grant west of the Pennsylvania Colony, offered to sponsor a number of convicts. I was one of the lucky ones chosen." He grew silent with his own reflections.

"And what happened?"

Almost like a pillow, his chest shifted against her cheek with the movement of his shrug. "Fortunately I was bound out to a Quaker couple, Ezra and Miriam. They sacrificed to send me to William and Mary's preparatory school in the winter months. And I was afraid of everything. Of the dark forests. Of the well-to-do planters' sons at college. Of the silent, fierce-looking Indians."

And *he* was fierce-looking, she thought. And roughly handsome with the sharply planed cheeks and broken nose. "And then?" she prompted.

He chuckled, his breath rustling the ugly tendrils of hennaed hair. She thought how deliciously disturbing his laughter was. It tickled all the way to the pit of her stomach. "Why, I grew, mistress. And grew and grew." His lips brushed away the tendrils to linger on the delicate flesh that planed her temple.

What he was doing was dangerously distressing. "How . . . how did you come to Virginia?" His lips nuzzled the black sweep of her brow, and she knew what was coming but could not help herself.

"Governor Dunmore awarded me this parcel for my scouting services with the Virginia Riflemen," he said.

Without her realizing what was happening her face turned up to that bronzed one so close. He kissed her lingeringly, softly, gently. He tasted her mouth, learning its shape and texture. His lips . . . they were warm . . . and the way they moved over hers . . . a pleasant creamy feeling eddied through her. Restlessly her fingers plucked his shirt's fringe. They itched to tunnel through the thickness of that red hair, to—

"Oh my goodness," she gasped, drawing back. "What are you doing?"

His lips twitched, but a self-anger played there also. "Thee has never been kissed, mistress?"

She had waited all these years for Terence. For her there had been no man, no kisses, no fondling—not even at St. James's Court where all manner of licentious intrigue went on behind the royal backs of His Majesty and the queen.

With a panicky need to escape she pushed herself to an unsteady stance. But she just stood looking at the man seated before her, his marred face mirroring wonderment.

She was intensely aware of Ethan from her frazzled carrot curls to the tingling tips of her toes. Her fingers uncertainly touched her lips. She wished he would kiss her again. Not just wished—ached. Ached for the completion of the kiss. She fled the room.

Chapter 14

Ethan's eyes scanned the letter the dispatch rider from Williamsburg had brought that morning. Ostensibly the letter from Massachusetts and Georgia's agent in London, Benjamin Franklin, was a light, newsy one.

> *Edmund Burke speaks in Parliament for conciliation with America, but his proposals are turned down. Mrs. Caroline Howard, Lord Howard's sister, has been playing a decisive game of chess with me. Like her brother, she, too, hopes that Great Britain and her American colonies can settle their dispute before events reach a point from which they cannot be reversed.*

Between the lines that were penned in the common yellowish brown ink Ethan knew he would find more important information. Fire, which would bring words written in lime juice or milk to light, would have no effect on Franklin's invisible ink. But potassium chloride would work wonders with litmus paper.

Below his bedroom Ethan could hear the *thwack* and *thump* of Jane's loom. Warning enough that she was otherwise occupied. He set to work with the chemical compound, silently cursing when some words did not develop or others washed out. But by the time he finished enough of the secret missive remained for him to forward its major import on to Dickey Lee in Williamsburg.

The last of the message brought another muttered oath from Ethan.

> *Intercepted letter to British Secretary of State*
> *received from your Lord Dunmore,*
> *emphasizing prudent measure should be taken*
> *now that the Virginia Colony has raised and*
> *trained militia. Dunmore suggests that*
> *gunpowder stored in Williamsburg magazine*
> *be removed.*

Hell and damnation! That explained the man-of-war, the *Fowey*, that had been reported standing in the York River off Williamsburg.

Ethan slumped back in the chair, his legs stretched out before him, and ran his fingers through his long, thick red hair, mussing the queue's arrangement. Patrick had been right. He would have to spend more time in Williamsburg, though the fledgling Committee of Correspondence there was not developed to the extent of that in Philadelphia's or Revere's in Boston.

From below came again the *thump* of the batten on the

weft of the loom, reminding him of another problem. His maidservant. The Lady Jane Lennox. Though she was performing her tasks better than he would have expected, and had admirably demonstrated a courage he had not suspected the day Mattaponi and his Powhatans visited, she was still the Lady Jane Lennox. She was not some maid to be tumbled in the hay. And yet that was what was too often on his mind.

She was thinner, with callused hands, strained features. That cool composure she maintained had finally cracked with Mattaponi's visit. And the cracking had not delighted him as he had expected. Instead, fingers of some curious emotion tightened his heart. He could picture the way she moved—like damned royalty with that proud walk and imperious tilt of her head. But it was her inner fire—that taunting spirit that so annoyed, so distracted, him from his daily work. And her chiming laugh—it did strange things to him.

For years he had told himself that if he could not have Susan he would wait to take to wife someone so similar that his loss would be muted. But the Lady Jane Lennox was no pale counterfeit. She and Susan were nothing alike. She could not be a substitution for Susan.

Yet he found himself drawn to this tall, haughty woman . . . found himself watching her as she walked from the well to the kitchen . . . found himself wanting to glimpse the occasional childlike sparkle that peaked through the veil of her damnably thick eyelashes . . . found himself foolishly bending to inhale the fragrance of fall's wild flowers or to run a finger along the downy cattails she set in vases about his house.

He reminded himself that her station in life was too far above his; that without the luxuries to which she was accustomed she would become miserable and make her husband wretched; that she was committed to another man.

Cabin fever was all it was. Obviously what he needed was to take a wife. He was as randy as a pastured bull. Come May and the General Assembly he would give Jane her freedom and rid himself of her. Then he would begin his search in earnest for a woman to take to wife.

Chapter 15

The American espionage network in Boston began as a volunteer group of amateur secret agents. Paul Revere, a silversmith who first set up the American intelligence net, and about thirty others held regular meetings at the Green Dragon Tavern.

This broke the one fundamental rule in all such organizations—that various agents must not know one another. True, all took an oath at every meeting, swearing to reveal their work to no one except John Hancock, Samuel Adams, and one or two others. And true, most of the spies were well-known citizens, established businessmen or tradesmen. But inevitably the personnel changed as a member would have to flee, either from imminent Tory persecution, British confiscation of his home, or because his espionage was exposed by British spies who kept dossiers on such myriad matters as waterfront pubs and dockside whores.

Ahmad was the most successful of the British spies, for he managed to infiltrate these Boston Sons of Liberty. With his gift for languages, it was easy enough to assume the Yankee dialect. And with his charm for women, it was even easier to convince the middle-aged wife of one of the lesser members of the American espionage network to hire him as a tutor for her two sons. That was how it all started.

The Yankee spy was a grocer named Horgan. Ahmad had readily found the rebel spy's house, spotting above the door the traditional sign of grocers—three sugar loaves. Horgan was not in that afternoon, but the wife, a little woman in a starched ruffled cap, greeted him cordially. He introduced himself by the name Nathaniel Rand and explained that he was a schoolmaster who left South Carolina to seek employment in Boston.

"Alas," Horgan's wife told him briskly, "few are lucky to be employed, what with the British Port Bill and the times being what they are. Best you hie yourself back to the Carolinas, Mr. Rand."

His eyes locked longing with hers before his lids lowered shyly. "The colonies farther south do not hold education in such high esteem as you Bostonians." His palms lifted in a hopeless gesture. "But, as you said, madam, it really is a futile effort, what with the times."

She hired him.

He lived in an attic room of the house, which reeked of fried fish and boiled cabbage. The two sons, aged eight and ten, were abominable monsters who shared their mother's prodigious lack of intellect. But Ahmad was able to watch the comings and goings of Horgan.

If, after the rotund little grocer left, the Tory spy's gaze seemed to dwell with a futile infatuation on the myopic wife—well, naturally, her innate generosity and kindheart-edness led her to do what she could for the poor bachelor.

And if at dinner the spy found it difficult to control his patriotic outbursts at the indignity Boston citizens suffered under the rude lobsterbacks, the grocer could well under-stand. From there it was only a matter of weeks until the Horgans were including the good-looking tutor in their small but close circle of friends.

With his droll wit and vociferous resentment of British tyranny, the lonely tutor found consolation in these Yankee bosoms—and, at last, a hint by the good grocer that he might be better able to help his country than by simply edu-cating the ignorant. The grocer's sly nudge in the ribs was followed by a mention of the Sons of Liberty, and Ahmad innocently responded with the expected question: "What can I, a mere tutor, do?"

Soon after that, with Horgan's sponsorship, Ahmad was accepted into that intelligence realm that frequented the Green Dragon Tavern. The leaders of the Sons of Liberty naturally held reservations about all newcomers. But then Ahmad knew that, with patience, he would be welcomed with complete trust; that information could quite often be gleaned from those who let things slip due to sheer self-im-portance.

He bided his time, sitting for the most part unnoticed in the tavern's wainscotted back room where a welcome fire blazed against the bitter winter-night cold. Silently he lis-tened to the general discussion among the members of the spy net—the vain and wealthy merchant, John Hancock; Dr. Joseph Warren, the probable leader of the ring; Samuel Adams, the rabble-rouser whose red cloak was invariably rumpled and spotted and his wig askew. The last was the most dangerous of the American spies, for Adams had the talent to inflaming the colonists through his pen, and to dis-tort events without actually lying.

Yet it was the shipper-merchant Hancock the spy found most cunning. Ahmad would not be surprised to learn that Hancock, who had quantities of tea chests stored in one of his many warehouses, had instigated the now famous Boston Tea Party for the sole sake of driving up the price of tea.

It was these three men, Ahmad deemed, whom Gage would be most interested in when the time arrived to permanently crush the rebellion fomenting in Boston. And that would be soon.

Chapter 16

A minor annoyance that was just the bud of the deep-growing tap root set off the argument between two people who for the past months had been warily circling one another like fighting bantams.

Jane finished playing the sentimental parlor ballad, "Rural Felicity," and launched into "Tally Ho." Her fingers flitted like fireflies over the harpsichord's keyboard, while One-eyed Peter played his fife to simulate the horn fanfares of the Virginia fox hunters. Icabod punctuated the fanfares with a jut of his parrot's nose, and Josiah, grinning widely, enjoyed the camaraderie of the impromptu gathering.

February's ice-cold rain had drummed out the day's work, to the delight of the three men who ringed the harpsichord. Ethan, though, was alone in his room—had been ever since that Powhatan, Mattaponi, appeared at the kitchen door that morning, asking in guttural tones Jane barely understood, to see Ethan. After nooning was past, she finally took the opportunity to fondle the keys, and one by one the three men drifted in from the kitchen, drawn by the lilt of the music.

The music was a balm to her lacerated spirit and lonely soul. The winter rains mired the roads, making them impassable, and the isolation could drive a woman to madness. With no visitors to worry about, she had not bothered to cut or rehenna her hair. Now the thick black mane cascaded in an unruly, unmanageable tangle that was dangerous prey to the candle's leaping flame, and she was forced to restrain the willful hair with a leather thong.

Where now were the diamond pins, the velvet ribbons, the loops of pearls that once graced her lustrous tresses?

With less work to do in the winter, her weight was returning, her face regaining its softer contours. She lifted her face now as her fingers stroked the keys; her eyes closed to savor this soothing product of civilization. She was unaware of the hauntingly beautiful expression she presented to the three men. And cared not. She was lost in the rapturous moment that took her away from the harsh reality that constituted her present life.

"The four of you have nothing better to do?"

The music ceased abruptly. Jane and the three men all turned toward the staircase, where the lower steps were just visible from the parlor. Dressed in a collarless, faded-blue kersey shirt, Ethan stood on the first step, his brown hands braced on the balustrade. His knuckles were ridged with white. She raised her eyes, colliding with his hot stare, and she experienced, as happened quite often these days, the force of its impact. Beneath his half-lidded gaze, she felt like butter left to melt in the sun. If his eyes did not soon release hers, she would be a little puddle on the puncheon floor.

After the night he had held her in the rocking chair, she was different, vastly altered in some subtle way. Under his kiss, she had softened, had yielded. Here was a man she could no longer dismiss with a sneer.

Under Ethan's annoyed glare, the three field hands sheepishly shuffled out of the parlor as they suddenly recalled pressing duties. Only she was left to face the big man. Guilt—and fear at his displeasure—whistled down her dry throat. She had been playing the instrument he had brought by wagon all the way from Williamsburg—for the sole use of his intended wife!

"Thy frivolity could better be directed," he snarled. She could almost hear his teeth grinding as he turned from her.

Frivolity!

For a long moment she sat rooted to one spot, the anger in her building. Did anyone in those backwoods even know what frivolity was? Her stunned gaze focused on her reddened hands that rubbed each other in agitation.

Without considering the rashness of her act, she let her feet march her up the stairs. She pushed the door open. Ethan, his back three quarters to her, leaned over the desk. His Bible lay open, and his forefinger seemed to scan verses as he periodically jotted something on another sheet. Sensing her presence, he spun in the chair. She could have sworn a guilty look flashed across his dark face, instantly replaced by one of righteous anger as he shoved back the slatted chair and rose to his enormous height.

Her intestines knotted before this visual sign of wrath, the way she quelled as a child before her father's explosive temper. Fear fired her words—unplanned, heedlessly spoken. "God-fearing man!" Her finger pointed contemptuously at his Bible. "You fear everything. Afraid to fight, afraid to rebel against wrongs, afraid to take a stand."

He advanced on her, and her tongue babbled on in alarm. "You're not much of a man at all. In fact, you make me ill." She retreated a step. "Your hypocrisy." The doorknob thrust against her hips. Closed! "Lusting after another man's wife!"

"Shut up," he said in a dangerously quiet voice, drawing perilously close to her all the while.

"She's not yours to have"—her breath sobbed raspingly in her throat—"so you would vent your lust on me!"

He came up short. His eyes blinked. "Lust . . . after . . ." Laughter. "That's what . . . thee . . . would like."

She hit then, her fist catching him square in the flat solid wall of his stomach.

He grunted in surprise, and the laughter faded from his strongly delineated lips. Then his large hands shot out, easily cupping her head. She dangled in his grasp, her shoes barely touching the floor, and she was forced to cling to his yard-wide shoulders.

Still, she spewed vituperations that had about as much effect as an axe cutting silk. "A pox on you—you oaf. You son of a sow. You—"

His fingers anchored in the abundant wealth of her hair and tilted her face to match the slant of his hard mouth. His angry kiss silenced her incoherent words, mashing her lips against her teeth. Uncomprehendingly, she welcomed the muted pain. His massive body flattened hers against the door, and she was intensely aware of the thick shaft that pushed against the soft cushion of her stomach.

Then she forgot even that phenomenon as her arms encircled the hard-columned neck. She had been achingly waiting for this. Since his last kiss months before. Too many months.

When his mouth opened and his tongue stroked the soft inner tissue of her lower lip, then shot forward to caress her paralyzed tongue, a thousand summer suns burnished her insides. His tongue thrust deeper, as if it would impale her—

and she wanted it to! She heard her own rapid breathing; smelled the musky heat of his body; felt her veins engorged by the sudden rush of blood; tasted the deliciously salty flavor of his wet mouth. Never had she been so acutely alive! And she wanted that life to be crushed from her by this man who had bought her body.

Please . . . let him do what he will. . . . Please— Was that her voice murmuring unconsciously?

He buried his face in the hollow of her neck. His beard-stubbled jaw rasped her skin, taunting her. "Jane . . . Jane . . . thee is a veritable shrew." His lips caressed her collarbone where it peaked above the drawstringed blouse.

Yes . . . yes. Don't let it end.

"An ill-tempered wench." His fingers found the drawstring, and the blouse veed open.

The translucent mounds of her breasts lay revealed. His tongue flicked the alabaster flesh. Her head tilted back, making it accessible even more for her master's perusal. "I should lash thee for thy disrespect," he rusked.

"Aye," she whispered, wanting the touch of his hand. Cream filled the hollows of her insides that were being dug out by this terrible want. In answer his hand cupped one heavy breast, taking the aching, dusky nipple into his mouth. The gentle suction stirred her from the induced languor. "Ethan . . . 'tis wrong. . . ." Yet her hands pressed his head against her softness. "I am a . . . virgin. . . ." Oh, dear God, what he was doing felt so good. ". . . could make me with child."

He lifted his head. Her lips wrapped around an *O*, and she looked up into black eyes glazed with passion. The back of his arm wiped across those eyes. "Jane . . . I'm sorry, Jane."

She heard the unsteadiness in his voice and knew that her legs were just as unsteady. If his body released its press on her by only an inch, she would slump ignominiously at his boots. She managed a cool, reproving look. "As well you should be!"

At that he threw back his head and laughed. "Ah, Jane! Thee wanted it as much as I did."

Her insides jelled. "Not until you made me want it," she said, each word spat through clenched teeth.

His smile waned. He stepped back, and she grasped the doorknob to keep from collapsing. "Thee is right," he said, turning away. His mammoth shoulders bowed. "Go away. Go on. Leave me, mistress."

That night Jane huddled against the seeping cold in the narrow bed that was too short for her unless she slept in a fetal position. Her toes were icicles, and she would swear it was because she was so abysmally tall that the blood never found its way to her feet. In the kitchen a fire burned, but the warmth that wafted down the short expanse of hall to her room was negated by the frigid draft that whistled under and between the kitchen's Dutch door.

In the dark she listened to the burning wood's heated resin pop and sizzle in the fireplace, while discordance rustled through her sleepy thoughts. She knew it was completely illogical to be bound beyond recall to someone she had seen so few times over the years. But fifty years could pass, and that bond would still be strong. As strong as the bond of blood.

She was bound to Terence by the shared past of her childhood and the future of her womanhood.

And Ethan? "He brings out my baser instincts," she mumbled against the blanket that scratched her chin. For her, Terence represented security. And Ethan, danger. She felt nothing for the backwoodsman—at least nothing until he kissed her.

Chagrined at her feminine weakness, she burrowed deeper in her blanket, then restlessly shifted on the thin bed ticking. Would Terence never come for her? His lean hand-some face was emblazoned on the back of her eyelids, when her name was spoken.

She sprang upright, clutching the quilt to her neck. Orange shreds of firelight flickered about a man's form. In the dark she was barely able to distinguish the intruder as Ethan. His arms were laden with something she could not make out.

"What do you want?" she managed to get out.

"When the ink froze in its well tonight," he said, mov-ing unerringly about her room, "I realized you and the others would need more blankets to keep warm."

So, even this late he worked at his desk. She was chagrined anew that paperwork so easily took precedence over any thought he might have spared to that afternoon and what almost happened between them. But then did he not own her? She meant little more to him than his other indentured servants. He only wanted her service in a dif-ferent way!

The scraping of flint could be heard, then a small flame flared on the candle's wick. Its light slowly filled the room and highlighted his face above it. He set the tinder and flint on the metal trunk that served as her nightstand and looked about him at the sparseness of the room—the dilapidated washstand with its ceramic pitcher and base on top and the porcelain chamber pot below; the hand-hewn press, little re-sembling her elaborately carved armoires that had bulged with watered silks and shining satins, with pearl-buckled pumps and beribboned hats.

"Quite bare for a woman accustomed to bedroom fire-places and woolen bed curtains to keep out cold drafts."

"You've brought the blankets," she said testily. "You can leave."

Shaking out a blanket's folds, he leaned over her to drape the cover across her legs. "I wanted to talk to thee for a moment, mistress."

Laughter crinkled lines at the corners of his eyes, and she snapped, "What is so funny, pray tell?"

"Thy night cap is out of kilter." His large hands caught its dainty edges, adjusting it about her face. "Do not henna thy hair again, mistress. Nor cut it."

His face was so close to hers that she found herself lost in the depths of those eyes. The eyes, she thought, were the entire man. Neither brown nor black, they were nonetheless luminous with the gentleness inside the man. She had hereto considered his face only roughly handsome, but now she also perceived the deep character sketched by its lines. There was still so much she didn't know about him.

Her gaze brushed the ravaged patch of skin. "How did that happen?" she asked without thinking.

His mouth twisted wryly. "Nothing so exciting as what your British soldiers must experience. I was but a lad, an ignorant lad, and very cold. I foolishly tried to start a fire by flashing powder in the pan of an old-fashioned gun. The powder exploded and"—he fingered the weltered splotch—"and left this to mark me as a dunce."

"Oh," she said inadequately. She could not bring herself to look at him again and instead studied the blanket as if its weave were of supreme importance.

His compelling presence forced her to raise her gaze. At the dark glitter she recognized in his eyes a slight breathlessness constricted her lungs. She was alone with him, separated from him only by her thin flannel night-clothes and the bed coverings. The wind whistled down the fireplace's great mortared flue, the only sound in the suddenly silent house.

Oh God, she had to escape soon.

"You had something you wished to talk to me about?" she asked, unable to hide the timorous quality to her voice.

The spell was broken. He rose, pushing back the dark auburn swath that fell across his broad forehead. "I have to call on the Fairmonts tomorrow. I thought thee might like to come along. We would spend the day. The night's heavens promise a sunny day tomorrow," he added, as if to tempt her further.

"What?" she mocked. "A servant gets a day off?"

His smile was impudent. "'Tis Sunday."

The idea was very appealing—until it occurred to her that this was her opportunity to escape. With Ethan gone for the entire day she might just make it to Williamsburg if she followed first the Chickahominy River then the James. There she could find a Tory home and explain who she really was. Once the situation was known, surely the family would help her get to Boston. From there it should be easy to locate Terence.

"I'd rather not," she said. "Being with people of their quality only reminds me of my present lowly station in life."

"Thee seemed to enjoy Susan's company, mistress."

"Go feast your eyes on your beloved, Ethan Gordon, but leave me alone!"

He eyed her narrowly for a long moment, then gave a half bow and left the room without another word. She was almost sorry for her spiteful words. But whatever attraction she was beginning to feel for this colonial farmer paled beside the vision of Terence. His face and voice had haunted her since childhood—as he would continue to haunt her until the day she became his.

Jane watched Ethan gallop off on the dun just after dawn, with the soft shafts of sunlight silhouetting man and beast as one. Quickly she performed her ablutions, this time not bothering with her usual muttered imprecations about the chilling water. Rolling a few of her belongings in her shawl, she fastened the mantle about her shoulders and closed the door on the cabin that had been her home for more than four months.

She was so deliriously happy at the prospect of a reunion with Terence that she wanted to find Icabod, Josiah, and Peter and plant a resounding good-bye kiss on each of their foreheads. Instead, she kept to the early-morning shadows of the trees and made her way down the withered-grass slope toward the Chickahominy.

All her senses were abnormally alert—pungent woodsmoke mingled with the sharp, crisp air that tingled her cheeks and vapored her breath. She could almost imagine she heard the sun pinging off the water. As she set off along the bank's path that was bordered with thickets bare of leaves, she wondered if she had ever felt this much alive.

Yes, when Ethan kissed her. The plague take the religious rogue!

Her strides were long and possessed an easy elastic grace that spoke of her ecstatic sense of freedom. Her skirts swung in rhythm with her legs. She hummed the little ditty Peter played on his fife—"Yankee Doodle Dandy," a song left over from the French and Indian War, until the rustling of dead leaves just behind her brought her up short. Ethan's warning of lynxes and Indians tore a gasp from her throat as she whirled. A raccoon stared up at her, his sharp little nose wrinkling with her scent.

"King George!" she breathed. She stooped and caught his furry body to hold before her face. "Now listen, you can't follow me. I'm not coming back. Ever." The raccoon stared back at her with eyes as black as Ethan's. "Don't look at me like that." She set the raccoon on the ground with a gentle whack on its rump. "Now go on back, King George. Return to your master."

For I shall not.

Turning she started off again, but the continued crackling of dry leaves behind her told her that King George was as stubborn as she. She did not look back but quickened her steps. The rustling in the brambles grew fainter, and her mouth curled in satisfaction. Nothing would stop her.

As the morning eased into midday, she felt the first pangs of hunger. Why hadn't she thought to pack something to eat along the way? By afternoon her stride shortened; the rhythmic swing of her legs was broken. At the confluence of the Chickahominy and the James, her feet refused to move another yard without rest, and she dropped to the earth, still damp from previous rains that winter. Wearily her gaze sought the sun's position in the sky. Would Ethan have returned to Mood Hill yet?

The thought of him, the sure knowledge that he would come after her, catapulted her to her feet. "You've wasted your fifty pounds, Master Gordon," she mumbled wrathfully. But even as she stalked down the trail she knew her English stubbornness had met its match in his Yankee obstinacy.

She studied the narrow path that stretched far ahead until it was lost in the overgrowth. How much farther was Williamsburg? She tried to recall the journey by gundalow, but that day she had been more aware of the man who had purchased her than of her surroundings.

Now her surroundings—and the very elements— seemed to conspire against her progress as she walked. Thorny thicket branches reached out to snag her skirts. A humped cypress root caused her to stumble. Her pace quickened. Mottled gray clouds scuttled across the sun, and the wind whipped her mantle about her legs. Her fingers clutched the hood against her cheek to ward off the sudden biting cold.

The wilderness had lost its initial intimations of beguiling innocence. Rather, a sinister gloom settled over that primeval forest. The Great Dismal Swamp—what if she were near it? Her feet slowed, cautiously picking their way over untried ground.

An owl's dismal hoot warned her that darkness would soon descend and she would have to find some kind of shelter in which to spend the night. Already it was growing bitterly cold. Her fingers and toes were numb, and she tripped again to sprawl in a mesh of moldering leaves and moss. The creeping wildness—suffocating branches and strangling vines—prickled her nape. Struggling to her feet again, she brushed the dirt from her hands, her teeth staying the bottom lip that threatened to quiver.

Then in the twilight she saw it—shimmering through the latticework of denuded, wind-tossed branches, a light beckoned in the far distance. A house! Refuge!

Her feet found new impetus. Gathering her bundle in one hand and her skirts in the other, she started to run, though she knew the cabin had to be a great distance away. At first she thought the sound of her feet was echoed by the labored pounding of her heart. But the reverberating thudding amplified until she could hear neither her own footfall nor her panting. Behind her. She spun. In that ghastly nether light of dusk she saw the horse—and the dark rider, with his surtout's many capes flapping, beat down upon her.

Simultaneously she threw her arm up before her face and cried out. The horse reined in, rearing slashing hoofs above her, and came down to one side of her to prance nervously under the control exercised by its rider. Jane's arm fell away, and she looked up into Ethan's ravaged countenance. He leaned forward on the pommel to fix her with an angry glare. "Did thee truly think I'd let thee go?"

Despair sapped her last vestiges of strength. She sank to her knees, her skirts billowing about her, and gasped little heartbroken cries that were much like King George's mewing noises. She had been so close to freedom. After walking all day—only another mile or so!

She heard him dismount to stand over her. Then he lifted her tear-stained face. Tension hardened his mouth in an unrelenting line, and she dropped her chin to her chest again. "'Tis said that those who run away secretly wish to be caught," he said in a low voice.

Her head snapped up toward him. "Not so!"

But the fierce light that pinpricked his eyes so that they gleamed like those of a night animal crumpled her defiance. Head bowed again, she whispered, "You can humble me no deeper than this moment. Free me from the bonds with which you hold me. Please."

She felt his hand on her head. Her hood was pushed back and her mobcap was lifted off. His fingers insinuated themselves in the silky black strands smoothed back sleekly and caught by the thong at her nape. Her scalp tingled with something that was akin to anticipation. She did not move beneath the stroking hand.

Suddenly it was withdrawn. "I cannot," he said hoarsely.

Her head snapped backward; her eyes beseeched him. "Oh, dear God, please!" she cried, flinging her arms about his knees. Her tears dampened his soft buckskin britches.

He made a sound in his throat and seized her shoulders, jerking her to her feet. His eyes were smoky. "Don't beg me. Thee is a lady, Jane!"

She twisted free of his grasp. "I am nothing more than merchandise! To be bought and sold as you will!"

"And I will not sell thee."

"You are unreasonable!"

"I am thy master!"

"My dearest life . . . since me aravil here, I write you with a feeling heart to inquire of you and me dear infants' welfare, this being the return of the day of the year on which I was obliged to leave you and my dear infants, which day will be ever remembered by me with tears until it shall please God to grant us all a happy meeting again. . . ."

The quill Jane had pilfered scratched hastily over the

page in order to keep up with Icabod's broad Scottish brogue and make the corrections necessary as he dictated the letter. At her feet, King George's paws alternately slapped at a raveled ball of yarn or snagged at her woolen hose.

"I am in perfect health, for neither the heat in summer nor the cold in winter gives me the least uneasiness. Only two months ago I laid aside my summer dress and put on a suit of new claret-colored duffle. . . ."

At that moment a draft of frigid wind swept into the kitchen as Ethan opened the Dutch door. Immediately Jane rose to stand before the table, her skirts hiding the quill and paper. Since the night two weeks before when Ethan brought her back to Mood Hill riding pillion behind him in furious silence, she had treated him with a civility that bordered on insolence. Sometimes she thought that the field hands could sense the tension that sparked between her and Ethan. Neither Icabod nor Peter ever made reference to her attempted escape, but, for a few days the songs Peter piped were mournful dirges. And deaf Josiah eyed her with unspoken sympathy.

The wintry gusts whipped Ethan's navy-blue surtout about his powerful body. King George deserted the skein he batted at and padded happily over to Ethan to brush his bristled tail around and between the man's damp jackboots. Ethan ignored the raccoon's playful plea for attention. His weary eyes moved beyond the startled Icabod to seek Jane's tall, slender form. "I have something for thee, mistress."

Curious, Jane tilted her head to the side to see that a slighter figure stood positioned behind Ethan's form. He stepped aside to present a dusky young woman, wrapped in a heavy blanket. Her hair, plaited into two braids, was as black and thick as Jane's, but with a brownish cast rather than blue.

Ethan murmured something to the girl in that language Jane did not understand, and the young woman raised her eyes—tilted brown eyes that were wide and dark with apprehension. "This is Porhatras, Mistress Jane. I've brought her to help thee."

A finger of renewed resentment prodded Jane. "Brought or bought, master?"

He shrugged his large shoulders. "She was to be left behind for the winter by her people. Four freshly killed turkeys purchased her."

"Left behind, you say, master?" Icabod asked. "A purty lass as that?"

"The Indian maiden is clubfooted," Ethan said flatly. "The Seneca don't waste time with infirmities."

"Where shall she sleep?" Jane asked.

"Porhatras will have thy room."

Jane's black brows lowered in confusion. Her bed was scarcely big enough for her as it was.

"And thee shall take the room upstairs across from mine," Ethan clarified. He turned on his heel to leave. But at the door he said, "Mistress, 'tis a sin to steal. Next time you need a letter penned—ask me. I will willingly give thee quill and ink and paper." With that he was gone.

The young Indian woman looked frantically after the closed door. Gently Jane touched the blanketed shoulder. "Come with me, Porhatras. You must be hungry."

The Indian woman understood nothing Jane said but obediently followed. The rest of that day Porhatras, her gait slowed by her limp, shadowed Jane as closely as King George did Ethan when the man was about the house. The young woman showed a willingness to work and a dexterity with the simple chores that Jane lacked. And this greatly pleased Jane, so much so that she gathered her courage to seek out Ethan that evening.

She found him in the vat shed, moving among the stacks of dye cake as he counted and marked on a ledger. The smell of fermented indigo swept over her, an earthy but not particularly pleasant smell. At her soft closing of the door, he glanced up. The lone candle in the wall's sconce cast a sheen on his red hair, setting his whole person aglow so that she remained transfixed inside the doorway.

"Does my disfigurement frighten thee so, mistress?"

"Nay." She forced her steps down the aisle of dye cake until she stood only a few feet from him. A blue glow seemed to envelop them. "But your unrelenting nature does."

He sighed. "Thee comes about thy indenture papers again?"

"Aye."

"I believe that it is thee who is unrelenting. Thee will hound me until the day thy indenture is completed."

"You have Porhatras. Her hands will fulfill their duties much better than mine."

"Porhatras is to stay here at Mood Hill. Thee is to go to Williamsburg this spring to serve me there."

Jane's mouth dropped open. She couldn't believe she heard right. Williamsburg! Civilization! Coffee houses and dressmakers, theaters and—and the opportunity to gain her freedom.

Ethan caught her square jaw between the large span of his thumb and forefinger. His eyes burned into hers. "But do not think to make another attempt at escape," he said harshly. "The pillory and stocks—or worse, a beating—will await thee at the public jail. Do not doubt my threat."

Jane's lids lowered to hide the excited gleam in her eyes. "If I can move among other people . . . pretend that I am one of them, not a commodity . . . I will resign myself to serving out seven years."

His eyes scanned her face, as if searching for truth on her parted lips or in her submissive eyes. At last, as if satisfied, he released her chin.

Chapter 17

The figures on the ledger blurred before Ethan's weary eyes. He knew well enough the standing of the accounts that March without looking at the numbers. With the Non-exportation Act against England, there was little hope of finding foreign buyers for this year's indigo crop. He could not blame the impending war for Mood Hill's financial woes. He hoped that the indigo warehouses he was establishing along with the Scottish merchant Angus MacAbee in the ports of Hampton Roads, Alexandria, and Norfolk would be new sources of income—and consolidate his nonpartisan image since MacAbee was of Tory leanings, as were most Scottish merchants.

Only that week at the Virginia Convention in Richmond Patrick Henry committed himself to liberty or death in a great speech that would mark him as an archrebel. The balance of political power in Virginia was slowly shifting from the Tidewater planters to the Piedmont farmers.

Ethan thought about his own part in the revolution—the probability of disgrace, most likely a dishonorable death. Hardly the kind of prospects that would entice a woman to marriage, particularly considering the abysmal state of Mood Hill's finances.

He had known when he cleared his acreage, his back protesting with each swing of the axe, that it would be difficult to make ends meet for those first few years. He had known that he would need help, and that it would be costly. But none of the indentures he had purchased had been as costly as Lady Jane Lennox. Fifty pounds! He must have been out of his head to bid that sum. And why he had done so, he still did not know.

Ethan's Folly it was called in Williamsburg, as Bram reluctantly divulged. Fifty pounds for a titled lady who knew not the first thing about labor!

And why did he go after her that day she fled Mood Hill? Could he be falling in love with her? No. He would attribute it more to his possessive nature. The hulking horror of the gray granite Kilmainham Jail had taught the child he had been to guard his few possessions—the scraps of food to ward off starvation, the lice-infested blanket to keep out the cold, the bartered clothing to hide nakedness. What was his, was his—and for that reason he had gone to reclaim his maidservant.

It was her damnable regal beauty shining through that disreputable maidservant's masquerade that tempted him far past his limits of restraint. The brutal way he had forced his kisses on her the afternoon she came upon him translating coded messages out of the Bible—they were not the gentle kisses he dreamed of giving to a wife.

Ezra and Miriam had rescued a guttersnipe, a boy of the streets who was wise in the way of stealing, of using a knife deftly when set upon. With patience they had taught him trust and kindness and love. With their love they had changed him. Yet where was that man now?

And to consider taking her to Williamsburg—aye, he was daft. He would have to rent a house, for he could not afford two separate rooms in an ordinary for what may be a month or more. Finding a home to rent would not be difficult with so many Tory families sailing for England. But at what expense a rented house? Mentally he tallied the cost it would run him to rent a house for a couple of months against taking a room at the tavern. Expensive. And money was dear.

And how would he find a wife to court, with a maidservant like Lady Jane Lennox on his hands? He did not doubt that she secretly laughed at his rustic simplicity, which remained despite the education old Eliza had afforded him.

Ethan's fingers gripped the quill. The mere view of her trim ankle encased in woolen stockings tantalized him. If he thought to turn her tart asperity into sweet, loving kindness . . . Ethan's Folly, indeed!

Lady Jane Lennox, thy cooked peas are like gun pellets.

Chapter 18

On April 19th, the day before Virginia's governor, Lord Dunmore, seized the kegs of powder from the Williamsburg magazine, General Gage marched on Lexington and Concord, Massachusetts, to confiscate the arms and ammunition cached there. The war materiel's location, along with Massachusetts Militia records—the principal officers, the number and location of units, including the "minute companies" and the general scheme of mobilization and planned resistance, was provided by the spy operating under the code name Ahmad.

However, word of Gage's planned march on Concord was inadvertently leaked—by, among others, the very servants of the British officers. These scurrying batmen, preparing their officers' gear for field service, dropped unguarded hints in billets. Something big was up.

Not only was the Massachusetts Militia alerted, but Revere himself rode to warn Hancock and Adams of their arrest orders, and the leaders of the American intelligence ring escaped just ahead of Gage's troops.

The battle that followed between the rebel colonial minutemen and the British soldiers resulted in a nightmare for the redcoats. They lost 273 men—more than twice the number of lost colonists, who, rather than fight in drilled formal formation, had chosen not only hit-and-run tactics but took aim when they did fire.

For Ahmad, the battle meant his spying operations would be that much more perilous; for as a result of that skirmish England's Whitehall declared the colonies in a state of rebellion against Great Britain and the second Continental Congress in Philadelphia that May voted to use that military confrontation in Massachusetts to put all the colonies on a war footing.

The Continental Congress picked a forty-three-year-old delegate from Virginia who had fought in the French and Indian War some fifteen years earlier as the commander of all the continental forces. And Ahmad's more primitive instincts sensed that his hope for the total abasement of the house of Lennox depended in some way upon this tall, rawboned man who carried himself with such great dignity, a man by the name of George Washington.

The spy lay on the tester bed of the small third-floor room he rented at 114 Elfreth's Alley in Philadelphia and absently perused the gilt curlicues that writhed across the ceiling. The city was the largest and most modern in the colonies, with finely cobbled streets paved with Belgian blocks. It was also the seat of the recently formed colonial government's congress.

And it was this Philadelphian society he would infiltrate, posing still as a tutor, this time fleeing British-held Boston. The limp he affected would prevent the indelicate question later of why he had not volunteered for the newly raised Continental Army.

He reached for the missive on the nightstand. His lids narrowed over pale-blue irises as he carefully reread the messages that were several months old. Jane's letter had only just reached him from Gage's headquarters in Boston by way of his own Philadelphian contact—the German baker Ludwig, who specialized in fancy gingerbread and intelligence notes.

Jane. Jane represented a supreme challenge for a bastard aspiring to possess a titled lady. And she represented revenge.

Now she was in the colonies. In Virginia. He wanted her as he wanted no other woman, not even her mother. For her mother had been beautiful—but very accessible in her loneliness. And he, an inexperienced youth of sixteen, had merely been infatuated with Lord Wychwood's wife.

Lord Wychwood, Robert Lennox, whose infidelities were legend, never expected to return home to find his own wife dallying—and with a sheer youth at that. Lady Lennox took her life with poison the next day.

Lennox took his revenge immediately. With the influence he wielded through King George, he was able to persuade the monarch to withdraw both the title and the Manor House estate from Lady MacKenzie. These had been reluctantly granted to Terence's mother by Lord MacKenzie upon their divorce—with the condition she would make no scandal by flaunting her illegitimate son in society. Manor House, awarded then to Lennox, was boarded up, and Terence's mother returned to live with friends in Scotland.

Next Lennox struck directly at Terence. At the time Terence was studying British constitutional and international law at the Inns of Court. Suddenly, Terence found that his application at the Inn's Temple was not renewed.

Terence joined Her Majesty's Dragoons. Lennox, too busy in London with both political and amorous affairs, did not suspect that over those next six years Terence was busy also at Wychwood whenever he could get leave, befriending the daughter who suffered the same neglect and loneliness as her mother had. He insidiously capitalized on the homely child's lack of affection, so that she willingly kept secret his visits to Wychwood.

But somehow Lennox must have discovered those clandestine visits, for Terence at last found himself posted to the worst hellhole in India.

Jane was no longer a child but a woman. And seduction was not enough. After his ultimate mission was completed, Terence would claim his rewards. He would take Lennox's daughter from him—and Manor House, and the Wychwood estates as well. Jane was not as tractable nor weak-willed as her mother. But he would yet bend her—and break her.

Terence held Jane's letter to the candle. Revenge was slow in coming, but it was nearing.

Chapter 19

The Tidewater plantation society of Virginia was for the most part a wealthy, semileisure class, a planter aristocracy that was able to devote time to pleasure: to reading, study, philosophy, the arts and writing, as well as to gambling, the fox chase, dancing, drinking, hunting, and social gaiety. And Williamsburg was the political and social metropolis of this plantation gentry.

Still, for most of the year Williamsburg was a small college town and marketplace. But twice annually, during "public times" when the legislature met and the courts were in session, the planters' capital sprang to life. The population of two thousand doubled or even trebled. The innkeepers often roused one customer from sleep so that another could take his place. Everyone met everyone.

Yet that spring session of '75 held little promise of excitement—or opportunity—for Jane. The first day, a warm May afternoon, she could only think of the handsome red brick house that Ethan had rented from the Tory, John Paradise, as Paradise Lost.

From the drawing-room window she watched the gilded carriages with their teams of four horses, a trademark of a prosperous planter, rattle along the wide, mile-long Duke of Gloucester Street. With longing for a society denied her, she gazed from behind the wooden Venetian slats upon the planters' wives. Dressed in fashionable satins and carrying lacy parasols, they sat talking on the stone benches randomly placed along the avenue or strolled with their Negro maidservants under the arching live oaks that bordered the wide esplanade.

An open carriage drawn by a pair of superb bays rolled to a stop before the house, and Ethan got out. Dressed once more in sober black broadcloth and black yarn stockings, he reminded her of the Dark Angel. His height and flaming red hair set him apart from all others on the street.

In mild surprise she watched as, tricorn tucked beneath his arm, he bent over the hand of the woman still inside the carriage. The woman's powdered hair was adorned with rose silk ribbons that were repeated on the wide paniered dress of pale-gray jaconet. But it was the woman's face that captured the attention—one of undoubted beauty with lips that formed a petulantly flirtatious *moue*.

Hastily Jane let the Venetian blinds slip into place. She had not yet dusted the house that had been closed up for several months, and Ethan was returning to catch her spying from the window!

She hurried from the parlor, mentally ticking off her chores that day. The plaid dust covers still needed to be changed, and the heavy brocaded curtain needed to be replaced with light silk gauze against the summer heat. Too, she must not forget the woolen bed curtains that needed to be exchanged for mosquito netting. She just reached the stairs when Ethan opened the door.

Hand on the dust-filmed black oak bannister, she slowly turned. His black eyes raked over her. Her butternut-dyed dress, bare of paniers and hoops, hung limply on her, her unpowdered hair straggled in wisps from beneath the unbecoming mobcap. What a drab comparison she must make with the anonymous lady in the carriage. Still, Ethan's expression reflected something other than disgust. Displeasure that she had accomplished so little in setting the house to rights?

No, that couldn't be the reason, because they had arrived too late in Williamsburg the night before to do much more than unpack his razor strap, shaving mug, and other personal belongings before retiring. But his mouth had flattened just as it was now when he passed the horn lamp to her before her bedroom door.

Later that night, lying on the linenless bed in her thin shift, she had heard him in the opposite bedroom, pacing the floor. Was it the evening heat that had kept him awake? Had his thoughts been wrapped up in the mercantile venture he mentioned he was embarking on? Or had he been dwelling on Susan, who would be coming to Williamsburg with Bram for the Burgesses' spring session?

And what kind of thoughts did he give to the maidservant he owned, the maidservant who shared an enforced intimacy with him? She knew he wanted her. And this afforded her no end of delight, for how it must go against his Quaker's grain to love one woman and lust after another!

And what of herself? Did she not love one man but lust after this one?

God help her, for between the two of them coursed the ultimate alchemy.

She dipped a mocking curtsey. "How can I please you, master?" Why did she feel pushed to provoke him?

He jammed his hat at her and strode on past. "Bring bread and cheese to the library."

"There is no bread and cheese. There is nothing in the pantry."

"Oh . . . yes," he mumbled and absently rubbed his clean-shaven jaw. Pulling the worsted purse from his black waistcoat, he handed her several pounds. "Purchase what is needed at the market."

At both Wychwood and the Lennox town house in London, the servants had done all the shopping. And at Mood Hill, Ethan had bartered for whatever staples weren't raised on the plantation. Jane had never shopped for food and had not the slightest idea what one bought. Still, her lips curled with scorn. "You are not afraid I shall make off with your fortune?"

"Thee has already cost me a goodly sum, mistress."

"I know—fifty pounds, no less. You have reminded me often enough, but I did warn you of your folly."

"Everyone has reminded me," he muttered, and turned on his heel for the library's double doors.

Curtseying to his retreating back, she muttered, "And good cheer to you now."

Morosely she repaired to the outside kitchen. Among the assortment of waffle irons, tea caddies, and coffee grinders she found a basket of split oak. Knotting her brown shawl scarf beneath her bosom, she set off in the direction of the market square, the center of every town.

It was a beautiful, warm spring day, and she felt a frantic liberty as she briskly walked the few blocks to the broad green. Her opportunity to locate Tory sympathizers had arrived more quickly than she could have hoped. Freedom might be as near as the hour! Forgetting her irritation with Ethan, she once again hummed to herself that silly ditty "Yankee Doodle Dandy."

As luck would have it, Saturday was one of the three days for the marketplace, and all the farmers were pouring in from the countryside. Only as she drew near Market Square, which was crowded with not only with farmers, hucksters, and shoppers but, alas, mustered militiamen, drilling, did she realize her error. The loyalists of Virginia hardly dared openly expose their political views in so radical a town.

Finding a Tory sympathizer was going to be more difficult than she supposed.

Despite her drab dress, which announced her lowly status, she found men doffing their hats or sweeping bows as she passed among them. A well-dressed older man in brown satin and a curly gray peruke fixed her with a quizzing glance that did not hide the prurient gleam in his eye; a farm boy, reeking of hogwash, gazed after her with a love-struck expression. She knew it did no homage to whatever beauty she might possess; for in that land where women were at a premium had she been as ugly as Medusa it would not have mattered to the men.

Ignoring the would-be swains, she picked her way through the pushcart vendors selling oysters on the half shell, the briny odor wafted by the day's heat among the sticky press of shoppers. As she neared the butcher's shambles and other market booths that offered green and yellow vegetables and luscious ripe fruits, she heard Ethan's name hummed by those about her. Belatedly she realized she was a part of that subject of discussion.

"A titled lady, for sure" . . . "Ethan's Folly" . . . "Escaping a forced marriage, 'tis said" . . . "What a bargain that Quaker struck!" . . . "Living together, no less!"

A heated blush flagged her cheeks. But she tilted her chin imperiously and marched on toward the dairy area. To have her name bandied about like she was a common slut! She looked over the array of cheeses, the thatched baskets of brown eggs, the quart urns of fresh milk; yet she heeded little, so strong ran her shame. "What have ye, dearie?" asked a farm wife with missing teeth.

"Nothing from the likes of yer prices!" quipped a woman's peppery voice behind Jane. "The king's treasury could take lessons from yew."

Startled, Jane turned to find the woman whose daughter had died aboard the *Cornwall*. "'Tis Lizzie," the little woman said.

Impulsively Jane leaned over to hug her. Lizzie represented part of that old world—and was a friend in that new world of total strangers. "Odd's blood, but I remember yew," Jane said, mimicking the Cockney accent, and stepped back. But she also remembered that Lizzie's hair had not been threaded with gray as it was now, and fewer lines used to pinch her mouth. Life apparently wasn't any easier for Lizzie in the colonies. "Are you 'appy, Lizzie?"

The woman shrugged bony shoulders. "Is anyone? Are you, Meg?"

Unable to meet the woman's discerning eye, Jane looked away. "Reasonably so. And Polly? Wot do you know of 'er?"

Lizzie shook her head sadly. "She was with child but lost the wee one."

"Then she found 'erself a 'usband!"

"Nay, not a 'usband. A brute of a master. She lost the babe when he cudgeled her. And he was the babe's father, Wainwright was!"

Wainwright! Jane shivered, realizing how much worse off she could have been. Then, "Lizzie, do you know any Tory families in Williamsburg?"

Lizzie cackled. "Aye. I work for one—the Widow Grundy. Treats me fair for all her queer ways."

"Lizzie!" Jane drew her away from the press of people making purchases. "Could you introduce me to her? It's important."

The little woman eyed her strangely. "She cannot 'elp you, for all that you are a titled lady."

"You know?"

"Everyone knows. But I 'ad it in me 'ead aboard ship even."

"And this Widow Grundy—"

"She be daft, Meg. She receives callers in a coach on 'er back porch. And me and the other servants—why, we 'ave to rock the coach to and fro while she talks with 'er callers. Can you fathom that!"

"Please—take me to her."

The Widow Grundy's house, a full two stories without dormers in the roof, stood at the shady intersection of Nicholas and North England streets. Nervously Jane paced the drawing room's worn carpet until Lizzie summoned her. Just as Lizzie had said, Jane was received in a green coach on the wide porch at the rear of the house.

When Lizzie opened the coach door, the odorous fumes of tobacco reached Jane. Inside an old woman sat on the fine green Moroccan leather seat. "Well, do get in, child. It's dreadfully cold to these old bones."

Lizzie nodded reassuringly, and Jane lifted her skirts to climb inside, ducking her head low. When her eyes adjusted to the dimness, she saw that the old woman's high-piled powdered hair was diamond-studded. The wrinkled cheeks were heavily rouged, and a beauty patch was pasted on one drooping jowl. Between the painted, funneled lips was a long-stemmed pipe. Jane remembered her now at the auction of the indentured servants.

The widow rapped Jane's knees with the pipe. "Don't gawk like a ninny. You've seen people smoking before."

"Aye," Jane said, thinking to humor the old woman.

"So you're Ethan's Folly." The old woman's gaze ran over Jane with a practiced eye. "Good lines. You'll weather the years well here."

"I don't plan to stay."

At that moment the coach began a gentle rocking motion, and Jane grabbed for the window strap.

The widow drew in on the pipe. "Fool to run away. Many a woman is setting her cap for Ethan Gordon."

Now she knew the woman was crazy. "I have to get to my—my fiancé. I believe he's with the British troops in Canada. Can you help me get there?"

A column of exhaled smoke spiraled upward. "Don't you know, child, that anyone who helps a runaway slave is whipped?"

Jane's shoulders sagged. Between the thick smoke in the closed coach and its rocking motion, she thought she would throw up. And the way the old woman eyed her, as if sizing her up—it made her stomach roll even more in a queasy nervousness.

"I think I can trust you, child," the widow abruptly pronounced.

"Trust me?"

"I'm not as loony as you think." The widow leaned forward and tapped the pipe against Jane's knee again. Then she spoke in a low voice. "A Scottish teacher in Westmoreland County wrote a letter to a friend in Scotland describing the scandalous hanging in effigy of Lord North. The letter was published in a Glasgow newspaper. When word about the letter found its way back to Virginia, the schoolmaster was fined and discharged from his job. I—and the network of loyalists I work with—helped him escape into Delaware."

Jane's eyes widened. Smoke exhaled once more in a neat little circle from the old woman's seamed lips, but Jane forgot her nausea.

"There are others like him I've helped," the Widow Grundy continued. "And so far I have avoided suspicion through inanities like this coach. And this ridiculous pipe. Though I've grown to like the taste of the green weed," she added with a chuckle.

The old woman paused to draw another puff, then said, "And I'm sane enough, child, to know that running away is not the answer. You don't even know for certain where your fiancé might be."

"If I could get to Boston, I am sure headquarters there could locate him for me."

"Fie! Boston isn't peaceful India where an officer's wife has her bungalow and servants. Boston is besieged. The people left in that city are tearing up the wharving planks for firewood. Go back to England. Wait for your fiancé there."

"No!"

"Ah! A parent who opposes the match awaits you in the mother country?"

Jane nodded miserably.

"Then wait out the war here. In the meantime do what you can for other, not-so-fortunate loyalists in Virginia."

Despair tightened Jane's clasped hands. She had counted on finding aid in Williamsburg. The widow laid a veined and spotted hand on her interlocked ones. "Help us, child. And I'll help you."

"How? I am almost a prisoner myself," she added bitterly.

"We want to find out who the Leper is."

She looked up, her brows lifted in bewilderment. "The Leper?"

"The Leper's Colony—the rebel intelligence network." The old woman tapped the bowl of the clay pipe against the door. "The Leper coordinates the various rebel spy rings—including those Committees of Correspondence—that operate between the lower, middle, and upper colonies. The Leper is the mastermind, and we feel he operates out of Virginia—the waist of the colonies. Discover his identity and we crush the most powerful link in the colonies' rebellion."

"But how could I do anything?"

"Your master is friends with skilled agitators and radicals—rebel leaders like Patrick Henry, Richard Henry Lee, and others in their revolutionary regime."

"Bah!" Jane scoffed. "Ethan Gordon is radical about nothing! He's too pious—too self-righteous—to lift a finger in any cause but his own!"

"We know that. But he does move in those political circles occasionally. You might overhear something. Listen. Watch. Think, gal—your fiancé's life might depend on what you learn!"

Jane drew a deep breath. To lose Terence—how could she go on through life? "If I find the Leper—you'll find my fiancé for me?"

The old woman drooped a wrinkled lid in a wink. "Agreed." She leaned forward and opened the coach's door. "Pay a visit to Lizzie here, child, if you have any information."

Only half consoled, Jane left. When she arrived back at Paradise Lost, she realized she had forgotten the marketing she was supposed to do. She turned in the hall to make the trek again to Market Square, only to find that Ethan loomed in the library's doorway. His normally placid expression was rigid with anger, the burn on his cheek almost scarlet. "Thy purchases?"

She swallowed. "I forgot."

He advanced on her. "Shall I beat thee for thy transgression?"

She remembered Lizzie's story of Polly suffering Wainwright's brutal beatings. She took an involuntary step backward but was blocked by the solid wooden door. "You would not!"

"I am sorely tempted, mistress." His large fingers wrapped about her upper arm, and he pulled her over to the parlor window, drawing back the Venetian slats an inch or so. Dust flurried in the shafts of sunlight. "Look, there, across the avenue."

She obeyed, seeing nothing out of the ordinary to account for Ethan's altered behavior. But she was aware of the way he dwarfed her, making her feel vulnerable—and strangely feminine. The knuckles of the hand that gripped her upper arm were pressed against the outside of her breast, and suddenly the room seemed stifling. She managed to swallow. "I see carriages and people strolling."

"The man by the nearest live oak—does thee not remember him?"

She stared. Beneath the black tricorn the man's face was narrow and pointed—like a fox's. "The man who bid against you for me," she recalled with a shudder.

"Uriah Wainwright—head of the Committee for Safety."

"And?"

He jerked her around to face him. "The Committee of Safety does more than just ostracize suspected Tories and cause them to lose their businesses and ultimately leave town. They tar and feather—very unpleasant, I assure thee. The skin peels off in painful patches." His forefinger reached out to touch the lone pox mark that clefted her chin. "Thy soft skin would never be the same again—and thee would be marked worse than I."

Marked! She shivered beneath his touch. "But I have done nothing."

"No? Then why does our friend follow thee? If not to the market, where did thee go?"

Her eyes looked up to meet his defiantly. "I met a woman who came over with me on the *Cornwall*."

"And nothing else?"

She shook his hand off her arm. She cordially hated the man. "We fell to talking, and I forgot my errand. That is all!"

"I would not take thee for an empty-headed goose."

"I wish you had not taken me at all!" she said, and flounced off to the kitchen.

Chapter 20

*B*ram and Susan came to call the following day. At least Jane, who had risen before dawn, managed to dust that morning, though she had yet to hang the Wilton carpet outside and beat it. The teatable and drop-leaf card table, the upholstered settee and tapestried daybed all shone with the beeswax polish. Likewise the spinet, which she didn't play lest she arouse Ethan's ire. She thought it strange, because initially he seemed mild-mannered. Only of late had his temper struck sparks.

Susan looked lovely in a mauve gown of the finest lawn with a matching parasol. A lacy little butterfly cap perched on her light-brown ringlets. Jane watched for signs in Ethan's warm greeting of any languishing lovesickness over the fair young matron. But she sensed that he was not the type of man to pine for what he could not have.

As Jane served the glasses of cool cider, Susan insisted she join her on the settee. "When I saw Ethan in the Apollo Room of Raleigh's Tavern last night and learned that you were here also, I told Bram we were not waiting a moment longer to call on you."

Jane knew Ethan had been invited to a reception and private dinner given by the Williamsburg Volunteers the evening before. She spent the evening alone, sulking like a child. Yet the very last dinner she had attended as the Lady Jane Lennox—a royal dinner, no less—had bored her. Until she entered into conversation with the marked man beside her, a conversation that changed her life drastically.

Setting the Paradises' silver tray on the semicircular side table, she glanced at Ethan. His face was noncommittal. Strange, she often forgot that he was marred. She took her place at the end of the settee, across from the two men, spreading her coarse, colorless skirts with all the grace of a duchess arranging her satins. She poured the cider and passed him and Bram the crystal cups with an assurance and elegance that was innate. She could have as easily been pouring tea at the Governor's Palace.

"I daresay his dinner partner was the lovely lady with the prettily pouting lips?" she asked of Susan.

Ethan's lids narrowed at his maidservant's drollery, but Susan took her cup with a merry laugh. "Margaret Peyton? Hardly. It was the slightly crazy Widow Grundy."

Jane's gaze flicked uneasily to Ethan.

"Thee has heard of her, mistress?" he asked casually.

A coincidence? Or was this man who owned her shrewder than she estimated? Cup in hand, she replied smoothly, "She is the mistress of the woman I spoke of—the servant woman who came over on the *Cornwall* with me."

Susan leaned forward. "Meg, you may have come over

as an indentured servant, but all of Williamsburg—nay, half the counties of Virginia—prattle otherwise. Your aristocracy is evident in everything you do—your speech, your movements, your fine bone struc—"

"Um!" Bram cleared his throat. Embarrassed by his wife's candor, he nervously fingered the buckle of his stiff stock. "We called on more important matters, Ethan. The pompous Dunmore removed the powder from the magazine this morning."

"It does not surprise me."

"Ethan!" Bram exclaimed. "Where is your rage at the governor's act? Where is your patriotism?"

Ethan shrugged. "This is what Patrick Henry has been waiting for—one more royal act of tyranny to spark revolution in the colony. This will alienate the colony from the Crown as nothing else has."

"Word is about that Patrick Henry plans to demand payment in exchange," Susan added.

"Thee may count on it," Ethan said with a wry smile at the young woman, a smile that did not quite hide that glimmer of affection that Jane had caught before. "Henry is Virginia's answer to Boston's Sam Adams."

The talk turned to the Second Continental Congress that was sitting in Philadelphia that month. Jane's concern was not whether or not the colonies would declare independence from Great Britain. Her problem was finding Terence. "What of this Leper and his Colony?" she asked casually.

"Now there is a patriot of the finest water!" Bram exclaimed.

Ethan ignored him and fixed his onyx eyes on her. "Why does thee ask?"

She shrugged carelessly. "My friend on the *Cornwall* was talking about the man—the mastermind of the inter-colony spy network, I believe she said."

"A daring man!" Susan said with a sparkle in her lovely gray eyes. "And quite dashing!"

"You have seen the Leper?" she asked, astounded.

"Well . . . no," Susan hedged. "But someone as courageous and patriotic and ingenious as—"

"Zounds, Susan!" Bram interjected. "You make him sound like a Greek god."

"A leper," Ethan said drily, "is a far cry from the imaginary beauty of the Greek gods."

"Well, Nox," Bram said, "was certainly not renowned for his fair beauty."

"Ah, but Hades," Susan interrupted. "Remember—he was a grimly beautiful god."

The subject went from there to Greek myths, and Jane was no closer to learning anything about the Leper than before.

When Susan and Bram prepared to take their leave, Susan suggested Jane and Ethan attend church that Sunday with them. "Your Society of Friends cannot disapprove a function intended to worship the Lord," Susan cajoled Ethan.

A look of amusement combined with tenderness crossed his face as he accepted. Jane almost declined Susan's matchmaking attempt until it occurred to her that Bruton Parish Church was Anglican, the official church of the colonies and controlled by the Crown. It was an opportunity to acquaint herself with any other Tory families in the county.

When she, too, accepted, Ethan's eyes narrowed in suspicion. "Would you deny me the right to worship?" she asked archly of him.

"Nay." His eyes mocked her. "I know thee has prayers for deliverance to offer up."

By Sunday morning Jane regretted her hasty acceptance of Susan's invitation. Standing in her shift and petticoat, she realized she had no formal dress to wear. Half an hour later she descended the stairs in a serviceable gray muslin dress, with a soft but threadbare fichu swathed at her throat. Her chin rose haughtily at the startled look in the ebony eyes of the man who waited below, dressed all in black as usual. This Quaker was the grimly beautiful Hades of the underworld who had ridden, not in a chariot as Hades pursued Persephone, but by horse to claim her the day she ran away.

"It had not occurred to me . . ." he rumbled, his hand motioning inadequately at her attire.

She faced him, their eyes barely on the same level, though she stood two steps above him. Her irritation at the situation she had contrived for herself combined with her humiliation at the role she was forced to play. "What? Concern for your humble servant's appearance? How noble is the master!"

His lips tightened, but his voice had that calming drawl. "Thee will not provoke me. Come—or stay—as thee desires."

With that he left. Fuming, she followed him. His stride outdistanced even her long one so that she was forced to quicken her pace the few blocks to the salmon-brick gothic church. From the white, wooden steeple a bell peeled out to the assembly. Only as they reached the entrance did Ethan pause beneath the shade of the towering magnolia to tuck his tricorn under his arm and let her precede him.

It seemed that all eyes were turned on her. From the large square of pews set aside for the governor and Council, there were audible gasps. Dunmore, who sat pompously beneath a canopied chair, whispered something behind his beringed hand to the attractive woman on his left—Margaret Peyton.

Ethan, his fingers firmly gripping Jane's elbow, guided her first past the pews filled by all classes of colonists, then past the north transept gallery, occupied by the Negro slaves who had their own separate entrance. At last he halted before the pew where Bram and Susan sat. These were the transept pews reserved for members of the General Assembly, most of whom were Whigs bent on separation from the Crown. The tension between these radicals and the Tories sitting with Lord Dunmore seemed almost palpable to Jane.

Smiling in delight when she saw Jane and Ethan, Susan moved her wide hoops aside to make room for the two. The dreary service seemed interminable to Jane—made so by the press of Ethan's hard flanks against her own. Had she worn a lady's paniers, there would not have been this intimate touching.

His weather-brown hand rested lightly on the hymnal—and was as large as the song book, large enough to cover her abdomen. At the forbidden thought her skin seemed to tighten over her bones.

Though it was customary after the rector's sermon to stroll about the grounds, socializing, issuing invitations to dinner, the governor and his retinue departed immediately, thus dashing Jane's hope of learning more of the parish's Tory families. In the brick-walled courtyard only Susan and Bram joined Ethan and her, though several children ran to tug on Ethan's coat skirts, crying, "Windmill!"

For them Ethan was a massive toy. And as the children clamored about him, he accepted his role genially, rotating a tow-headed toddler up in the air like the blades of Robertson's windmill. Did Ethan long for the children that Susan might have provided him?

When half a dozen colonists wearing belligerent expressions gathered before the church's entrance, the romping halted. Among them was Uriah Wainwright, dapperly dressed in a suit of minister's gray. Though his countenance was benign as a rector's, Jane could tell by the way his head occasionally jutted in her direction that he was plotting like a pharisee. A sinister tension slowly pervaded the air.

Ethan set the boy down, and the children scurried away like frightened field mice. A fierce glare replaced the laughter in Ethan's eyes.

"Pay no attention to the niggling tongues," Susan counseled, laying a comforting hand on Jane's arm.

Yet, it was difficult to ignore the rising voice of the little man. "A Jezebel, she is." His bony finger pointed undeniably at her. "A Tory temptress baiting this God-fearing patriot with the sin of fornication!"

Ethan's arm flexed beneath Jane's hand. "Ethan!" Bram warned. "No. Not here."

Jane's lips curled in scorn at Wainwright. "So speaks the sanctimonious Brutus!" Head high, she sailed majestically from the churchyard. Tears blurred her eyes, and she was not even certain which direction lay the Paradise house.

Ethan caught up with her before the courthouse. He jerked her around by her shoulders. "Never leave me like that!"

She would not look at him but fastened her shimmering gaze on the King's Arms affixed to the courthouse door. "It stings your pride?" she cut. "That a mere maiden would battle when a man of peace will not?"

His fingers gripped her shoulders. "Do not bait me, mistress."

"I tire of the whispers behind my back, of having my name bandied about as the Whore of Babylon!"

"Shall I marry thee then and make honorable thy name?" he ground out.

Her lids flared. "I—marry you? Never! Better your servant for seven years than your wife forever!"

Chapter 21

The next few days Paradise Lost became a prison to Jane, for Ethan studiously ignored her by remaining away as much as possible—attending elegant dinners and balls at the governor's palace and the assembly balls and suppers given at the taverns for all who cared to purchase tickets.

Who was his dinner partner? Margaret Peyton? Susan had casually mentioned that the woman was married to a doddering but wealthy man. At church, the woman looked small and soft, like Susan—except for the eyes. Jane had caught the laughing challenge Margaret's dark-brown eyes had issued to Ethan. But Margaret could not know that his heart belonged to Susan. How droll that the populace believed Ethan to be enamoured of his maidservant!

Within days Jane received the first of a trickling stream of anxious, wary callers who had heard in that colony of shifting and uncertain political ties that Ethan Gordon's maidservant was loyal to the king. Always they inquired if the master was away before the tightness eased from their faces.

There was Lucy Barnes, whose husband was a cobbler. Jane sat in the parlor with the sloping-chinned woman and listened to the hesitant words accelerate until the woman's speech became like a runaway carriage.

"We—me husband and me—don't want to take sides . . . we love this land . . . my second-born is buried here . . . but we love England, too. Why, we were raised there, don't you see? Like yourself, mistress. We celebrated the king's birthday and rejoiced at his wedding. We don't want killing between our own blood. Me husband keeps saying there must be some way we can work this out. . . ."

Jane found it incredible that bitter Tory fathers could battle against equally rabid Whig sons. Then again, she also found it unusual that in Virginia it was mostly the rich planters, the colonial aristocrats, who were for the revolution and not the have-nots, as in the other colonies. This gentry was not composed of ambitious men on the make, rebels against the establishment. They were the establishment. Of all the colonies, Virginia with its House of Burgesses had been the closest to self-government, and the aristocrats who served in the House of Burgesses were not about to give up that autonomy.

Jane contained her observations before her visitors. Other Tories came. The short, balding William Dribble, a Tory gunsmith who that first hour fell to one knee in courtship of Jane; Cornelia MacAbee, the wife of the wealthy Scottish merchant who was even at that moment negotiating to sell Ethan's indigo to French concerns; and the Wormelys, the aristocratic planter and his wife who professed they were but passive loyalists—"which is only a little better," Ralph Wormely announced frankly, "than those who ride the fence—such as your master. One day he will be forced to take sides."

She refilled Wormely's cup. "No one forces Ethan Gordon to do anything, Mr. Wormely." She should know.

She subtly prodded each visitor for information on the Leper's Colony. All had heard of the underground intelligence organization, but few knew facts of any worth.

Two other visitors came regularly—Uriah Wainwright, who never called but remained across the street before the Lightfoot house, watching; and, of course, gentle Susan. Jane would lead her to the back porch where it was cooler and offer her a cup of cider or julep.

She admired Susan's sensible accomplishments. The genteel young woman was schooled in the fine arts of the kitchen as well as in the preservation and storing of foods. Jane knew not the first thing about the planting and harvesting of the kitchen's garden, but Susan was generous in sharing her knowledge. But their conversations did not always concern domestic issues.

"I am afraid Ethan's reckless actions have earned you Uriah Wainwright's everlasting hatred," Susan said during one of her pleasant visits.

"Ethan—reckless?"

"Aye. When Uriah Wainwright baited you before the assembly in the Bruton Parish churchyard. After you walked away, Ethan grabbed the odious man's stock and cuffed him on the jaw. Bram and the others had to restrain Ethan. Can you imagine?" She dimpled. "Ethan Gordon, a man of peace, forgetting his Quaker doctrine?"

On another visit Susan asked her about her fiancé. "Did he ever return your billet?"

Jane looked out across the dwarf box garden. "No."

Susan called again at the end of the third week, but this

time as they sat chatting on the back porch, they were interrupted.

Ethan, ducking his head, was framed by the doorway.
His smoky gaze aimed first at Susan, then shifted to Jane.
Since that episode at Bruton Parish, the formality between
the two of them had grown so stiff that any outsider could
see that virulent emotions seethed just below the eruption
point. The right spark and—

"I'm pleased to find it is not another Tory thee enter-
tains, mistress."

Jane rose. Stiffly she took the tricorn he cradled beneath
his arm. "I will return to my work. I'm sure you have much
to talk about with Susan."

"Ethan!" a man's voice shouted.

From the front of the house came running feet. All
three people on the back porch watched in dismay as Bram
threw open the porch door. "Ethan!" His breath came short.
"A ship has arrived. British." His stubby-lashed eyes darted
a glance at Jane. "A Lord—Woodwick or something—is
seeking his runaway daughter."

"Wychwood," Jane corrected. Her heart thudded dully.
Her father was as obstinate as she. She looked at the other
three. "My father can do nothing. I am of age."

Bram leaned against the red brick, closing his eyes and
breathing heavily. "He travels to Williamsburg. With six of
the king's royal guard, mistress—Lady—"

"Lady Jane Lennox," Ethan supplied.

"Lady Jane!" Susan echoed, gray eyes wide in astonish-
ment.

"You are a subject—of the Crown," Bram continued
with labored breath. "The king's order for your return—the
royal governor to enforce it—the lobsterbacks to make the
arrest . . ."

Jane sat down again. Her fingers gripped the chair's
wicker arms. Her thoughts spun like the blades of Robertson's windmill across the way. She could run again.

Susan's small hand reached out and touched her rigid hand. "There must be a way, Lady Jane."

Jane rose. "I'll need a horse."

"You'd never make it out of the colony, much less to British headquarters," Ethan said flatly. "There is but one alternative."

Jane's eyes left Susan's troubled face to meet his indecipherable gaze. "What?"

"Recant thy refusal of my offer the Sunday we attended church."

Jane sprang to her feet. "I won't."

He shrugged. "Then return to England. I rid myself of a contentious maidservant."

"But you would settle for a contentious wife?" she snapped.

"Not happily. But thee is in trouble."

Both were oblivious of Susan's and Bram's bewildered gazes. Jane's mind searched frantically for another escape. But she seemed boxed in, with no alternative but to accept the big man's honest offer.

"Ethan's right," Bram offered. "Not even the king would dare defy a rite of the Crown's own Anglican church."

Jane bowed her head to hide the tears of frustration. "Aye," she said at last.

"Aye—what?"

"I shall marry you."

"Nay. Ask me, Lady Jane Lennox. Here before witnesses. Ask me to wed thee."

Her hands clenched. Her pride was shattering. "Continually you have humbled me. I will neither forget nor forgive you."

"So be it." He turned to leave. "Come along, Bram. I want to show thee my newest warehouse. Since hiring MacAbee as my agent, my indigo business has doubled and—"

"Wait!"

He turned. His eyes bored into hers. "Aye?"

Her lids lowered over belligerent eyes. Her voice, when it came, was as demure as Susan's, but no submissive quality colored it. "Will you wed me?"

His gaze did not leave her face. "Fetch the rector, Bram."

"I'll go with you, dear," Susan tactfully volunteered at once.

When they were alone, Ethan said quietly, "This marriage is not entered into on either of our parts with any of the love that flows between Susan and Bram."

Jane turned her back to him. Her anguish made speech impossible.

Ethan's hands cupped her shoulders from behind. His voice—low, bereft—stirred the lace on her mobcap. "But we must do all we can to make work this mockery of what marriage should be. On my part I shall do what I can to be a pleasing husband in thy sight. I will not ask of thee what thee is unwilling to give. Yet I would desire that thee would attempt the same, Jane. Forget thy anger . . . forget thy Terence."

She turned to face him. "As you shall forget your Susan?"

The two stared at each other with the emptiness of years stretching between them. When Bram and Susan returned with the rector, Ethan was in the library and Jane changing into her one suitable dress.

The marriage, once decided upon, came about swiftly and inevitably. Like any news of import, word of Jane's identity spread rapidly, and neighbors began to filter into the Paradise house to watch the wedding that was about to take place. Williamsburg had not experienced this much excitement since Dunmore proclaimed Henry an outlaw for demanding payment for the confiscated powder.

The colonists parted for Jane, head held high as she descended the stairs and entered the library. Susan gave Jane a brief hug before she went to stand at Ethan's side. The hand she placed in his enormous one was icy cold. The walls of books seemed to close in on her, and her breath came shallow and fast. Marriage with Ethan Gordon was not what she had waited for, dreamed of, and plotted out all those years. She was afraid of him, more so than even her father. Yet she feared herself also. How could she keep her body from betraying Terence?

Yet Ethan had promised not to ask of her what she would not willingly give.

She spared her future husband one glance but was given only that view of his profile that could make a child's heart shudder.

The plump little rector cleared his throat. "This is— rather irregular. The banns haven't been posted. Neither of you is a member of Bruton Parish Church. Rushing into something like this could only—"

"She is with child."

Jane's gaze snapped to Ethan. He did not even bother to glance at her, but said, "Please get on with the ceremony, Reverend."

The vows were barely exchanged, before the library doors opened and Lord Wychwood entered. Behind him pressed the curious colonists, and flanking him were scarlet-coated soldiers, above whom he towered. There was no doubt in the mind of anyone present the relationship between him and the woman just married. Their inordinate height clearly announced their blood tie.

His eyes slowly raked over the five people as he digested the scene before him. "I see you have proceeded without my blessing, daughter."

Ethan's hand, warm and possessive, pressed Jane's. "Thy daughter is now my wife."

Lord Wychwood threw back his handsome head and laughed, showing his bad teeth. Jane shivered, but Ethan's custody of her fingers reassured her. When the laughter ebbed, her father chuckled, "You have spared me my confession, Jane, and cost me a needless trip."

Chapter 22

Daylight. A new day was beginning. Ethan uncoiled his length from the bed where he had lain awake for the better part of an hour and strode to the window. His naked torso was silhouetted by the faint gray-pink that tinted the windowpanes. He braced his hands on either side of the window's sash. Below, Williamsburg's town crier passed, calling in his German accent, "Basht four o'glock, und Lord Dunmore hast fled the gobenor's palace. All isht vell."

Was it? Virginia's 169-year history as the first permanent English colony was now ended, and its status as a free and independent commonwealth was beginning. The day before, the General Assembly had appointed an eleven-member Committee of Safety to act as executive of the newly created commonwealth until such time as a governor was elected. God grant that the commonwealth would fare well—God grant that his own new life would fare better than it had the past three days.

It was too late to unsay those halting words on the back porch. He reminded himself that marriage was a step that had to be taken sooner or later. Across the hall slept his wife. Did Jane, too, suffer the restive days and sleepless nights? Did she agonize over what was lost to her? Did she hate him—or was she merely indifferent to him as her husband, as the hours since their marriage would seem to indicate. And would they ever come to terms? They had to.

He straightened, plowing his fingers through the long rumpled hair. Without its ribbon, his hair flicked the sun-browned skin of his shoulders like a vexing horsefly.

Vexing. The encounter with Lord Wychwood had been vexing. The man had crossed an ocean to prevent his daughter from marrying a certain British officer, this Terence, only to accede to her marriage to another with a satiric humor that was without rhyme or reason. Lennox's pride was as stiff as his daughter's, and it made no sense he would yield her so easily to a colonial farmer.

Like Lord Dunmore, Lord Wychwood had boarded a man-of-war that morning in Chesapeake Bay. Wychwood's ship would sail with the tide without a word of farewell for his daughter.

And Dunmore's ship? Henry reported that the *Fowey* would doubtless remain in the Bay until reinforcement came. And it was the task of the Committee of Correspondence, who ultimately reported to the Leper's Colony, to ascertain when, from where, and with how large a reinforcement.

That other committee—the Committee of Safety that sought to rid Virginia of her Tories—they now had another loyalist to persecute. Jane. And this time Wainwright and his host of fanatics were entrusted with the power to carry out their vigilante programs.

Ethan sighed and began to dress for the day, pulling on a ribbed cotton stocking over each muscled calf. For Jane's safety, it would be best if they returned to Mood Hill. When his work necessitated his absence, he would have to depend on Josiah, Peter, and Icabod to protect his wife.

His wife. His wife in name only.

Chapter 23

The principal event of Philadelphia's most popular ball in years, held that August at the country estate known as Walnut Grove, was the exchanging of the black and white cockades—badges that the rebel soldiers wore on their hats. The exchange signified the union of all the colonial armies, of which the New England Militia was the core, under General Washington. At that moment the general continued to besiege Boston like a persistent and nagging fly.

After the exchange of the cockades, the guests adjourned to the vast dining room. Two tables covered with an incredible assortment of food stretched the length of the room. In addition to fifty pyramids of jellies, syllabub, cakes, and sweetmeats, there were over a thousand other dishes, not including the great tureens of soups and stews. All of this was served by black slaves dressed in Moorish costumes with silver collars and bracelets. Many toasts were exchanged, but the spy Ahmad picked up little information he did not already know. Most of the talk now concerned Virginia's Declaration of Rights, which George Mason introduced that month. But the rumor went that most members of the Continental Congress thought the idea that all power was vested in and consequently derived from "the people" too radical to be passed.

The most prestigious of patriots graced the hall—John Adams, Randolph Peyton, John Hancock, Samuel Adams, and Benjamin Franklin, who was recently recalled from England. Ahmad had reason to be wary of Hancock and Adams, for they certainly recalled his participation in the Boston Sons of Liberty meetings. But his clever tongue deceived even the discerning Hancock. From the outset Ahmad reassured Hancock and other patriots that, like them, he had been forced to flee Boston by Gage's subjugation of that city. He told them in his most humble manner that he sought only the opportunity to serve the colonies here in Philadelphia.

However, Hancock was an exceedingly cautious man, and Ahmad was invited only to the patriotic functions and not the private councils that were usually held immediately afterward.

At midnight a set of doors was opened at one end of the dining room to reveal an enormous ballroom elaborately decorated with flowered arches. The orchestra struck up a minuet, and Ahmad began his enchantment of one patriot lady after another. And at last he was rewarded for his efforts. As dawn broke, he danced the quadrille with Esther Reed, the pretty wife of one of Washington's ablest officers. Esther was the heroine of a transatlantic romance, for she had been courted in London when her colonial husband was a law student at the Middle Temple and boarding with her father.

And though she was a converted patriot, London was still dear to her.

Ahmad capitalized on this, mentioning his own studies at the Temple Bar. The two reminisced, with Ahmad never touching on politics but bringing London to life again: Turk's Head Tavern in Soho where intellectuals like the slovenly Samuel Johnson, Oliver Goldsmith, and rakish John Wilkes met; Westminster, where deer still grazed in St. James's Park and the wealthy were moving to escape the horrors of the city; London's thick, grimy haze that forced one to walk to the middle of London Bridge to try to find a breath of fresh air off the Thames.

At one point the spy permitted himself the merest of smiles as fragile Esther unwittingly divulged, with his skillful prompting, information he was seeking.

"You are too tempting, Madam Reed. Your husband is unwise to leave such a beautiful wife in a city full of men far from home and family."

She dipped as called for by the music and dimpled a smile up at him. "Ah, but you do not have a family," she said mischievously. Then, as they straightened, and their hands joined, she added somewhat forlornly, "And I sometimes wonder if Joseph remembers he has a family. His letters seem more preoccupied with Benedict Arnold's planned march on Quebec than with letters about his newborn son."

The spy's pale-blue eyes raked over her appreciatively. "Madam, you are much too slender to have recently given birth to an infant."

The daring compliment brought a blush to Esther's fair cheeks and a babble of words to cover her flustered state— "the horrible war and all these desertions!"

At the first light of dawn Ahmad left the ball, quite satisfied. By midmorning he was on his way to Quebec—this time dressed in the soutane of a Catholic priest. The journey took him three weeks by canoe and horseback. There were reconnaissance patrols to avoid and the wilderness to contend with—its unyielding forest and frustrating rapids and falls.

One afternoon at dusk he came upon the body of a British soldier, most likely a deserter. A mongrel dog hovered near. When, a few minutes later, a Yankee patrol passed near, he had to silence the animal's yelping with the soldier's bayonet. A messy business for one of his fastidious nature.

At the citadel perched on the sheer cliff of Cape Diamond, General Carleton received him. With the general was a swarthy Indian dressed in the civilized garb of knee breeches and doublet but wrapped in a foul-smelling blanket. The spy guessed immediately the Indian's identity. The educated Iroquois chief, Joseph Brant, who had sometime before thrown in with the English. The chief's eyes met Ahmad's direct gaze, then shifted away.

"Welcome back to Quebec," General Carleton said, indicating to the spy the other chair opposite his desk, which was littered with papers and maps.

Ahmad placed the chair in a position that kept the other two men in his line of sight and spun it around to straddle it. His black soutaine hiked up to reveal buckskins. Carleton said, "I see you come this time as a man of God rather than a soldier of war." It was an uncomfortable attempt at jocularity to cover an uneasiness about the secret agent that the general could not identify.

The man's lips smiled, and Carleton thought he looked more like a satyr than the priest he was disguised as. "If he were still here, the good Father who last wore this soutaine would no doubt have appreciated the irony, General."

The general's mouth flinched, but the agent continued on in that same easy vein. "However, I come as the Angel of Death. The Continental's Colonel Arnold is marching on Quebec now with two battalions."

The general sucked air through his false teeth. "How much of a head start did you have?"

"Benedict Arnold has the head start, by a week. But he has sixty-five tons of provisions and ammunition to haul with him."

Carleton grunted. "It'll take him at least two to three months then. We can easily fortify ourselves for a long siege."

"Can you?" Ahmad asked with a touch of malice. "You have less than four hundred men. I passed settlements all along the Susquehanna Valley that not only will aid the rebels but will join them. Even your Canadians will abet Arnold's troops. You might succeed in turning Arnold back, but eventually another rebel contingent will attempt the invasion again."

Carleton drummed his fingertips on the desk, rustling the papers. His small mouth pursed. He did not know whether he was irritated more by the news or by the arrogant man who brought it. "You have a better suggestion, I assume?" he asked sarcastically.

Ahmad's gaze flicked to the Indian chief, who had remained stoically silent, then settled again on Carleton. "Have your allies—the Iroquois and Butler's Rangers—stir up trouble in the valleys as a warning. If every man, woman, and child is killed in—let's say, just one selected settlement, perhaps the Mohawk Valley, I can assure you that you will never have to contend with an insurrection in other settlements."

Carleton's puffy lids flared. "I am not a barbarian to order the scalping and murdering of helpless people! A war is waged between armies!"

The spy shrugged his wide shoulders nonchalantly and smiled. "A war is waged to be won."

Chapter 24

Making of the winter's stock of candles was a dreaded household duty, for the great kettles were tiresomely heavy to handle and the kitchen, despite the open upper half of the Dutch door, was stifling. Worse, neither Porhatras nor Jane knew what they were doing. Ethan had simply said over dinner, "The candle stock is running low, mistress," assuming she knew what to do.

Or, knowing full well she did not, was he merely trying to provoke some emotional response from her?

How could a man and woman who cordially detested each other live in the same house? Year after miserable year? She and Ethan had only been married a couple of months, and already the strain was beginning to tell. The tension, the unhappiness—she knew it showed in both their faces.

If only they could have remained in Williamsburg, where the crêpe myrtle was just beginning to bloom. Where there was some hope of learning about Terence. The many activities of the public session would have kept Ethan too busy to pay her much notice. As it was, the two of them seemed to snap at each other like curs over a bone.

Yet she owed him an allegiance, difficult as it was to come by. He had saved her from her father's wrath. The day her father sailed back to England, after discovering, too late, her marriage with Ethan—that day she was able to put her bitter childhood behind her forever.

She pushed the hair from her face and furiously stirred the fragrantly simmering bayberries. Other women might waste their lives in such a miserable union, but she would not! When this ridiculous war was over—surely, with England's military power, in the next several months—she would divorce Ethan Gordon. Scandalous—but then she had faced down scandalmongers often since her arrival in the colonies. She would do it again. Whatever it cost to be at Terence's side, she would pay.

Both One-eyed Peter and Josiah leaned on the lower half of the Dutch door. Josiah's large, expressive brown eyes sought out Porhatra's slender form, and not for the first time Jane wondered if Ethan also took an interest in the docile Indian maiden. When he entered the house, he would only nod dutifully at Jane but greet Porhatras in that low, guttural language so unlike his usual soft-spoken drawl.

Did he seek company for his empty bed in the arms of the Indian maiden? The thought stung Jane's pride anew—and set off dissonant images in her mind. Images of Ethan winding Porhatras's braids about his hands, of him kissing the delicate Indian woman's soft, full lips.

Jane held up the ladle for Peter to see the transparent green wax drip. Not wanting to display her ignorance to Ethan, she had once again turned to the one-eyed servant for help. Josiah had explained patiently that bayberries were the best source for candles, since bayberries did not melt in the summer heat as did tallow candles. "Is it the right consistency yet?" she sighed.

"That it is, mistress. Now all that remains is pouring it into the candle rod molds. Here, let me tote the kettle."

He pushed open the door and crossed the brick floor to heft the kettle for her. His large hands carried the weighty cast-iron kettle over to the molds as if it were a wicker basket. King George, who entered on Peter's heels, sniffed curiously at the mixture that bubbled over the sides.

"Oh, mistress!" Peter chuckled, "you forgot to tie the wicks above the cylinders!"

The strain and tension that had been steadily building were released in her laughter, which bordered on hysteria. Josiah and Porhatras stared at her, for they failed to see the humor in the situation. "No wicks, no candlelight!" she gasped, wiping the laughter's tears from the corner of her eyes.

"Peter! Josiah!" All four in the kitchen turned to find Ethan standing in the hall doorway. His dark eyes moved from one to another, glaring at them in reproof. "Icabod cannot hoe the cornfield alone."

Peter ducked his head with an "Aye," and, putting down the kettle, shuffled around Jane and Ethan. Josiah and Porhatras, with King George trailing, his tail tucked under him, slipped out the door to leave the two alone.

Jane's eyes narrowed. "There was no reason for you to growl at the men. They were only helping me."

"I won't have my wife making eyes at every male in the vicinity, mistress. This is Mood Hill, not a jaded English salon."

Her nails dug half moons into her palms. "This is not a jail!"

"For all that it may be, thee is my wife, Jane. And thee will behave in a seemly fashion."

"Your wife in name only!"

The stringent line of his lips eased slightly. "Would thee have it otherwise?"

"No! Do not twist my words. I meant that only a rector's recited words bind us. No love, no duty hold me here. I shall leave when the time is right."

He caught her shoulders, his thumbs anchoring beneath her collarbone. His eyes were whorls of black smoke. "Thee shall never leave. God, not a rector, has joined us together."

The unrelenting edge in his voice severed all the plans she had been weaving. "What do you know of God?" she struck out in her fear. "You pious hypocrite—reading your Bible while you covet your neighbor's wife!"

She saw the pain that flashed across his face, followed by a sardonic twist of his lips. "That is the second time thee has made the accusation. Do I detect jealousy in thee, Jane?"

She swung back to the kettle. "You detect absolutely nothing. I feel absolutely nothing."

"Really?" His fingers touched the tendrils that curled at her nape beneath her lace cap, and her flesh tingled in a not unpleasant reaction. "Sometimes"—his breath warmed her neck—"sometimes, I would swear otherwise."

She whirled, her lips parted to refute his statement, but he was already striding out the door toward the stairway.

Later that afternoon, in the beautifully furnished bedroom that was now hers, she drew back the lace-ruffled curtain from her unshuttered window and watched her husband stroll from the far field with the men who worked for him. From that distance, she could not see his marred visage; but she could make out his straight carriage, his light tread, and his solid build that made him seem a Goliath.

Never did he mistreat her, and before the others he addressed her with the high respect a husband would his wife. And alone? She did not know; for they managed to avoid being alone. A pang of guilt pricked her, for in her own painful dilemma, she had given no thought to what he must be suffering. Longing for one woman denied him, marrying another because . . .

As the thought slowly took form, she chewed on her lip in agitation. The laughter of the men's camaraderie drifted up to the open window—and she knew then. One-eyed Peter; Icabod, who had to leave his family to find work; the deaf-mute Josiah; the club-footed Porhatras; and herself, a titled lady reduced to a servant's station when she fled England to complete fate's prophecy—*why, we're all misfits—misfits like himself.*

The curtain material wrinkled between her fingers. Her husband's compassion had purchased all of them! The thought was devastating to her pride. Her pride had enabled her to hold her head high in the worst of the times she had faced since indenturing herself. By looking down on him, castigating him, she could retain that pride. And now . . . what had she left?

The afternoon sky darkened, and Josiah pointed to the heavens. She glanced upward in expectation of a thundercloud. But the cloud she beheld was not spawned by a storm.

A cracking noise came with the black cloud as it neared, and only then did she realize that the indigo field, as well as the smaller fields of crops were suddenly aswarm with locusts. Below, the men ran for the fields, tearing their shirts off as they went. Stunned, she watched while they began beating at the tender indigo stalks, infested now with the locusts.

The men smashed at the insects, and she was sickened by the crunching noise that could be heard even from the distance of the house; yet, inexplicably, she turned to fly from the bedroom. She skimmed down the stairs, yelling, "Porhatras! Come!" Not even waiting for a reply, she grabbed up the Indian corn broom from the kitchen corner and dashed outside toward the fields.

The bodies of the feeding locusts cracked beneath her shoes. She swung the broom to ward off the hideous insects that lit on her arms and shoulders. Her skin crawled with revulsion. Still, she soon forgot herself, to flail at the plague of locusts devouring the indigo plants. Their clicking drone drowned out all other sound. As she grimly beat the air and ground, their wings seemed to saw at her face. She kept her lips clinched tightly, more afraid that she might vomit than that a locust might fly in her mouth.

She looked up once to see Porhatras on her knees between rows of indigo, deftly scrunching locust after locust between her thumb and forefinger. Shudders shimmied up Jane's spine, and she knew for certain she was going to be sick. Yet somehow she continued to kill the locusts.

Time ceased for her, and her body moved automatically. Sometime later she realized that the droning had ceased. In a daze, she looked around her. Porhatras was rising to her feet, a savage look of triumph distorting her handsome features. Icabod crooked a tired grin, and Peter slapped Josiah's back. "We did it, my friend! We beat the locusts!"

The sickness she had thrust from her rose rapidly in her throat, and she spun from the others, one hand clamped at her mouth, the other clutching at her stomach. Ethan caught up with her before she reached the nearest sycamore and held her by the waist as she doubled over. Her stomach retched in painful dry heaves. She began to cry. Tearless sobs wracked her body. She hated her weakness, always crying in moments of crises.

"'Tis all right, Jane," his low voice consoled. "'Tis over with."

"Oh, God!" she wept. She tore from his grasp, running for the house.

At the well she dipped her hands in the bucket and washed her neck and face and hands feverishly, as if by doing so she could rub out the revulsion of the afternoon. Ethan found her there. She looked up as, shirtless, he strode toward her. "I hate it here! I hate it, do you hear me!" she gritted.

He caught her wrists and drew her to him. "I know. I know," he soothed, pressing her head into the hollow of his shoulder. "'Tis not an easy land. 'Tis only for the strong of heart. And thee is strong, Jane."

She realized he understood what she was feeling—the horror of the afternoon, the shame at her weakness—and sensed he was trying to make her feel better. His large chest was bare, and his flesh, the color of cognac, glistened with sweat beneath her fingertips. For a long moment she allowed herself the pleasure of being held this way. His smooth skin made her forget the crackly bodies of the locusts, the brown slime that oozed when they were crushed. But she doubted she would ever forget the clicking noise their wing sheaths made at her ears.

Almost regretfully, she pulled away from Ethan. The sudden longing for Terence was a bittersweet pain. With a tremulous smile, she said, "I'm all right now."

But she wasn't. She would not stay in that hated land a day longer than need be! Reaching the kitchen door, she turned to watch Ethan head back toward the others who trudged out of the fields. His warm, resonant voice, thanking them for their efforts, reached her ears. She pivoted and rushed inside. There was time.

Speeding up the staircase, she reached Ethan's room and crossed to the secretary. She took a sheet of parchment and dashed out the same letter to Terence as before. Though he might not receive this letter either, by writing it, by corresponding, she was doing more than marking time. Emotionally the writing of the letter was a catharsis for her; yet intellectually she recognized that little could be done until the silly war was over. Silly, because Parliament in its obstinacy had provoked it.

When she went to look for the blotting sand, her fingernail snagged on something. Curious, she drew out the offending object—a mere sheet of blank paper but with an hourglass hole cut from its center. Why would Ethan—

"I told thee to ask before rifling through my desk."

She whirled, thrusting the cutout behind her into the drawer. Ethan, with that soft, Indianlike tread of his, had managed to come within a foot of her without her hearing. "I'm—I'm sorry. But I wanted to write a letter—to my father—assuring him that all was well—tell him about the episode with the locusts."

She knew she was stuttering, but she could not help herself. Ethan's dark gaze was formidable. "Odd," he drawled. "Because I would have sworn thee did not have a close filial relationship with thy father."

She colored. "He is still my father."

"I see." He reached around her and picked up her letter from the desk top. "The salutation is to Terence, mistress," he said in a sardonic tone.

His calm self-assurance angered her. She tried to snatch the letter from his hand, but he held it out of her reach. "You have your Susan to yearn for," she spit. "Leave me my own dream!"

"Jane, I will never leave thee. Thee is my responsibility. Just as thee shall never leave me." With a quiet deliberation he shredded the letter and, walking to the hearth, tossed the shreds into the fireplace.

She wanted to fling herself against him. For an instant she wished she were a man that she might call him out in a duel. "You're more of a tyrant than King George could ever be! You—you beast!" The last she flung inadequately at his broad back and stalked from the room.

He was not to let her forget her parting volley.

Chapter 25

Ethan was leaving. He and Icabod were to drive two wagonloads of dye cakes to Ethan's warehouse in Williamsburg. Jane approached the wagon parked near the shed and watched the men load the layers of dye cakes. Ethan straightened and looked down at her from his elevated position in the wagon's bed. September's early-morning sun mellowed the angles of his face, casting that corduroyed portion of skin beneath his cheekbone into shadow. The faded brown cotton tunic clung with perspiration to the wide span of his chest.

"Aye, mistress?"

Suddenly shy before the three field hands, she smoothed her apron. Why didn't she ask him that morning, when he came into her bedroom to tell her he would be gone for three or four days? But he had caught her relacing the drawstrings of her bodice. Lazing in the doorway, he had been unable to repress the twitching of his mouth as she struggled to close the gaping material that revealed the deep plunge between her breasts. And she had been too distraught at his presence to pose her question then.

She shielded her eyes with her hand and looked up at her husband who hunkered down on the wagon's bed. "I—may I ride into Williamsburg with you—Ethan?" There, she had said his name in a wifely manner for the benefit of Icabod, Josiah, and Peter.

Fists planted on narrow hips, Ethan drew a deep breath and let it out slowly. She knew he was not fooled by the warm inflection she gave his name. "'Tis impossible, mistress. The Secret Committee is demanding the Oath of Loyalty from every citizen now. And from certain seditious statements thee has made, I do not think thee will willingly give the oath."

"I shall say nothing to betray my feelings."

"Without saying a word, thee betrays thy feelings. The look in thy eyes—the way thee holds thy head—'tis enough to set off a man like Wainwright. To set off any man," he added, almost as an afterthought.

Then, at a curious glance from Icabod, he said more briskly, "'Tis more than that. Dunmore has seized Norfolk. Detachments of British soldiers are raiding nearby villages and plantations. 'Tis not safe to be on the road now. In my absence Peter will defend Mood Hill from the marauding soldiers."

Concern for Mood Hill but not her. Stung, she struck back through the safer subject. "The Crown is only doing its duty. What would your Quaker teachings have a parent do when its child rebels? Sit idle while the child throws a temper tantrum?"

"There is something absurd, mistress, in a continent continually governed by an island."

Neither was really listening to what the other said. They were at it again. Baiting each other. "The colonies can still reconcile themselves," she declared heatedly. "It's not too late for harmony to be restored."

His mouth tightened. "Can thee restore prostitution to its former innocence?"

Icabod cleared his throat. They both looked at him, then realized they were not alone. Ethan turned his back on her and hefted another skid of dye cakes into place. Clearly he considered the discussion—and her request—put to rest. She threw a contemptuous glance at his back and stalked off to the kitchen.

Yet she stubbornly refused to give ground. Before the wagon with its cargo of indigo could roll away, she strategically grabbed up a farmer's felt, wide-brimmed hat and hurried outside, handing it to Icabod. "For the sun," she explained, eyeing his pink balding head.

"Why thank ye, lass," he said gratefully.

She slid Ethan a glance. But he kept his hands on the reins and his eyes straight ahead. He was not going to give her a chance to ask again. Arguments obviously did not work. She walked around to Ethan's side and stood on tiptoe, her hand braced on the brake. "Good-bye, Ethan," she said sweetly, offering her face up for a kiss.

Her husband's startled expression delighted her. But the swift peck he rendered was not the thorough kiss of before. And he snapped the reins over the team, as if the Hounds of Hell were on his trail.

Over the next three days she moved about the house in a huffy mood. King George prowled restlessly with her. Even Porhatras forsook her beloved mistress to seek consolation in the perfect afternoon. The fair Indian maiden, clothed in a sleeveless buckskin shirt and a pink plaid calico

skirt, sat outside the kitchen in the shade of the roof's over-
hang and strung on linen thread the harvested apples intended for drying.

In the kitchen Jane pared the sweet and sour apples into
the brass kettle suspended from the stout crane in the open
fireplace. From her view through the open upper half of the
Dutch door, she saw Josiah's lanky frame approach with another barrel of apples. She could hear Porhatras's musical
voice greet the field hand and saw the way his thin face lightened. Did he truly understand anything the Indian woman
said? Or did it matter to him? Doubtlessly not. His crinkly
eyes announced his lovesickness.

Jane peeled ruthlessly at the apple. Another Indian
summer was upon Mood Hill, and she was more a prisoner
than ever. She would have it out once and for all with Ethan
when he returned. She would declare her intention to go to
Williamsburg more often. After all, she was no longer a servant. She was a wife. She now had the freedom of choosing
what she wished to do. She would no longer bow before his
autocratic behavior.

But her resolution to confront Ethan was forgotten
upon his arrival the next afternoon. Obstinately, she remained in the kitchen, refusing to go outside to greet him.
She could hear him talking to Porhatras in that unintelligible
language, and a few minutes later the two of them climbed
the stairs together.

An unidentifiable emotion she labeled anger—anger
that he would ignore her, his wife—infused her. She looked
down at the apple she was peeling to discover there was little
left but a mangled core. Nearly half an hour later when Porhatras appeared in the kitchen to collect a scuttleful of char-
coal, Jane was nearly speechless with rage. She slammed the
knife on the table and passed by the startled Indian girl without a word.

Ethan's door was closed. She knew at that moment she

was too furious to storm in and vent her wrath. Incoherence would be the disastrous result. And she intended to serve Ethan Gordon an articulate eloquence that would put Patrick Henry to shame.

Instead, she repaired to her room, bumping her head on the door's low lintel. She muttered an expletive. Massaging her bruised scalp, she looked up to find dress after dress laid carefully across her bed. Simple gowns of cotton, wool, linen, and muslin, gowns of demure colors but with exquisite stitching and lovely embroidery. With the gowns were other apparel—stockings, Moroccan pumps, an ivory fan, a pair of long kid gloves. So this was what Porhatras had been up to— laying out the exquisite articles.

Stunned, Jane looked from the wealth of clothes on the bed back to Ethan's closed door. Reluctantly her feet carried her into the hall. Without knocking she opened his door.

He was dressed in formal breeches of dyed black buck- skin with black stockings and brass-buckled shoes. A fine lawn shirt that ruffled at the wristband was his one con- cession to elegant dress. He turned from the oval looking glass to face her.

"The dresses . . ." she murmured.

"Sorry that I could not purchase them new."

"Why?"

"Why, because imports from England are forbidden."

"No. Why did you purchase them for me?"

"I would not have my wife dressed like a pauper."

"Thank you," she managed beneath his close regard.

"Will thee help me with my stock, mistress? I can't seem to get it buckled."

"You are going somewhere?" The idea of going any- where sounded heavenly. But then he had not invited her.

"I am attending a meeting of the Society of Friends"— his large fingers wrestled with the neckcloth—"at a farm not far from Mood Hill."

No doubt close enough to the Fairmonts', she thought sullenly. Her lips set in a mutinous line, but she walked up behind him and reached over his shoulders to take the muslin neckcloth edged with narrow lace. She was close enough to detect that pleasant scent unabetted by a gentleman's usual jasmine powder or perfume. She first noticed that clean scent the night he rode after her to bring her back and she had ridden pillion behind him.

"It's your queue." Her words were spoken grudgingly. "It's in the way."

He reached behind his neck to move aside his clubbed hair, and somehow her arms about his neck awkwardly entangled with his hands. "Oh!" She couldn't drop the stock. "Wait. I think I have it." Nibbling at her lower lip in concentration, she tried releasing one end of the stock, but her free hand caught in the crook of his lifted arm.

"Drat it!" she muttered.

His responsive chuckle was infectious, and she quite forgot her vexation. Over his shoulder she dimpled in the looking glass at him. When she saw the grin tilting the corners of his mouth she couldn't help herself, and the smile she'd been attempting to stifle overtook her. "What buffoonery!" she quipped. "Here, turn about . . ."

Still holding the stock, she maneuvered around him. Now their arms were locked about each other's shoulders, and she was looking into eyes that darkened in a suddenly serious expression. Her lids lowered against the heat of his gaze, and her own came to rest on his mouth. Its lines were strong, the bottom lip taut with restraint.

In a purely automatic response, her lips parted, and he murmured, "Jane."

Slowly, wonderingly, her gaze rose to meet his. She found it astounding that the eyes of such a simple man could hold such plummeting depths. For one timeless moment she forgot she had been a titled lady, forgot he had been a convict. Her hand touched the square line of his jaw, just below the burned patch of skin. "You have been only good to me," she whispered. "I will try to be all that you want in a wife."

"All?"

Something in his expression made her uneasy, though his eyes reflected a steady calm. Hastily she dropped her hand, shuddering. "I cannot refuse you, I know. But . . . please . . . do not ask that of me."

Too late she saw the import of her words mirrored in his eyes. He had misunderstood the reason behind her plea—not her fear of surrendering what was meant for Terence but a supposed revulsion of him.

Living with him daily over the stretch of months, she was no longer repulsed by his disfigurement. Yet unwittingly she had stung his pride.

His voice held its level, drawling quality. "You once called me a beast. Does the beauty fear the beast? Do not worry, mistress, I do not want *that*—nor expect that—of thee."

Chapter 26

In the dark Ethan let the dun pick its own way through the deep forest undergrowth. From overhead a yellow sliver of a Southern autumn moon filtered through the fern-needle branches. The surprising interlude with his wife made him late for the assignation, and he chafed at the slow plodding dictated by the heavy underbrush.

She was constantly surprising him. Stubborn . . . resourceful . . . sweet . . . volatile . . . and definitely unpredictable, which held a ridiculous though undeniable charm for him. Did that charm, did those bewitching eyes and beguiling lips, cause him to underestimate her as a potential enemy? His mind reached back to earlier that week when he had caught her at his desk with the mask. Did she recognize the coding device for what it was? He thought not. The mask looked little more than a paper cutout. Still, he had to be more careful. It would not help to have his own wife spying on him. He hoped the disagreement he provoked over her letter had distracted her from her discovery.

But then she certainly distracted him tonight. He did not expect to find her capable of humor. Her laughter . . . there was a pleasant quality in it. Just as there was a most pleasant sensation in the pressure of her breasts against his back when Jane and he were so ludicrously entrapped with his damnable neckcloth. Unfortunate, he thought with a melancholy sigh so foreign to his nature, that his wife was repulsed by his face.

And her Terence? No doubt a highly attractive man. Ethan cursed his jealousy. And his acquisitive nature that would not allow him to give up what was his—and which chained him for life to a highborn woman who loved another man.

A pine branch snapped across his shoulder, reminding him that he needed to keep his wits about him. The moonlight brightened as the trees fell away at a crossroads that was little more than an Indian path. Four miles farther east was the Sergeant of Arms Tavern and the Post Road—at one time a heavily beaten Indian trail, like the Great Wagon Road that ran southward all the way from Pennsylvania to the colony of North Carolina.

He would not be visiting the tavern that evening. The black handkerchief he wore about the lower half of his face precluded any social discourse; rather it insured his anonymity. He thought about Emma, the tavern's chambermaid. She would readily welcome him to her bed again. His need for release was almost overpowering. Like the Biblical Onan, he could resort to the spilling of his seed. But that only parodied the miraculous union of the flesh, the union of the spirit at that moment when mortality was transcended.

The French agent he was to meet was waiting beneath the tree's shadows, his horse shifting about impatiently. At Ethan's approach, the agent said, *"Il auberge est proche. Vous a soif por thé ou café?"*

Ethan had studied only a little French at William and Mary before summer chores necessitated his final absence. But his ear told him that this was not the native Frenchman he was to meet.

Still, he went along with the prescribed exchange. His reply to the question of whether he preferred tea or coffee at the nearby tavern was to be, of course, coffee. *"Café, monsieur."*

The agent's horse picked its way across the path, and in the moonlight Ethan could see beneath the shadows of the cocked hat that the man's mouth—thin lips that twitched nervously. "You are the Leper?" the man asked in English.

"Aye," came Ethan's voice, muffled by the handkerchief. "And the message you bring from France?"

"This!" The man's hand drew the horse pistol. Ethan's hand was a flash of white in the darkness. Twin explosions shattered the night's stillness. His opponent's horse reared, and the rider toppled to the earth with a thud and did not move again.

The dun, trained against Indian warfare, had not stirred. Neither did Ethan. He drew deep breaths, afraid that he would be sick. He had thought—hoped—that for him killing had ended with that last Mingo attack a lifetime before. In the darkness passed the vision of a frantic fourteen-year-old's pistol still smoking . . . of the Indian dead scattered about the blackened ruins of what had been his home . . . of Ezra and Miriam, who had lifted no weapon in their defense . . . of Miriam's blood that splotched the charred Bible beneath her outstretched hand . . . of the tomahawk buried in Ezra's chest.

Ethan wheeled his mount back toward Mood Hill. Only

with the pressure of his thighs against his horse's barrel did he feel the flash of pain in his left flank. A quick glance revealed a mere flesh wound that could be easily dressed without alerting anyone at Mood Hill.

His thoughts turned to the more pressing issue. Where was the real French agent? Most likely waylaid and murdered by the now equally dead Tory. The Tory spy had posed as the French agent, hoping to discover the identity of and dispose of the mysterious Leper.

Cautiously Ethan chose a different route back to Mood Hill. There could be more than one Tory; another waiting to ambush the Leper if the first plot went amiss. Danger was his constant companion. Yet his work also jeopardized his wife's safety, and with disgruntling clarity he realized she was as unsafe at Mood Hill as she was in Williamsburg. He would have to keep her near him at all times. The added responsibility entailed by his marriage vexed him anew.

From his wife's unshuttered bedroom window candlelight shafted down on the dead leaves strewn across the earth. He reined in his mount, watching for a minute the pacing of Jane's shadow against the wavy windowpane. So she knew no rest or peace, either. His shoulders slumped with fatigue and desolation.

Chapter 27

The same priest's cassock that enabled the spy Ahmad to pass unsuspected up the Susquehanna River Valley to Quebec facilitated his penetration of the rebel troops that ringed Boston, already beset by October's wintry storms. With incredible daring, he even paused at the marquee tent, with its arched chambers and dining and baggage tents attached, to deliver the last rites to a soldier dying of dysentery—one of General Washington's own bodyguards.

Though Ahmad was able to observe the size of Washington's troops, their condition, and the food and munition stores, he knew Gage would not be overly interested in the information. The commander of all British forces in America already had a number of spies wandering up and down the

Hudson River Valley procuring just such information. Indeed, Ahmad discovered some months before that the official doctor for the Continental Army, Benjamin Church, was also a trusted spy for Gage.

No, Gage wanted something he could not obtain from an ordinary spy. Ahmad permitted himself a thin smile as the young sergeant ushered him into Gage's office. His victory over Robert Lennox drew nearer. "Bless you, my son," he told the departing sergeant.

Two people, a grizzled man in a rumpled greatcoat of brown velvet and a hook-nosed gentleman dressed in a fashionable royal-blue satin frockcoat and breeches, sat in chairs that flanked Gage's desk. Both eyed the visitor curiously—skeptically—but made no effort to introduce themselves.

Since no other chairs were available, the spy hooked a leg over the low red chest near the hearth, where a fire burned against the room's damp cold. He faced the two men with a benign expression that at the same time seemed to mock all that was sacred. Their identities were unknown to him. But he had been expecting the meeting.

A moment later the portly Gage entered. Usually genial, he wore a preoccupied frown today. All British authority had collapsed outside his lines around Boston. And the political scuttlebutt predicted if he didn't subjugate the rebels soon, General Howe was waiting in the wings to succeed him.

He wedged himself into the chair behind the desk and faced his most dependable spy. "From various reports, I find that you have been successfully waging a campaign with the Mingos against the settlers along the Monongahela River."

"Conducting a campaign," the spy corrected.

He preferred not to take any actual part in the bloodbath the Mingos perpetrated, not because of any squeamish reluctance but because of self-preservation. Once the Indians worked themselves into a killing frenzy, he knew that neither political allies nor color guaranteed safety, and often the Mingos even fell to massacring one another over such trivialities as the possession of a woman's petticoat or a child's corncob doll.

"We lost another of our agents," Gage announced without preamble. "To the Leper again."

"But it is not because of the Leper that you have asked me here," Ahmad stated.

The spy's uncanny discernment never ceased to rattle Gage. The man had the instinct of an animal. "I have a more important assignment for you. An assignment of such delicacy that you are the only one whom I feel capable of carrying it out."

The spy raised a sardonic brow. "An assignment of such danger, you mean."

Gage hesitated, pulling at the lower fold of his chin. "Yes." His glance slid questioningly to the man dressed in elegant satins, who nodded his assent. Gage's two visitors had come directly from a meeting at 10 Downing Street, if one could exclude the six-week voyage.

Gage's rather nasal voice dropped to a conspiratorial tone. "Parliament is getting a backlash from our businessmen in England. Not only are the businessmen taxed to support a war they didn't want in the first place, but they have lost the profitable trade they were doing in the colonies. They want an end to this war before it drags out another year."

"And?"

Gage looked again to the man in satin, who spoke for the first time, in a falsetto voice. "We represent an important segment of Parliament that feels without this General Washington, the rebel army might disintegrate for lack of leadership. We want the man assassinated."

"So the Roman Senate wants to do away with Caesar?" the spy asked with a caustic smile.

The grizzled man shifted uncomfortably. "We want to execute a treasonable man," he snapped.

"Are you interested in the—enterprise?" the man in satins persisted.

Ahmad delayed, knowing that by doing so, he would drive up his bargaining price. "I am quite certain you have other agents, Gage—other fanatics willing to risk their lives for the Mother Country."

"England has such patriotic men," the grizzled man injected. "Men willing to die for their country."

"True," Gage said, "we have patriotic men willing to die. But Washington has bodyguards. Any attempt that is unsuccessful will just alert and prepare the rebel general that much more. We must succeed the first time. We need someone unencumbered by patriotism," the general finished drily.

The spy gazed indifferently out the window, where windblown snow obliterated the landscape. The interview was following the course he had foreseen long ago.

"What about a mercenary?" the man in satins asked of Gage. "One of the Hessians?"

Ahmad chose the moment to speak, and all three men listened. "A mercenary does not act out of idealism. Thus he is more calm and less likely to make mistakes. Neither does he have reservations at the last minute about a bystander who might get hurt in an explosion or killed by a stray bullet. A mercenary calculates every conceivable hazard."

He paused and asked coolly, "Yet none of the men have come forward, have they?"

"But if we could find a patriotic man willing to attempt the assassination," the grizzled man insisted.

Ahmad did not bother to look at him. "Your spy system is filled with more holes than a sieve," he said. "Boston is crawling with agents and double agents. General Washington would be alerted before the would-be assassin could prime a pistol or draw a sword." The spy came to his feet. "Gentlemen, we've discussed this long enough, don't you think?"

Gage looked to the two men on either side of him. Both nodded. "All right. Will you do it—will you assassinate George Washington?"

Ahmad stared at the three for a long moment. "Yes. But it will be costly."

"A gentleman who looks after his own interests," the grizzled man sneered.

"How much?" asked Gage.

"Wychwood Estates and Manor House."

"Impossible!" pronounced the man in satins.

The spy leveled his pale blue gaze at the man. "My price is high because I am risking all—and because I shall accomplish that which you wish."

"Wychwood and Manor House belong to Lennox—one of the king's own favorites," the grizzled man said. "The king would never consent."

The spy shrugged and turned to leave.

"Wait!" Gage said. He looked at the two political representatives from Great Britain whose faces wore expressions of strained uncertainty. His own military career lay on the chopping block. "Our king, I'm sure, is well aware of prior history—of monarchs like Charles I, who pushed Parliament too far and lost his head for it. I think when His Majesty is better acquainted with the facts, he will accede to this demand."

"Naturally, gentlemen, before I undertake the task, I will want the king's own signature on a proclamation deeding the estates over to my name upon the successful conclusion of the assassination."

"These two gentlemen will return immediately to London with your instructions," Gage said.

"Also, once I have the proclamation, I will not be in

contact with your office again. I will make and carry out
what plans are necessary on my own."

"But suppose something goes awry? Our intelligence
operations could help out."

"Nothing will go awry, unless it occurs from your end.
Once the proclamation is delivered into my hands, I will
carry out the task. Good day, gentlemen."

Chapter 28

*J*ane sat on the bed, brushing out the tangles that snarled her hair before she retired for the night. King George pawed at the wooden hairpins scattered carelessly over the quilted coverlet. The flames in the fireplace that occupied her bedroom's north wall burned low. The bedroom was the only room in the house with wallpaper—a soft design of blue and brown leaves that ended at the dark oaken wainscot.

The large tester bed, the cane-back rocking chair, the chest of drawers topped by a framed looking glass, the painted floor canvas—they added a warmth to the room. Not for the first time she reflected that Ethan had gone to a great deal of work to build and furnish Mood Hill. Had he vainly hoped that he would find someone like Susan to share Mood

Hill with him, to grace the house and bring warmth and lighthearted laughter to its rooms?

She looked down at the dress of soft blue wool she wore. Buttoned to the neck, the dress was unadorned but for the simple swaths of linen that fell in graceful folds from the three-quarter sleeves. The dress was one of the many he had purchased for her. That morning at breakfast he idly commented that its color had reminded him of her eyes. Compliments those days were rare from those silent lips, and she flushed with pleasure under his scrutiny.

The abrupt knock on her door halted the sweep of her brush. "Yes?"

"I would like to talk with thee, mistress?" came Ethan's muffled voice.

"Wait—I—just a minute." Her fingers scrambled to retrieve the scattered pins. "I don't have my cap on," she threw over her shoulder. Where did she lay the frivolous lacy embellishment?

Ethan opened the door, and she saw his gaze catch on her unbound hair. Before her hair had been either powdered or cropped and hennaed. This was the first time he had glimpsed the heavy length and black luster of her hair without its concealing mobcap. After a moment's hesitation, his gaze slid up to meet hers, and she found only indifference registered in his sulfuric eyes. "I think it's permissable for a husband to see his wife without her hair covered," he drawled.

Nonplussed, she asked, "You wanted something?"

He strolled across the room to lower himself to one knee at the bedside, near where she sat, and scoop up King George in one large hand. The candlelight danced on his rich auburn hair, and she almost forgot herself in the temptation to run her fingers through its thickness.

His hand stroked the raccoon's back. "It seems that thee has captured King George's affection."

His direct gaze, on a level with her own, disconcerted her. Flustered, she returned to brushing her own hair, delighting in the sudden latent flare of his pupils. "You are surprised that I could capture someone's affection?" she asked archly.

An amused grin curved his lips. Marvelous lips, she thought. "I am surprised that thee could return that affection—as unhappy as thee is here," he added with a sly glint in his eyes.

"There is no place else for me to go now—not until the war is over."

He set the raccoon aside and braced the heel of his palm against his bent knee to face her squarely. "Not even after the war is over, mistress."

She opened her mouth to protest, and he silenced her with, "I come to inform thee I have to leave tomorrow for Williamsburg. My agent informs me that the market for indigo has greatly increased, and there is much paperwork to be done—accounts to be seen to, negotiations to be made. And, of course, the General Assembly is to be convened to officially transfer the power of the royal government to the revolutionists."

She had to convince him to take her. She knew that during Williamsburg's public sessions diplomats, spies, self-seeking businessmen, witty philosophers, scheming politicians, flaming revolutionaries, and courtiers abounded.

If the Leper and his Colony operated out of Virginia, then the Leper would be there for the public session. Only when she discovered his identity could she dare hope to be reunited with Terence. Discovering the Leper's identity—it would be difficult, but she did have entree, through Ethan, that most Tory sympathizers did not. By watching and listening and asking discreet questions, she meant to succeed where no one else had yet. She faced him fully, the brush gripped tightly in her hand. "Please, may I go, also?"

His mouth hardened. "Thy Tory tongue would make the trip unwise."

There was something in his expression—was he baiting her again? She could not tell. "I'll say nothing," she entreated.

His eyes seemed to show no leniency. "I find that difficult to believe. By the end of the month thee would have us both in the jail's stocks."

"At the end of the month?" she echoed, dismayed. "You shall be gone that long?"

"Thee will miss me?"

"Hardly."

"Alas!" He made to rise, and she caught his shoulders, restraining him from leaving her. Tears glistened in her eyes. "Ethan, please—please let me go with you. I—I'm so unused to the loneliness here."

His hands came up to remove hers from his shoulders. Abruptly, he turned them palm up, and his thumb rubbed the calluses that ridged the once-smooth skin. He frowned. Still rubbing her palms, he said, "Thy life has greatly changed since coming to Mood Hill. Thee is in need of thy own chambermaid, Lady Jane."

The gentle pressure of his thumb sliding over her palm set off turbulent sensations in the pit of her stomach. "Not Lady Jane," she said softly, tremulously. "Madam Jane Gordon."

He sighed. "Aye. I will take thee to Williamsburg."

The statement was said so smoothly that it almost seemed planned. She was impulsive with gratefulness and unthinkingly threw her arms about his neck. "Oh, Ethan!"

Unexpectedly she slid off the bed's edge, and he caught her in his arms. Knee to knee, her hands splayed against his shoulders, his hands encasing her rib cage, they faced each other. Her hair tumbled down her back, somehow finding its way into his hands and wrapping about his fingers. He tugged gently, tilting her head back. His face blurred as it moved closer. She stiffened, but his lips, brushing lightly against hers, did not demand, did not insist, only gave of their wine-scented warmth.

That human need to be held, to be touched, was her undoing. Over a year had passed since she had felt the security and reassurance of Terence's arms. She responded, her lips easing into a pliancy that admitted the unanticipated shaft of Ethan's tongue. Her lungs constricted in surprise. A sinking feeling sapped all strength, and she clung to this man, her husband, as he took his fill of her mouth.

His mouth tasted of honey and wine. Kisses were given in a wild, hot desperate need. They swayed together in that flickering candlelight, fused mouth to mouth, belly to groin. She wanted to get inside him, she wanted him to crush her. Fiery wine bubbled through her veins. She was drowning. Drowning in her own body's liquid.

"Jane . . . Jane . . ." he groaned, his mouth moving to press against that sensitive spot where her jaw curved just below her ear.

What was happening to her? Even now she was wantonly arching her neck to offer his lips access to her flesh. His right hand freed itself of her entangling hair to loosen the top button. With surprise she heard the soft mewing she made involuntarily as his lips plundered the hollow at the base of her neck. Her fingers had their way and slipped through his hair to press his head to her chest.

Her will seeped from her. She was melting again, would melt into little pools on the canvas floor covering if he did not stop stroking her flesh with his velvety tongue. "I want you to . . ." Oh, the shame!

"Tell me what you want me to do to you," he grated. His fingers loosened several more buttons, and his hand delved beneath her stays to free one alabaster breast, revealing the sweet cocoa nipples.

"I want you to . . . to . . ."

"Tell me!" His tongue licked tantalizingly nearer. "Oh, sweet, sweet Jane, tell me."

" . . . to kiss me . . . there . . . please."

His mouth complied and engulfed the aching tip, and her head lolled backward. His lips tugged, his tongue flicked, his mouth suckled. Her body was fluid, trying to flow into his, no muscle, no bone.

"What do *you* want to do?" she asked daringly, delighting in the delicious talk, her inhibitions shattered by the mouth that flexed on her nipple and the hands that were everywhere—stroking her aching belly, cupping the curves of her hips, palming her heavy breast. She must be mad! Oh, but a sweet madness.

"You know what I want, Jane." Low, guttural, heated.

"Tell me."

"I want to take off every piece of your clothing, I want to hold your bare flesh against mine, I want to kiss you—everywhere, I want to bury my face lower in that fragrant patch of hair that—"

King George's paw, snatching at a curling swath of her hair, jerked her back to reality as nothing else could have. She pulled away, hearing her ragged breathing that echoed his own. Her eyes were glazed, her mouth trembled and her body shuddered. "You would have taken me," she whispered.

"Thee would have given thyself to me," he stated unequivocally.

Her hands struggled with her stays and the buttons of her gown. "No!"

"Thee would have given thyself and thee will, Jane." His fingers anchored in her hair again and drew her face near his own. "Thee will yet surrender to thy husband."

Rage at his profound self-assurance sputtered in her like a hissing candle. "I will never surrender that part of me to you! I find you—"

"Repulsive?" he asked with a mean leer.

"Coarse and crude."

"And thee is rude and spoiled. Someone should have delivered thee a thrashing a long time ago. It's too late now," he muttered, releasing his hold on her hair only to grab her shoulders a second later. "Hell, it's not too late!"

"What—!"

She found herself shoved face forward over his knee, her petticoat tussled by the hand that proceeded to whack her exposed rear soundly. "There!" he growled. "That is for thy disobedience as a maidservant. And that"—another smarting whack on her rear—"is for thy disrespect as my wife."

"Ohhh!" She pushed away from him and sprang to her feet. "You are—are abominable!"

He rose from his knee, and she sprawled ignominiously at his feet. "Good. Then thee need not accompany me to Williamsburg."

He turned away, and she caught the lace at his cuff. "Wait!"

He looked down over his shoulder at her. "Aye?"

She swallowed the pride that burned in her throat. "I— I meant no disrespect."

"Oh? And thee does not find me abominable?"

She shook her head in a negative gesture, her loose hair swaying against her back.

His eyes glinted. "Prove it."

Her breath sucked in. Once again he was humbling her. "'Tis not fair!" she blurted out.

"Life is not fair, Jane." He shrugged. "Besides, thee does have a choice."

Closing her eyes, she rose to her feet. She took a tentative step toward him and tilted her face up, her mouth puckered as if prepared to taste a lemon. He caught her shoulders. Disgust hardened his voice. "I am not interested in bartering for goods grudgingly given."

Her eyes snapped open, and he set her from him. "Thee may come," he tossed over his shoulder as he strode to the door. "Only thee must behave in a respectful fashion, or I shall pack thee back to Mood Hill."

Chapter 29

During her absence Jane found she had become the talk of Williamsburg. *Imagine, a titled lady, the Lennox lady no less, residing in Virginia! . . . And such a romantic marriage, my dear. . . . Rescued her from being returned to a convent, Ethan Gordon did. . . . No, no, Ethan rescued her from a forced marriage with a gouty old earl, 'tis said.*

The last lady of nobility to reside in Williamsburg was Governor Dunmore's wife, who made a visit from England, only to be sequestered the last five months of Dunmore's term as governor when it became obvious she was with child. And now almost a year later, Lady Dunmore was sequestered on the *Fowey*, standing off Norfolk in the James River.

That very first morning in Williamsburg Jane approached Ethan, who worked on his accounts in the library, with her request. "You mentioned once I needed my own maidservant. I would like to purchase one now."

He laid aside his pen and leaned back, tilting the scrolled chair on its rear legs. "Thee has someone specific in mind, mistress?"

Still the formality, despite the unbridled passion that his torrid caresses had unleashed upon them. Just talking with him made her weak all over, made her want to feel his mouth hard on hers again, his hands roaming her body's contours. Oh, dear God.

"Yes. The indentured servant I came over with on the *Cornwall*. She is unhappy with her master."

She would not add that Polly's master was Uriah Wainwright. She could handle the obnoxious man despite Ethan's misgivings.

Ethan flipped a page of the ledger, his eyes traveling down the boldly penned column. "It would seem that the revolution has financially blessed Mood Hill's indigo venture, mistress. The proceeds are at your disposal."

She took Susan with her, though she would have never admitted that by doing so she bolstered her own courage. Susan seemed to have a homey genius for cosseting.

The day was cloudy. Horses waited at hitching bars, tail end to the cold wind that rustled the brittle leaves along the street. Jane buried her hands deeper in her woolen muff. Wainwright's house was a small, quaint cottage on Frances Street.

"It once served as slave quarters," Susan said in a hushed tone that bespoke her own uneasiness.

Jane's stays did not seem quite so constraining after Polly answered the door. But the girl was changed drastically. "Polly!" Jane breathed, astounded.

Tall, almost as tall as Jane herself, and robust, Jane recalled, Polly now looked gaunt, gaunter than after the five-week voyage across the Atlantic. The pink flesh seemed to hang in folds upon her large bones. Gone were the brilliant butter-churned curls, replaced by tarnished yellow strands. Fear held sway in the once spunky gleam of the Dresden-blue eyes. And a faint black shadow smudged one broad cheekbone.

"'Tis Meg?" Polly asked, then drew back a step. "Nay. I forget meself. Ye be the Lady Jane, hain't you?"

"Nay, Polly. I'm Mrs. Gordon now. Jane Gordon. And this is Susan Fairmont."

Polly glanced cautiously at Susan, then back to Jane. "I can't ax you in, mistress. The master—'e don't take to me 'aving visitors and sech."

"Your cheek, Polly—"

Polly's hand flew to her face. "I fell—cleaning the book-case shelves."

Jane glanced down at Susan, then said, "Polly, would you be interested in coming to work for me—if I can per-suade Wainwright to sell me your indenture?"

The gaunt young woman covered her face with work-worn hands and burst into tears. "Aye, that I could! But 'e'll never let me go."

"Can we come in out of the cold, Polly, and talk about it?"

The raw-boned woman's eyes widened. "The master might come back hany time now."

"Then I'll talk to him," Jane said and stepped past the tearful woman. "As one civilized human being to another."

"The man haint civilized!" Polly bit out. She closed the door, and watched Susan and Jane go to stand before the fireplace that lent little warmth against the eerie chill of the room. The house had a clean appearance but was musty, redolent of the Oxford Museum.

"Then we'll make sure your papers are purchased," Jane said, turning herself like a fowl on a spit to warm her back.

Polly paced before the worn horsehide sofa and wrung her hands. "You don't know 'im. 'E delights in tormenting people. Making 'em feel as small as 'e is." She stopped pacing to look with wild eyes at the two women opposite her. "Sometimes I think I would kill 'im with me bare 'ands." She shuddered. "But killing hain't in me soul."

Susan's face paled a ghostly white. In the warmth of the muff Jane's hands went sweaty. "We'll do something, Polly," she managed to say with a false bravado. "I'm sure that—"

The front door opened, and Wainwright stepped over the threshold. Once again Jane was struck by the little man's almost saintly face, but the meanness in his small foxlike eyes betrayed a malignance that made him loom like a specter over the room.

At once those slitted eyes shifted to Jane. "So the Tory maid comes to visit me," he said in a tone that slithered its way up Jane's spine.

"I come to purchase Polly's papers."

He removed the battered felt tricorn and passed it to Polly's trembling hands. Now that he was close enough, Jane could see the sparse tufts of black hair that grew atop the rim of each ear. Even the man's spidery hands were hirsute. "I won't sell the gal."

"We'd best go, Jane," Susan whispered at her side.

"I think that you will," Jane said in what she hoped was a steady voice. "Because the other members of your Executive Committee might not approve of your inhumane treatment of your maidservant, should the word get out."

Wainwright smiled congenially and drew forth a pipe from his frockcoat's pocket. He was so short his eyes were on a level with her breasts, and he did not raise his gaze as he said, "It's not against the law to beat a servant."

"But it's twenty-one lashes for fornicating with one."

Susan crimsoned at the taboo word, and Polly gasped at Jane's boldness in confronting the fox-faced man.

"It's the lazy wench's word against mine," Wainwright said. His furry hand almost caressed the pipe's bowl.

"No, it's my word against yours."

He chuckled. "A Tory's word?"

She smiled contemptuously. "Williamsburg has not left the mother country's ways that far behind. Its Tidewater gentry is still an elitist society and still stands in awe of nobility. If you don't believe me, then wait. By the end of the month and the public session, I shall have the rest of the Executive Committee, for all its pretensions at egalitarianism, eating out of my hand, and you, sir, locked in the pillory for fornication!"

Wainwright's small, slanted eyes narrowed as he considered her statement. She was showing a bold front, while her insides quivered like quince jelly. Something in his crafty expression alarmed her, but it was too late to back down. "All right, Mrs. Gordon, the servant woman is yours," he sighed in a nearly pious voice, like King Herod giving up Christ to the mob.

She almost sighed herself, until he added, "But your threat shall cost you your lovely neck." His small furry hand reached up to stroke her throat, and she jerked back. He merely smiled, baring small, pointed teeth. "I mean to expose you as the Tory spy I know you to be, Mrs. Gordon. And before you are hanged, I personally shall brand into the flesh of your forehead the letter *T*."

Her scalp prickled. *And you, too, shall be marked.* Dear God, let the old Hindu's prediction be wrong.

Jane's own prediction was coming true. Every available inn, tavern, and private house in Williamsburg was packed to overflowing, and all who came for the public session that autumn watched and talked about and copied Jane Gordon.

Out of perversity, she chose to wear the simplest fashions. Yet on her tall, slender build, with her erect, graceful carriage, the bombazine and moreen dresses were like silk and brocade gowns. If she wore a simple, inexpensive gorget collar, the women who paraded along the Duke of Gloucester soon sported one.

A milkmaid hat tilted at a provocative angle over her classic brow caused the milliner's shop the next day to be besieged with customers wanting just such a hat made. The milkmaid hat soon dislodged from fashion the calash bonnet that, with its cane ribs, was large enough to house the high coiffures.

Her hollow cheeks caused a marked drop in the purchase of plumpers—cork balls stuffed in the cheek pockets that prevented stylish ladies from uttering more than six or seven words at a time. Her brilliant, even teeth brought back a rash of fans, despite the cool autumn weather, to be spread concealingly before the mouths of the many cursed with imperfect teeth.

Even the general's lady, Martha Custis Washington, was not so talked about, so stared after, when she arrived from Mount Vernon in the gilded and scrolled chariot with the diamond-cut glass, the coat of arms on the painted panels, and pulled by six magnificent cream-white horses. With her sister Nancy Bassett, Martha would stay in Williamsburg at the Six Chimney House, the house her first husband, the late Daniel Custis, kept for the round of festivities that occurred twice a year.

Jane did not meet Martha Washington until the Executive Committee hosted the first ball of the new Virginia Commonwealth. The ball was the initial social function she and Ethan attended as man and wife.

Given in the governor's palace, which looked more like an English country estate with its fish pond and holly mazes patterned after London's Hampton Court, the ball was attended by people as far away as Alexandria and Fredericksburg. All the guests came powdered and turned out in their best finery. And the two women—the general's lady and the Quaker's wife—were the main draw.

Jane stood at the entrance to the marble-tiled hall at the side of Ethan, who was dressed all in black, as she had known he would be; thus as a foil to his black broadcloth she had worn a white dimity petticoat with a heavy corded gray overskirt shot through with silver threads and a matching gray fichu to discreetly cover her décolletage. Compared to the pearl-studded slippers and gold-buckled shoes and the yards of Alençon lace and rippling satins and silks of the other guests, both men and women, her manner of dress was understatedly elegant. A white velvet love ribbon encircled her throat and matched the ribbon looped through her unpowdered hair, setting off its ebony sheen. By the following week natural hair would be the fad.

When the liveried footman took her pelisse, Ethan's gaze slid boldly over her. It seemed to her the first time in the week they had been in Williamsburg that he bothered to cast more than a preoccupied glance at her. The strain between them colored their every moment together, so that she was relieved that his business kept him from the house so much.

His eyes lingered on the rise of her full breasts—the flesh was the color of champagne against the white silk. "Thy love ribbon—for whom is thee wearing it?" he asked with a sardonic twist to his lips.

"Why, for the gallant Leper."

His hard gaze flicked to hers in intense scrutiny. After a moment he said, "Then thee has converted to a colonial patriot?"

She smiled brittlely. "Hardly." She splayed her fan with a snap of her wrist. "I am merely intrigued by a man of such courage and do him honor."

"Far better the Leper," he said derisively, "than thy

Terence." Before she could form a suitable retort, he took her elbow and led her past the two footmen stationed at the ballroom doorway.

As she and Ethan passed among the guests, gentlemen swept bows, ladies curtseyed. She ignored the women's glances of envy and the men's coveting gazes. Ethan introduced her to men whom she recognized as leaders of the Virginia revolutionary movement. Who among them was the Leper or a member of his Colony?

Tom Jefferson? He was lean and sandy-haired with a light, boyish voice that Bram said failed him in Assembly debates.

Richard Henry Lee? Certainly a prime candidate, as the silver-tongued Cicero of Virginia. A tall, spare man with a profile that belonged on a Roman coin. He wore a neat black silk bandage round his crippled hand.

Daniel Franks? A shy but handsome Jew. Competent, it seemed, if his conversation were any indication.

Patrick Henry? Most likely a member of the Colony, but hardly the Leper, for he was too visible to carry on the essential underground work, especially if he dressed as flamboyantly as he did that evening—in a velvet coat as scarlet as sin.

Bram hauled Ethan off to the supper room for refreshments—mainly from the long table's centerpiece, a silver fountain that cascaded with wine. Susan loyally remained with Jane, introducing her to those arriving guests she had not met. When the name of Martha Washington was announced, it seemed as if everyone in the room ceased to breathe as they waited for the confrontation between the general's lady and the famous Tory beauty.

Jane did not know what she had expected in Martha Washington, but it was not the short, middle-aged woman with the wise hazel eyes who greeted her so serenely. If the general's lady was dumpy, plain, sharp-nosed, as the gossips described her, Jane never noticed. The woman's graciousness settled like a magic net over the person in her presence.

"At last I meet the Lennox lady," Martha said after they were introduced. "The story of your marriage with Ethan Gordon is a most romantic one."

Jane curtseyed deeply. "As is yours with the general. I understand you have been married almost seventeen years."

Martha's plump cheeks deepened in a melancholy smile. "Yes, but we have been apart for so long this last year. I depended so much on him for everything, and now the war has demanded an enormous adjustment of me."

At the mention of the war, the faces of those about the two women lit in expectation. But Martha continued quietly, "Still, I am sure that it is just as difficult for you to adjust to a new place and different people."

"Ah, but she adjusted so well to her work as a common servant," a feminine voice said.

Smothered gasps and titters erupted at the calculated spite in the voice. A small frown puckered Martha Washington's rice-powdered nose. Susan laid a warning hand on Jane's arm.

Jane drew herself up to her full regal height and faced the woman who joined the gathering, her doting husband in tow. She was not surprised that it was the sultry beauty she had seen in the carriage talking with Ethan and later at Bruton Parish Church. Margaret Peyton. The woman was dressed in a robin's-egg blue satin gown with gold sequins clustered about the low-curved neckline. She waved a feathered fan as she openly assessed Jane with glittering green eyes that were set off by her white-powdered coiffure.

Was this the woman who was taking Susan's place in Ethan's heart—who filled his arms when he was in Williamsburg? The thought annoyed Jane. But then, with a bony old husband like John Peyton, she could understand

Margaret's need to flout society's mores, though she could not approve.

Jane's chin tilted imperiously as she said quietly, "You should know about the common quality, Mrs. Peyton."

Triumphant with her riposte, she sailed off with Susan. However, she later realized that it was Margaret who was ultimately victorious, for more than once she saw her engaged in intimate conversation with Ethan. "Join them and cut her throat," Susan urged.

Jane had to laugh. This gentle woman, this loyal friend, had a savage side after all—at least when it came to those for whom she cared. However, Jane chose to ignore her husband and his companions.

When the guests entered the dining room with its three-trestled table set for fifty-five, Margaret somehow contrived to be seated next to Ethan. Her haughtily held head was inclined close to Ethan's brilliant red hair in intimate conversation.

A stream of lackeys passed about the table, setting tempting dishes of tarts and meat pies and hothouse fruits before the guests, so that Jane's view of the two was often blocked. Despite the noise of cut glass clinking with pewter and porcelain, Margaret's silvery laughter could be heard at that end of the table. Susan sent Jane a sympathetic glance that did little to soothe Jane's irritation.

When, later, Margaret's clear voice asked for the pepper, Jane was using the caster. It was a childish thing to do, but too marvelous an opportunity to deny. A simple loosening of the hinged top before she restored the caster, along with the salt cellar, to the butler's tray accomplished her purpose. A shame Margaret had not asked for the vinegar cruet.

Moments later a shriek of distress, followed by a violent fit of sneezing, broke the table's conversation. Innocently Jane glanced down the length of the table to see Margaret holding the now-empty caster and looking down at her ample bosom in dismay. Pepper flecked the pale-blue bodice. Immediately the surprised butler was dusting her bodice with a napkin, which only made the embarrassing situation worse.

"Oh!" Margaret cried. Holding her skirts high, she dashed from the room.

Innocently Jane turned her devastating smile on the gentleman to her left, Dickey Lee, whom she had maneuvered to be her dinner partner. The man possed a *savoir faire* that reminded her of the Old World. Was he the Leper?

"So you are Ethan's Folly," he said, his dark eyes laughing. He knew of her prank!

"So you are Ethan's friend," she returned with a mischievous smile. "Odd that we have not met before."

Dickey Lee sipped at the sangaree, but his gaze held hers over the glass's crystal rim. "I cannot blame him for the lack of introduction. If I were he, I, too, would keep you fast in the dungeons of my heart."

She almost made a lighthearted reply, then realized the man's words were no flirtatious jest. He was sincere, and she honored his sincerity with the truth. "I am afraid you are wrong about Ethan. My Tory views disrupt his life, and for that I am sequestered at Mood Hill."

"But you are here now at the most conspicuous of places for a Tory, the governor's palace—and at the most auspicious of times, the public session," he pointed out gently.

Dimples formed in the hollows of her cheekbones. "I was persuasive, Mr. Lee."

His dark eyes glinted with laughter. "I imagine you were, madam."

Margaret eventually rejoined the dinner guests. After the meal, when the guests adjourned to the ballroom, a solicitous Ethan offered Margaret his arm. Jane had accomplished nothing with her prank.

Infuriated at being so easily ignored by her husband,

she proceeded to dance every minuet and quadrille, never dancing with the same partner twice. Her eyes entranced. Her smile enslaved. Every man there was drawn to her—but one, her own husband.

With those partners who were deep into their cups, she mentioned casually the legend of the Leper's Colony. "Is it true? The Leper is a real person? Who could he be?"

And no one knew. Oh, there were plenty of guesses. *The saddle and harnessmaker. . . . No, 'tis the glover. . . . The butcher, most certainly.*

Once she glimpsed Uriah Wainwright with staunch patriot cronies of his, and her stomach churned with a sickening feeling. *Branded. Marked!* Quickly she looked to the nearest man—Daniel Franks, as it turned out—and asked pertly, "Will you not ask me to dance, sir?"

"I was but waiting for the opportunity, madam," he said with a quiet but intense gallantry. "You have danced with all but me."

"Not all," she said pointedly.

His gaze followed hers to the dice-scarred tables that had been set up in the smaller supper room. In addition to hazard, games of piquet were in progress. Margaret Peyton and her husband sat at the same table with Ethan. Margaret's senile husband partnered the Widow Grundy, while Margaret's eyes gleamed most provocatively above the tops of her cards at Ethan.

"Ah, but his religion prevents him from dancing, does it not, Mrs. Gordon?" Daniel inquired tactfully.

"But not from playing cards?"

Daniel smiled shyly. "Well, you can't deny a man everything."

"His piquet partner does not deny a man anything!" she quipped.

Uncharacteristically, Daniel Franks threw back his head and laughed, causing both of them to miss a step. "You will certainly enliven Williamsburg this session, Mrs. Gordon."

Chapter 30

Hair brushed out but still unpinned, Jane sat before the cherry-wood secretary in her Grecian-style robe of gauze and belladine and sorted through the pile of invitations that mounded on the silver platter. Having proven herself that month a formidable opponent in any battle of wits as well as mistress of mischievous gaiety, she was firmly established as the reigning queen of Williamsburg society.

Invitations to private parties, marathon whist games, and teas poured in—hosted by aristocratic planters, wealthy businessmen, and legislators. No homes were closed to her. The elite merchants of Williamsburg, who were for the most part Scots of Tory leaning, had heard of Jane's loyalist temperament and were only too happy to have the famed Tory beauty grace their homes. And the patriots welcomed the diversion from boredom she afforded.

Even her critics grudgingly admired her for her obvious intelligence and the air of complete independence with which she seemed to move through the world.

Jane found what she was looking for—a boxed gift along with an invitation to a whist party given by the Widow Grundy. It was the third such gathering of Tory women that Jane attended that month, and naturally most of the talk concerned the sorrowful situation their families were in—outcasts in a decidedly patriot city.

But for Jane the parties were more. The Tory families had friends and relatives in the British-held Boston area, and she gleaned scraps of information about conditions there. Nothing so far about Terence, though she continued to hope.

Her fingers fumbled as she opened the gift the Widow Grundy had sent. In the long, narrow box was a quill pen, as Jane had expected. Quickly, her fingers twisted at the quill— and it came away from the plume. Inside the hollow quill she found the coiled strip of paper. Eagerly she withdrew it and read the minuscule writing. "Terence MacKenzie arrived in Quebec last fall. Since then his name has completely disappeared from the rosters. He now serves the loyalist cause as a spy."

Slowly Jane wadded the strip of paper. S Terence was a spy. She disliked the sound of the word. But then, wasn't she one? In return for this information, was she not committed to passing along any political information she acquired at the various functions she attended—especially information regarding the Leper?

The idea bothered her. The broad intellectual stimulation she was exposed to as a child made her mind open to all avenues of reasoning. Thus, she could too easily understand and sympathize with both England and the colonies.

To get in touch with Terence she would, of course, correspond with other Tory sympathizers; yet she felt a niggling sense of guilt at deceiving her patriot friends. And what of her husband? She tried to tell herself that since his Quaker's religion prevented him from being a staunch patriot, she need not feel any sense of betrayal.

She was in the midst of resealing the quill to the plume when Ethan entered, his blue camblet coat's long skirts flapping with his brusque stride. He tossed his tricorn on the japanned chest. His face was set in tense lines that had been there since the ball at the governor's palace. Because of her prank or her flirtations?

Though he had said nothing that night, she saw the displeasure in his eyes when he returned from his card game to find her dancing once more with Daniel Franks. Rebelliously, she had smiled up at the Burgess member, laughing at some story he related and replying some inanity that she couldn't even remember.

"Is business not going well?" she asked with a formal politeness, anything to put a distance between herself and the man who was her husband. She was thinking about him too often when alone at night in her bedroom.

He crossed the room to stand before her. "Business is going excellently," he said in a harsh tone.

"Marvelous," she prattled, growing more nervous by the moment. "I was afraid that buying Polly's papers would put a strain on finances. You know, Polly is marvelously happy here. Even now she's doing all the marketing, and you know how badly I was at doing the mar—"

He dropped a knotted rope on the desk. She looked down at it blankly. Her name was written on a small scrap of paper tied with string through the rope's knot. "It's a hangman's noose," he said flatly. "I found it draped outside on the doorknob."

She swallowed and looked up at him. "I don't understand."

"I think thee does," he growled. "'Tis a warning—from our friend, Uriah Wainwright, no doubt. Has thee been meddling in Tory politics?"

Obstinately her chin shot up. "I have attended parties given by loyal British subjects."

"'Tis time we went back to Mood Hill," he said, and turned to leave.

"I won't." She sprang to her feet, toppling her chair. "I won't go back."

He whipped around and grabbed her arm. His free hand swept up the rope, and, before she knew what he was about, he looped it over her head, drawing the noose so tight she was forced to stand on her toes. He looked down at her with eyes that scorched. "If thee doesn't go with me, thee will not be received here by the patriot families. And if thee can find a Tory family to take thee in—ultimately this is what thee can expect."

With that he pulled the noose upward until, straining against the bite of the rope, her mouth touched his.

Something happened. Something intangible—a current of devastating intensity—passed between them. Her lashes fluttered closed. Her lips parted. The rope burned at her neck, but she would suffer the pain—if only he would kiss her. And then his mouth was crushing her lips. His breath flowed into her, filling her, so that she was a part of him. Her hands clutched at his shoulder blades, pressing her breasts against the steel plate that was his chest until they hurt, and moving her hips against his hard groin in a wanton manner.

But, oh, she wanted him.

"Ethan . . ." she rasped, when he pushed down her gossamer sleeve and kissed the inside of her arm just below her shoulder. The kiss was a blow in the belly. Her body flooded with liquid rapture.

"Jane, honey, thy skin, it's like cream—soft, tasty." And he wouldn't stop kissing her. His mouth returned to claim hers with a hot, exultant pleasure. He backed her against the desk and buried his face in her cloud of hair. "Sweet Jane"—his hands romped along her curves—"I can't get thee out of my mind." Her breast filled one large hand. "At night—" His other hand entangled in the rope's noose. Abruptly he released her, and she had to grab for the desk's edge to keep from losing her balance.

For a long moment he looked down at the rope he held, then he passed the back of his hand across his eyes. "Thy— charms make me forget the danger." She watched with a sick heart as he turned from her. "Pack," he ordered, and left.

Chapter 31

He could hear her in her bedroom, opening and closing drawers resoundingly as she went about packing. He sat at the edge of the bed and rubbed at his tired eyes. Trying to understand his wife was like trying to understand ciphered codes. He knew she was in love with Terence MacKenzie, so why the amorous flirtations with Daniel?

And why was he jealous of her flirtations? He had wanted a demure wife, a gentle woman to make the house he had built into a home—the home he had not known as a child. And through his own folly, he was married to a hoyden who could neither cook nor sew but who could entice every man within miles. His knuckles stood out in ridges when he thought of Jane's lips bestowing her coquettish smiles, her vivacious laughter, on other men, but not on her own husband.

He gained very little information at the piquet table the evening of the ball because of his preoccupation with his spirited wife. Still, he doubted if old man Peyton was that involved with the loyalists. Margaret, fortunately, was too free of tongue, and he could not let such a useful intimacy cool. And the Widow Grundy—he suspected she was a minor agent in the Tory movement. And she certainly was not as daft as people seemed to think.

Yet he was. He was daft for wanting Jane Lennox like he did. Nay, Jane Gordon. And he was afraid for her. She was courting danger. Consorting as she was with the enemy, he was powerless to protect her.

Chapter 32

Ahmad stared at the list of names that lengthened daily—names of Washington's military family, mostly the officers who made up the headquarters personnel and ate at the general's table.

Joseph Reed and Thomas Mifflin—two young Philadelphians who act as secretary and aide, respectively. Both experienced men of the world.

Charles Lee—adventurer with a new major general's commission in the American Army. Already unpopular and difficult, the man was being touchy about his rank and privileges.

Schuyler—landowner and Indian War veteran like Washington.

Knox—former Boston bookseller whose hobbies are military history and engineering.

Gates—recommended by his past military experience with Braddock.

Billy—Washington's faithful black body servant.

The staff officers: Robert Hanson Harrison—the writing aide; Colonel Baylor—carries out trivial military duties.

While the spy waited for word from Parliament declaring Wychwood and Manor House his with the completion of his assignment, he mingled with the American soldiers who patrolled Cambridge, Washington's headquarters. Since there were no uniforms, it was easy enough to pass among them undetected, gleaning information pertinent to his forthcoming operation.

He knew that in the absence of uniforms to identify the American officers, a system of colored ribbons, worn diagonally across the breast between the coat and waistcoat, had been worked out: light blue for the commander-in-chief, the brigadiers wore pink ribbons, the major generals purple, and the staff green. The field and company officers had colored cockades and shoulder knots.

He also knew that simply waiting for Washington to appear on one of Cambridge's streets involved both the problem of a shot going wild and escaping an entire army afterward. No, the assassination would have to take place in close quarters and with only a few bodyguards to contend with. Washington wisely surrounded himself with a number of bodyguards, whom he rotated on an irregular basis.

Ahmad learned from one of the former guards, who was only too willing to drink to George Washington's health a goodly number of times, that the general had been headquartered in the home of Harvard's president. But that had been inconvenient for everybody and embarrassing to Washington, as Dr. Langley was allowed to retain only one room for his private use.

Surreptitiously Ahmad had scouted out the new headquarters, a house belonging to a loyalist named Vassall who left it with its furniture intact when the Colonial Army first appeared. The general's own washwoman, a middle-aged mother who had been abandoned by her husband, revealed after subtle prompting during a pleasurable night of lovemaking the headquarter interior. A handsome dwelling, she said, with paneled rooms on either side of a central hall and space enough for the aides and secretaries to work.

Specifically, which rooms did they use? And was there an established routine? With cunning and patience Ahmad eventually ascertained that Harrison, the writing aide, spent his life at a cluttered table in a room behind the general's study. But much more detailed information was needed.

Ahmad pulled from the sheets of scribbled notes the house's floor plan he had sketched from the miscellaneous information he had accumulated. The general's bedroom was on the second floor—accessible only by the one stairway inside the house and a window. Both inside and out, the house was heavily guarded. He wadded up the map, ruling out the possibility of assassinating Washington from within.

He rose from the desk and went to the narrow window of the room he rented above the Lion's Head Tavern. February's snow swirled by, obliterating Cambridge's streets. In the reflection off the windowpanes he saw in his mind's eye the man Washington. Tall, large, raw-boned. Unpolished, but charismatic.

The washwoman had related the general's personal habits—that Washington had a passion for black walnuts; that his toilet, plain and simple, was quickly made. A single servant prepared his clothes and laid them out at night for use in the morning. The servant always combed and tied his master's hair, but Washington preferred to dress and shave himself.

Ahmad called up the man's daily routine, when the general left and returned to the house. But there was no uniform schedule. Only in the evening was the man reliable, as he took his stroll through the gardens at the rear of the house to seek the privy. And only then was the general without guards.

That seemed to be the one viable option; still, there remained the fact that when Washington did not return within the half hour, the alarm would go up. And there was too much rebel countryside to negotiate between Cambridge and Boston Harbor. His chances of living weren't worth a tuppence until he was safely aboard ship, bound for England. He needed more than a half-hour start.

Then the spy's eye fell on the day-old newspaper lying on the bed. Twice he had read the article about Washington. Long ago he had learned that every detail could serve its purpose—yet . . . impossible! In his preoccupation with the man, he had forgotten the woman. He grabbed up the Pennsylvania *Gazette* and once more read the article.

> *Yesterday the Lady of His Excellency General Washington arrived here, on her way to New England. She was met at the Lower Ferry by the officers of the different battalions, the troop of the Light Horse, and the Light Infantry of the 2nd Battalion, who escorted her into the city.*

The spy tried to recall where the general's home was. Mount Vernon, that was it. The odds were good that at some point the general would pay a hurried visit to his home and wife—and certainly not with his entire army. A few personal bodyguards, maybe a troop. But these, Ahmad knew, he could deal with. Better yet, Mount Vernon was located on the Potomac River where a British warship already plied.

And if Washington did not journey to Mount Vernon in the near future . . . well, there was the general's lady.

There was also Jane. His sources in Virginia reported she had married a colonist and was acquainted with Martha

Washington. Ahmad swung away from the window, balling the list he held and flinging it against the cracked plastered wall. That she was sharing her bed with another man shouldn't sting. But it did. And he would yet have her, even if it meant killing her clod of a husband in order to take her back to England when he was ready to escape.

He retrieved the wadded paper from the knot-holed floor. One by one he held it and the other sheets to the candle flame. His homework was done.

Chapter 33

"A Valentine's party!" Polly sighed and fastened the powdering gown about Jane's shoulders. "To be sure, yew'll be the finest lady there, mistress."

Jane covered her face with the mask, muffling her voice. "For all the good it will do, Polly."

"Now wot makes yew say a thing like that?" The girl sifted the powder dredger over Jane's coiffure of elaborately arranged curls, and slowly the ebony sheen whitened. "The master 'as 'is eye on yew. Last time we 'ad visitors—New Years 'tis was—I seen 'im looking at yew with that look, if yew get my meaning."

"Aye," Jane muttered. "Only because he was afraid I would flirt again with Daniel Franks."

"The man 'as the sweets for yew, he does."

"Daniel came to Mood Hill with Mr. Lee on business." She laid the mask on the dressing table and, smiling wryly, looked in the mirror at her maid. "Besides, I think 'tis Peter who has the sweets for someone."

Polly's ruddy color actually deepened. "Peter's a fine bloke, 'e is, mistress." Rapidly the chambermaid changed the subject. "Speaking of fine blokes, I 'ear tell that Lizzie 'as a gentleman caller—Mr. Critcham, the butcher. Wants to buy 'er papers from the Widow Grundy, 'e does." She held up the Spanish wool that was saturated with carmine. "Yew want the rouge fer yer cheeks?"

Critically Jane studied her image in the looking glass. As a young girl, she had stood in the shade of her mother's brilliant beauty and despaired over her own awkward height, her nondescript hair coloring, her thin, bony face. She thought her mouth was still too wide, her face too sharply angled. But, still, a vibrantly lovely woman stared back at her. "I think not, Polly." Her finest asset was her eyes, and the rouge would only detract from her eyes' color.

"Is thee ready?" Ethan asked from the doorway.

Jane's gaze met his in the looking glass. He was dressed in a dark-brown frockcoat with white facings cut into the standard wide, stiff skirts reaching midthigh. His clothing was trimmed with simple pewter buttons and knee buckles, and he carried buckskin gloves. The buff-colored nankeen breeches, a trifle too tight, and white, ribbed cotton stockings showed the muscular turn of his thighs and calves. No padded rolls needed there. Too easily she recalled her thighs pressed against the solidity of his and wondered what it would be like to lay crushed beneath. . . .

"Almost," she replied with that distant politeness toward her husband that she knew Polly found quite confusing.

Rising from the padded stool, she brushed off some of

the powder grains flecking the charcoal-colored crêpe gown. A narrow lace ruffle trimmed the high neckline. The dress was tight across the bosom, and from beneath the black tangle of lashes she saw the way her husband's fierce gaze locked on the evidence of her femininity. She repressed a curiously pleasant shiver. "Polly, get my pelisse, will you."

"Thee will need the greatcoat, also," Ethan drawled. "The spirits in Fahrenheit's thermometer are dropping."

The late afternoon was growing colder, and the horizon was layered by giant gray puffs of clouds portending snow. Riding pillion, Jane sorely missed the rented carriages of Williamsburg. She huddled against the lee of Ethan's broad back, seeking the warmth it afforded. Her fingers locked in front about the hard wall of his stomach, and her palms picked up the knotting of the stomach's muscles as he shifted in rhythm with the dun's movements.

As the dun picked its way in the direction of the Fairmonts' house, soft snow flurries dappled the silent forest on either side of the traveled road. She couldn't help thinking that were she in love with her husband, this delightfully romantic mode of traveling would rival the warmer comfort of the coach. In a coach there would be no excuse to cuddle so close to her husband.

Evening had settled in by the time they reached the Fairmont house. A smaller-scale model of the great Georgian plantation mansions along the James River, it stood at the end of a long avenue of gnarled and denuded paper mulberries that were flanked by cultivated fields lying fallow in the winter months. The crushed-oyster-shell drive crunched beneath the dun's prancing hooves. At the end of the drive welcoming lights illuminated the many windows beneath the snow-capped roof.

Before the ringed hitching post, Ethan held up his mammoth hands to help her dismount. In the light of the porch lanterns, her eyes met his, and she saw the snowflakes that dusted his thick lids—and the lust that burned in his dark eyes. It shook her all the way down to her Moroccan pumps. Whatever he might still feel for Susan, Jane recognized with a frightening clarity that she was no longer safe from him. He wanted her.

Worse, she knew she was no longer capable of denying him.

She slid into his waiting grasp and quickly stepped back, avoiding his questioning gaze. He turned the dun over to the old Negro groom, who shifted from one foot to the other in the cold, and led her up the expanse of stairs. Laughter and good-natured shouts greeted Ethan and Jane when a little black boy admitted them inside. He took their greatcoats before ushering them into the large drawing room warmed by the marble fireplace's leaping flames. It was a pleasant room, with cream-colored walls and pewter-blue woodwork.

A game of charades was in progress, the men grouped on one side of the room in competition with the women on the other. Susan, spotting the newly arrived couple, left her place on the needlepoint-covered settee to hurry to them. "Jane, Ethan—I'm so happy you could come. I was afraid the weather would keep you away."

"You know nothing would keep us away, Susan," Ethan said. Jane heard that tender warmth his voice lacked when he addressed her. Anger boiled in her—anger at her husband for loving Susan and anger at herself for being angry. What should Ethan's feelings matter to her as long as they were not directed at her?

Bram detached himself from the males to offer a hot cider toddy to the couple. Soon she and Ethan were separated and towed over to reinforce the opposing sides as a new game of charades got underway. In the merriment she forgot that the guests were rebels and she was a Tory. Startled, she realized that there was a gradual shifting in her loyalties.

When the dandy, Harry Gramble, humped his padded shoulders and brandished an imaginary sword, Ethan was the first to accurately guess Goldsmith's popular *She Stoops to Conquer*.

Jane could not have been more surprised at this indication of Ethan's literary knowledge. She herself had a more difficult time trying to discern the pantomime performed by the pug-nosed Ida Mayhill. Ethan's deep laughter goaded her to try harder. Only when the wall-eyed matron, Lucy Knowles, guessed that it was a gate and not a door that Ida pretended to open did Jane come up with the correct answer of Newgate Prison.

Pleased at her success, she turned a triumphant gaze on Ethan but saw only the bleak look in his eyes. She instantly guessed the reason for it. Someday she would like to ask him about that period of his life at Kilmainham Prison.

During the intimate dinner served on a linen tablecloth stitched with red lace hearts, Bram talked of politics, naturally—"Dunmore's burned Norfolk and sailed away for England" . . . "Washington, they say, lost half his army New Year's Day when enlistments were up."

She saw Ethan flash his friend a guarded look, but a few minutes later her husband was speaking quietly with Susan. Was he still enamoured of his neighbor's wife?

When Harry Gramble sought to monopolize Jane's attention with droll conversation, light laughter pealed from her inviting lips, bringing a slashing frown from Ethan. Ethan owned her, had paid for her, and obviously did not like sharing his property. Perversity prompted her into beguiling the handsome dandy only that much more. Once she leaned close enough for Harry to whisper some inanity in her ear, and she thought Ethan was going to bolt out of his chair.

Later, the guests adjourned to the parlor again for a game of Judge and Jury, which called for the forfeit of kisses.

When Jane was appointed the judge, she called on Ethan. "Who is the Leper?"

His eyebrows rose. "I do not know."

When Jane replied, "Then, good sir, you must forfeit a kiss," the guests grinned and wall-eyed Lucy cackled aloud.

As Ethan rose to his feet, Jane's heart pumped wildly in expectation. But when, amid the cheering, he bestowed a simple kiss on her forehead, where errant tendrils curled, she barely managed to conceal her disappointment behind a merry little laugh.

A while later Bram announced that it was snowing heavily, and it would be best if the guests spent the night. Jane realized this meant that she and Ethan would be forced into occupying the same bed. She looked at him with eyes that pleaded, but he also seemed at a loss for words.

"It could get worse, Bram," he offered up. "I think Jane and I should start back for Mood Hill tonight."

"Nonsense. An expert woodsman like yourself knows as well as I do how easy it is to wander off the road in a snowstorm. Besides, we want the pleasure of your company for another day, don't we, Susan?"

"Of course! We have room enough for everyone." The dainty woman clapped her hands. "Oh, it shall be a delightful weekend!"

Delightful was hardly the word Jane had in mind as the guests dispersed to their assigned bedrooms. At her side Ethan arched a cynical brow. "Truly delightful," he muttered beneath his breath. With trepidation she followed Susan to the rear bedroom on the second floor.

"There now," Susan said, lighting the candle in the brass wall sconces. "Since this bedroom faces the south side of the house, you two will find it the coziest of the guest rooms."

Ethan flicked a rueful glance at Jane. "I'm sure we will, Susan."

When the young woman had departed, the two looked at each other over the length of the Oriental carpet. "What can we do?" Jane whispered.

His fingers loosed the waistcoat's pewter buttons. "Nothing at—"

"What are you doing?"

"Getting undressed."

She swung away, her hands covering her face. "You promised."

"Thee didn't let me finish." She heard the frockcoat and waistcoat flop across the back of a chair. "I'll take the chair. Thee can have the bed."

"You would sit up all night?"

He unbuckled the ruffled stock and tossed it on the dresser. "I've spent many a night sleeping in the saddle when I rode with the Virginia Riflemen."

It was just one more aspect of her husband of which she was unaware. "You patrolled the frontier against the Indians?"

"After Ezra and Miriam were—after they died." Settling his tall frame in the flounced chair, he stretched his long legs out and rotated his stockinged feet with a grunt of contentment.

She eyed him warily. His hands were clasped behind his head, and his lids had already closed. Quickly she began to disrobe, feeling the rush of the room's cool air about her shoulders as she slid the gown off. She unknotted the stomacher's strings, stepped out of the side hoops, and untied the ribboned garters about her cherry-colored stockings. When she stood clad only in her camisole, stays, and underpetticoats, goose bumps surfaced along her arms. Something prompted her to look up. Ethan was watching her with a less-than-sleepy look in his eyes. With a small cry her hands flew up before her barely concealed breasts.

"Get in bed," he muttered, closing his eyes again. "'Tis cold."

Wasting not another moment, she smothered the candle's flame and in the darkness sought the concealing covers of the bedstead. Ethan rose from his chair, and her heart thumped like a loom's waft. But he merely drew the heavy brocaded bed curtains. Enclosed by utter darkness, she shivered between the cold bed sheets. How much colder and uncomfortable must Ethan be. If only the bed had one of those New England bundling boards.

"Ethan?" Was he already asleep? "Ethan?" she called in a louder whisper.

"Hmmm?"

"Come to bed."

If possible, the bedroom seemed even quieter than before she had spoken. After an eternal minute, his voice asked, "Is thee certain that is what thee wants?"

Her tongue stumbled. "'Tis not fair that you should be uncomfortable."

"Thee desires only my comfort?"

"Yes . . . of course."

In a moment she heard his white linen shirt slither to the floor and felt his weight sag the mattress. She lay rigid, afraid some part of her would touch him. His body heat stole over her. For a long time she waited to hear the even breathing that signaled he was asleep. Yet eventually it was her own breathing that filled her ears and lullabyed her into sleep.

In the deep of night she stirred to find herself cuddled against the warm flesh of his side, her head pillowed on his arm. Instantly she stiffened. Her husband had shed all his clothes!

When after a time he made no move to embrace her, she relaxed. A little later she drowsily slid her arm about his wide, barrellike ribs and pressed her entire length against him. Her leg slipped up to wedge between his heavier, more muscled one, and her cold toes snuggled against the hair-matted calves. In her sleepy state, she thought contentedly that this was a decidedly pleasant aspect of marriage that she had almost missed.

She did not even feel alarmed a little later about the lips that kissed her widow's peak then dropped a tenderly brushed kiss in the soft hollow just before her ear. And when his tongue teased the pox pit in the center of her chin, she dipped her chin to seek that warm, wet mouth in a quite unconscious manner. The pleasurable kiss changed imperceptibly, though she could not identify that moment she came wide awake to the exquisitely sensual arousal that claimed her, to the liquid excitement that coursed through her. She only knew she almost hurt with some deep, insatiable need.

She lost the arm that had been her pillow when he raised on his elbow to look down at her. His eyes glittered. He drew away from her and kissed her forehead. "Go back to sleep, Jane."

"But . . ."

"Go to sleep. With the first light of day sometimes come regrets."

Her hand sought his shoulder only to come in contact with the hard mound of his chest. She left it there, savoring the crisp tangle of hair beneath her fingertips. "But Ethan . . . I liked you kissing me." She was glad that the darkness hid the color that surely flooded her cheeks at the bald admission.

"There's more to loving than kissing," he told her in a harsh tone.

"Show me," she taunted softly, unwisely.

A guttural rasp tore out of his throat. He rolled half over her, pinning her on the goosedown mattress. His callused hands gripped her bare shoulders, and he slanted his

mouth down over hers. His lips crushed hers like an unheeding bootheel would fallen rose petals. His tongue filled her
mouth, and she wanted to feel its slashing tip sabering clear
down to that aching pit in her stomach.

She slid one hand behind his neck, loosening the queue
so that his thick hair swished free, tickling her wrist. Her
other hand slid around his waist to press against his back,
pulling him against her. Against her own volition, her fingers
followed the fine hair that veed down into the firm, rounded
buttocks.

A small gasp fluttered up her windpipe, but his mouth
silenced her sudden modest outcry. "Jane," he growled low
against her lips in a voice that she hardly recognized, "'tis too
late . . . all is lost."

Now an undefinable fear crept up her spine as his fingers worked nimbly at her wooden pins and tumbled loose
her heavy hair. Remnants of its powder flurried about them.
His fingers buried in the thick tresses, tugging to arch her
neck, and his mouth traveled down the creamy column to the
base of her throat. But she was insensitive to the feverish
kisses. The thick, engorged organ against the inside of her
thigh, announcing its inevitable intent, terrified her. The
swollen, tumescent member was incredibly large; as large,
surely, as that of Wychwood's brood stallions.

"No," she whispered in a tight, panicky voice.

But there was no stopping Ethan. He was far stronger
and beyond the reach of pleas or hands that shoved ineffectually against his chest. For too long he had repressed his
volatile desire for her. And that desire was damning her. He
was a volcano erupting. His violation of her was inescapable,
unavoidable.

God, let it end, let it end soon, she prayed.

But neither God nor Ethan seemed to hear her. Instead,
Ethan took his time. Anchoring her wrists at either side of
her hips, he slid down her, his thick silky fur brushing her

breasts, her belly, the insides of her thighs. He kissed her nipples softly, harshly, tenderly until the aureoles' nerves became so taut they hovered on the threshold of pain. He worked his way down past her navel until his breath warmed the furred flesh.

Shocked, she tried to thrash her hips up out of reach, but his viselike grip on her wrist prevented but the merest movement, and that movement only intensified the action of his tongue. Her hands began to go numb from the lack of blood, but after a moment she did not notice because there was nothing else for her but the steadily rising pleasure he was engendering within her. His tongue softly worked up and down her, its stiff tip like a searing branding iron on the taut knot between the folds. Her body began to respond. Warm fluid mingled with saliva.

She was sobbing weakly at her helplessness—and her pleasure in the humiliating act; her rage at helplessness and her pleasure were all drawn from the same well.

"Jane, Jane," he rasped against her flesh, "let go—try to enjoy it. I am thy husband."

She attempted to repress the lust rising in her and maintain her revulsion and anger, but it was impossible. The sexual arousal he stirred in her overcame her efforts to isolate herself, to turn herself completely cold. The sounds of sucking and licking and nibbling joined with her inarticulate mouthings. She was laughing and crying. And then a pulsation started deep within her. The soles of her feet planted themselves against the mattress, and she raised her hips, offering herself to him.

He slid up her, pressing her down, and the hot cylindrical flesh drove beyond the ring of muscle, deep, deep with rhythmical thrusting. She felt her jaws go slack and her eyes begin to glaze. Then abruptly Ethan collapsed on her with a hoarse outcry.

She lay rigid, afraid to move for sudden pain—and un-

able to move beneath his colossal weight. Tears brimmed behind her tightly squeezed lids. Surrendering her virginity to
Ethan extinguished her hope of going to Terence pure in
body.

Between her legs she could feel the slow seep of wet-
ness—her blood mixed with his semen. The mere thought
enraged her, burned away her tears of self-pity.

"Jane," his voice husked at her ear. "Jane, I'm sorry . . .
I had gone too long . . . it will be better next time."

"Next time!" she spat through clenched teeth. "What in
Heaven's sweet name makes you think there will be a next
time?" Fury rendered sensible speech impossible. "You—the
smell of—of your lovemaking—revulses me. Your giant's
body has—has no beauty—is repugnant. Dear God in
Heaven, get off of me—no, don't touch me again!"

His hand dropped from her cheek, and the mattress
shifted as he rolled from her and turned his back.

With first light, she was still considering his statement
about regret coming with the morning. Her regret knew no
bottom.

She tried to conjure up Terence's face as a source of
comfort. And to her consternation, she couldn't recall its
handsome lines at all.

Chapter 34

With both Porhatras and Polly to help around the house, idle time weighed heavily on Jane. Beckoned by the shafts of warm sunlight on the wooden floor, she left the harpsichord and went to stand in the doorway. Spring had come early to Mood Hill. In the snowy blossoms that kissed the plum trees, in the scent of the tender indigo shoots, and in the way of a man with a maiden, March brought the promise of life renewed.

In the fields she could see deaf Josiah pause in his hoeing to watch Porhatras walking toward him in that uneven gait of hers. The Indian maid had eagerly volunteered to take a pitcher of water to the men, and Jane knew the reason. For some time now it had been evident that Porhatras and Josiah were in love. And for the deaf mute, Porhatras' language presented no problem.

Likewise, Peter was courting Polly. Or as the blushing Polly so delicately put it, "The Peter, man-of-war, and the Polly, frigate, wot soon shall be moored 'ead and stern along side of each other in Blanket Bay, missus."

With the summer Icabod's term of indenture would expire. But rather than going back to the Old World, he was sending for his wife and children—bringing them to settle on the fifty acres that was the freedom dues given a servant at the expiration of his term. The Scotsman was in love with that primeval land with its spring carpet of brilliantly colored yarrow, trumpet creeper, and Queen Anne's lace growing in riotous profusion about the fields and woodlands.

And Ethan? Did he feel any of the stirrings that marked the rites of spring? She hardly knew, since the two of them said little more to each other than was required. Her anxious eyes sought out his huge figure. He was nowhere to be seen, and she felt a vast sense of relief. That night with him—at the Fairmonts'—had changed her. He had implanted within her the seed of desire. She was angry with this new side of herself only slightly more than she was angry with the man who had violated and mastered her.

Images of her stretched beneath him hounded her so that she knew no peace. He had dominated her, and in her submission she had discovered within herself a sensuality she had not known existed. Now her fingers surreptitiously touched her aching breasts at night; the soft globes which had once seemed foreign appendages. Now they were a part of her, had come alive beneath the lips of a man, the lips of her husband.

"Mistress Gordon," Icabod said, rounding the corner of the house.

Jane jumped guiltily. "Aye, Icabod?"

He removed his cap and rubbed his round, balding head. "The master kinna make it for the nooning."

Icabod was clearly embarrassed. Everyone at Mood Hill seemed to know of the estrangement between the master and mistress. Had Ethan found her so clearly lacking in matters of intimacy that she held no appeal for him at all? She cared little if he did, for she had no desire for a repeat of the crude, painful performance. But she did want a demonstration of his respect before the others!

"Try rubbing rosemary on your head for baldness," she snapped at Icabod and, oblivious to his startled glance, stalked past him.

King George nipped at her heels as she crossed the yard toward the log vat house, where hammering could be heard. At the vat house's door she could make out Ethan, naked to the waist, kneeling before the lower vat as he hammered at the yellow-pine siding. In the vat house's dimness his flesh glowed like polished copper. She stepped inside and the smell of the fermenting indigo swept over her. Flies buzzed incessantly about the small room.

Ethan looked up. "Aye?"

She knotted her hands at her side. "I will not have you ignoring me."

His eyes flicked past her to the sunlight streaming through the doorway. "'Tis for thy own good." He turned back to his work, sticking an extra nail between his lips.

"I am your wife, and—"

His shoulders rose with a deeply drawn breath, and he took the nail from between his lips. "Mistress, thee—"

"Jane."

"Jane," he amended without turning to face her. "Thee is courting trouble."

She knelt at his side, wetting the hem of her skirts with the excess water that sluiced into the bottom vat to form a muddy-looking sediment. Her voice was low, strained. "We can't go on forever with this farce of a marriage."

He looked down at her, his glance taking in the soft rise of her breasts beneath the thin gauze shade of the pale-yellow dimity dress. "Leave me, Jane," he commanded sharply. "Go back to the house."

"Certainly, milord," she spat out.

Furious, she rose to dip a mocking curtsey—only to catch her pump's heel on her hem. Too late his hand grabbed for her as she toppled over the vat's edge into the shallow mixture of lime water and steeped indigo sediment. Sputtering she pushed herself upright. A bluish red coated her bodice and skirts and ran in rivulets from her hairline down over her cheeks. The rank smell of the fermenting indigo oozed from her straggling hair and clothing. "Ohhh!"

Then she heard Ethan's deep chuckle, and her lacerated pride exploded. "How dare you laugh!" Her hands balled and she sprang at him.

He caught her pummeling fists. "'Tis not my fault, Jane," he said, but his mouth was crimped trying to restrain his laughter.

"You swore to humble me!" she raged, still thrashing ineffectually in his more powerful grip. "Does this not delight you?"

His gaze dropped to where the drenched gown clung to her breasts, revealing the small button nipples. "Aye, that it does, Jane," he rasped.

Renewed fury swept over her. She gave a sudden jerk of her wrists, so that both of them went sprawling into the vat, splashing the indigo on King George, who made a frenzied dash for the doorway. Jane braced her arms behind her and sat up, her soaked skirts tangled unladylike about her thighs.

Ethan wiped away the colored water that clung to his thick eyelashes. His red hair was plastered across his forehead, and the indigo's sediment splotched his upper lip like a mustache. With visible effort she tried to preserve her grave demeanor. But it was hopeless. She began to laugh, unable to stop despite the unholy gleam she saw in his eyes. "We are a pair, aren't we now?" she managed between laughter-stricken gasps.

"Oh, that we are," he growled. Then, unexpectedly, his hands gripped her shoulders. His mouth captured hers in a ravenous kiss. This elemental passion was what she had wanted, had been starved for, and she returned the kiss, her hands sliding over his shoulders to draw him near, to feel his heart thudding against her own erratically beating heart.

The primitive odor that enveloped them was like a sensual stimulant, so potent that she cared not when he pressed her down into the wash of indigo. The blue-red sediment lapped gently about her ears and streamed her loosened hair to the foaming surface. Yet she was aware only of the intense urgency that filled her. She understood now that powerful drive to mate.

"Ethan, my husband," she murmured against the rough-textured skin of his jaw. Her fingers slipped up to caress that shriveled spot that marked his cheek. "I want—I can't help myself. I want you, Ethan."

His brilliant eyes searched hers. "Thee is certain?"

Her laugh was low and husky. "You have to ask me?"

Startling her, he swept her up against him and rose to his feet. He staggered beneath the weight of her sopping wet skirts. "I'm not a little woman," she said in a small voice.

"So I notice," he groaned as he carried her from the vat house. "But thee is just right for me. Between us," he puffed, "we shall breed Goliaths."

She blushed, then despite her embarrassment and his frankness, laughed. One buckled pump fell from her bobbing feet. Another few yards and the other pump plopped. Through eyelashes spiked with indigo she saw Icabod's double chins drop in surprise as Ethan strolled past him. Farther on, Peter paused in his hoeing to stare.

"Everyone is watching," she said, burying her burning face in the hollow of his shoulder.

"Good," he grunted. "Jane, thee weighs more than a cask of rum!"

Her head snapped up. "Sir," she said with exaggerated dignity, "the bigger the better!"

He chuckled, and her breath caught at the beauty in his smile. How—when—had he bemused her, bewitched her, so that she forgot all else, even Terence?

His boots echoed on wood planking. "In you go."

"What—?"

Suddenly she was sailing in space to splash unceremoniously in the river. Shock raced through her. "Ethan!" she floundered. "I can't swim!"

A heron took wing at her screech. Above her on the dock, Ethan laughed. "The water is only waist-deep."

She got her footing. Her skirts billowed about her with the lily pads. Pushing her wet hair off her face, she looked up at him. The shirt and boots were already stripped from him. Astounded, she watched as he shucked one stocking at a time—and then his breeches. "Ethan!"

"'Tis time thee knew." He grinned.

"I already know!"

A small grimace pleated his mouth. "Thee knew the pain, not the pleasure."

From between splayed fingers she peeked at the nude giant above her. The mahogany skin ended at his pelvis. Then pale white—and the thick brush. His organ stood boldly erect, throbbing, taunting her. Her mouth parted. A strange hunger took hold of her. Her tongue flicked at her wet lips.

His mouth curled in a pleased smile, a smug smile, that irritated her. Still, she could not take her eyes from that veined, tumescent object of male beauty. He dived smoothly, shallowly into the water and surfaced just beyond her. "No," she sputtered as he waded purposefully toward her. "Not here, surely!"

"Aye, here. Now." He caught her shoulders and steadied her. His eyes held hers while his fingers began to unfasten the myriad buttons. "This time I intend to make it right between us, Jane."

She could not answer. The water lapped coldly about her thighs. What if it was to be a repeat of that first night? He unhooked the dress and drew it down over her shoulders and past her hips. His arm encircled her waist as he lifted her, drawing the gown and undergarments from her legs. They floated free, then buoyed with the eddying wash of the river toward shore.

She stood paralyzed before him, while he lowered his head to nuzzle the narrow valley between her breasts. Arms hanging lifelessly at her sides, she stared sightlessly at the great willows and red oaks that bent from the river's far side toward them, as if to share in this tryst. His lips found one turgid nipple, wrinkled with cold and fright. But his mouth was warm, sucking the fright from her. Tentatively her hands laid across the wide expanse of his tendon-ridged shoulders. Without conscious thought her pelvis arched toward him, only to spring back at the press of the hard shaft.

He lifted his head. "'Tis right. And natural. And it will be beautiful. With thee it will be as never before for me. And for thee."

Desperately she wanted to believe him. She trustingly let him take her hand and move it downward to encircle the girth of his rigid member. He was well favored by nature. Her thumb and forefinger could not meet, but when hesitant, she moved curious fingers along its great length, he groaned. "Ah, Jane." He caught her wrist. "Thee must stop, or my seed shall be spilled vainly."

She grinned, hating to release this newest wonder, but his questing fingers found that cavern that had once before known pain. Her thighs squeezed tight. "No," she whispered, feeling a wave of humiliation wash over her.

He disregarded her plea. His arm, a steel bar now, balanced her against the lazy lap of the water, while his leg prodded her thighs apart. "Aye, Jane," he husked. "Hold me. Put thy arms about my neck and kiss me. I need to know thy love."

She did as he instructed, for she needed him, too. There was no denying her need, for his finger encountered the moisture, which was so much more viscous than the water that swelled and rippled about them. Now two fingers lubricated her, and her lids fluttered closed, her lips parted with the exquisite feelings that creamed through her.

He withdrew the source of her pleasure, and she moaned discontentedly. "Not yet," he murmured against the base of her throat.

With her anchored against him, he waded ashore and lowered her onto the grassy slope. The sun fingered her sparkling-wet flesh, until Ethan's magnificent body blocked out the sunlight, blocked out everything. "Ethan—"her arms raised to enfold him against her—"hurry . . . please."

Yet he teased her, testing the still virginal-tight entrance with the tip of that pulsating part of him until she arched and embedded him deep within her. They came together in the flare of mutual need and response. Later her soft cry of fulfilled passion mingled with the raucous evening song of the swallows and robins.

And, as she drifted in that mellow world of his afterlove, a love that left her soft and melting, she knew it mattered not that he might love another. It was her that Ethan would be coming to each night.

Chapter 35

E than stared at the message from Samuel Adams in Philadelphia, forwarded by Dickey Lee. But Ethan's thoughts drifted elsewhere—to the river earlier that afternoon. Once again he felt the way the tension eased from Jane's limbs, and he remembered thinking that he liked the way her slender body molded his in all the right places . . . her head fitting perfectly into the hollow of his shoulder, her breasts lodging just below the rise of his chest muscles, her hip bones cushioned by his thighs. Susan was so much smaller—it would have been difficult to turn his head and find her lips waiting as close as Jane's had been.

For so long he had wanted this woman who had caused him such trouble from the very beginning; who tempted him and swore at him, and fled from him.

His hand trembled as he recalled the flatness of her belly and how the muscles there flexed at his touch, not in recoil but in response. His mind's eye saw again the full, faintly veined breasts and the spun black hair that whorled softly at the apex of her legs. The mating with her had been as none he had ever known.

Susan . . . it was the last time he would think of her . . . Susan would have been crushed beneath his weight. But Jane—surely she had been meant for him.

He forced his attention to the communiqué—innocent-seeming if intercepted. Without the mask, the entire letter read:

You will have heard, sir, I doubt not long before this that Sir Thomas Gage's armies have retreated from Boston. We all feel that Gage's spies learned that the French may help us. However, we know Gage has commissioned his armies to occupy New York. Also, a highly trained spy reports that the British have been planning to execute our soldiers that they hold prisoner. Of course, Washington is furious at this breach of war conduct. No one knows the general's grief at this act. As to our agent's identity—keep your tongue still. Thus we hold our eyes and ears ready to serve the United Colonies. And thus through your efforts and ours we shall bind together to form a network of one indivisible nation.

When Ethan placed the mask with its hourglass cutout over the letter, a different message took shape:

*I
have
learned that
Gage has commissioned
a highly trained spy
to execute
Washington
No one knows the
agent's identity—keep
eyes and ears ready
through your
network*

Tiredly Ethan rubbed the back of his neck, while he assimilated the import of the message. This wasn't the first time a rumor was out about an attempt on Washington's life. Several months earlier the story went around that there was a conspiracy to poison him with green peas, a dish of which the general was especially fond, but that the housekeeper warned him in time to send the peas away untasted. Instead, the story went, the peas were thrown into a chicken pen and all the chickens died.

And there were other tales of assassination plots and planned kidnapings. But Adams specifically mentioned a highly trained spy this time. Apparently this was not to be one of the heretofore inept assassination plots. Nor a conspiracy. Only one man. A man willing to give his life? No, that kind was a fanatic who in most cases bungled the plot. A highly trained man did not waste his time—or endanger his life—with idealism. He would strike only at the moment that afforded success and a good escape . . . a time when Washington was the least guarded . . . a place that offered the quickest and surest flight.

The last—the place—was the easiest to determine. The place would have to be near the coast, for the assassin would be hounded down if he remained on the continent. He would be—

What if the he were a she? What if . . .

Ethan closed his eyes. His clever wife possessed the most ingenious talent for prevarication. She was the mistress of magnificent mendacity.

God help him, could he trust her?

Chapter 36

For the women of the plantations along the Pamunkey and neighboring York and James rivers, wealth and its related social position were measured in terms of the careful façade of elegance and civilized manners that hid the tenuous nature of the economy that supported them. The sight of graceful ladies in heirloom jewels and old silks moving daintily beneath crystal chandeliers and the polite conversation emanating from formal drawing rooms were enough to establish Virginia society as a true child of the best society that Europe had to offer.

On a particularly warm June evening in 1776 the older daughters and sons of New Kent, on the Pamunkey, were gathered in the ballroom of the Chamberlaynes' plantation, where George Washington first met the widow Martha Custis. The home of Martha's family, the Dandridges, was only a few miles to the north, and nearby was the White House, an immense plantation where she had lived with her deceased husband, Daniel Custis. More Dandridge kin resided at the close-by Chestnut Grove, and her sister, Nancy Basset, and her husband and children lived at Eltham.

These Tidewater families watched their sons and daughters dip and curtsey as they performed the minuet, the Virginia reel, and the quadrille. The instructions had taken weeks, but the parents were extremely well satisfied with the results. Bartholomew Dandridge, Martha's brother, watched with a critical eye while his young son bowed, as the dancing master instructed. Perfectly executed!

Thirty-seven-year-old Nancy Basset's eyes beamed proudly while her nine-year-old Fanny moved faultlessly through the minuet's intricate steps. The dancing master was a marvel! Handsome, obviously well bred, with an intelligence that could cover a wide range of subjects—and a perfect decorum with the older daughters of the Tidewater gentry.

She turned to her hostess, the Widow Chamberlayne, at whose home the itinerant dancing master was residing during the period of tutelage. "I do declare, Mr. Carter should be the master of a plantation rather than a mere dancing instructor."

The widow raised her fan before her mouth. "My dear, word has it that he is the scion of some titled lady. He was touring the colonies, when war broke out, and—can you imagine—he swore his allegiance to us. Forfeited his inheritance, rather than return to his Manor House, he did. We must do everything we can to make him welcome in the colonies."

"Oh, most certainly," Nancy assured her hostess. "When his instruction period is finished here, I shall recommend him to friends elsewhere. The Public Assembly will begin soon in Williamsburg, and the planters would be delighted with a gentleman of Mr. Carter's stature and accomplishments. Why, when my sister returns to Mount Vernon, she could sponsor him in the Alexandria vicinity."

Her gaze drifted back to the tall, aristocratic-looking dancing master who had given up all to side with the American colonies. "How romantic and noble a gesture he made," she murmured. "How romantic and noble a man."

Yes, most certainly she would make sure that Martha was informed about the dancing master.

Later when the dancing master, Richard Carter, learned of Nancy Basset's intentions, his lips curled in a lean smile. General Washington, he knew, had driven the British from Boston and was fortified now in New York. And the general's lady was in Philadelphia with his old friend's family, the Hancocks.

The dancing master found it quite convenient that she would very soon be returning to Mount Vernon. There was nothing to stand in his way now.

Chapter 37

The cannons boomed on the green outside the governor's palace, signaling that as of June 29, 1776, Virginia declared itself officially a free and independent commonwealth with Patrick Henry as its first governor. It was generally expected that the other colonies would declare their own independence the following week at the Constitutional Congress in Philadelphia, though the war with Britain had sputtered for fourteen months now.

Before the cannon's smoke could drift over the green, the boats on the James River shot forward in the annual Tidewater Race. Sloops, yawls, shallops, ketches, and bateaux boiled the water. From the docks the ladies watched and cheered from beneath lacy pastel parasols, while the men and children loped along the river banks, trying to keep pace with the bobbing boats.

Jane strained to see Ethan's gundalow, the very sailboat that had brought her to Mood Hill, tack with the sudden shift of breeze. Even after nearly two years in the colonies she still had not become acclimated to the heat of the Southern summers. The sultriness of the late afternoon brought a sheen of perspiration to her temples and upper lip. Certainly such an unladylike bodily function never overtook Margaret Peyton.

At the gala barbecue picnic earlier that afternoon the woman flirted outrageously with Ethan. Jane had returned from a stroll with Susan to a nearby quilting booth to find Margaret's hand clasped about Ethan's upper arm as she leaned into him, laughing saucily.

And that was another thing that bothered Jane—Ethan's attitude. He had changed since that afternoon he took her on the banks of the Chickahominy. Those moments when their bodies blended together in incredibly beautiful lovemaking, she experienced his profound tenderness and that undefinable joining of their two spirits. She was close to him then. Yet mere hours later she had found his dark, luminous eyes watching her . . . watching her as if part of her displeased him in some inexplicable way.

Faith, she knew he desired her. But a caution lurked in those sulfuric eyes. Perhaps she too obviously enjoyed those moments when he made love to her; perhaps genteel ladies such as Susan did not respond in such an uninhibited manner. But she could not help herself. She had sworn Ethan would never enslave her spirit, but he had done just that by mastering her through his lovemaking. She did not know if she loved him, but she did know that she wanted him with a desperation that equaled that illogical need she felt for Terence.

Even now she felt shamefully weak in her knees just

thinking about Ethan. He merely had to look at her with those expressive eyes, and she found herself witless.

The boats reached the turn-about point far up the river, and were hauling about for the final leg downriver to the docks. Hand shading her eyes, Jane could make out Ethan's gundalow two boats back from the fast-paced little catboat in the lead. Her heart raced with the gundalow. For those eternal moments he was her knight, his boat carrying her colors. Slowly the gundalow gained and passed the yellow-canvased sloop. The first two sailboats were close enough now for her to make out Ethan's mahogany-red hair and his billowing black shirt. The catboat and gundalow were running stern and stern, and the cheers of the people about the docks were deafening. She found her hands locked about the parasol's handle in a death grip.

Only at the red-flagged wharf did the gundalow nose out the catboat, and a roar went up from the crowd. Ethan was the winner of the regatta! He was hauled from the sailboat with a hero's welcome. Several men pressed forward to pound his back, and Daniel and Bram offered their hands in a hearty shake. Susan stood on tiptoe to bestow a sisterly kiss on his cheek. Standing apart, Jane waited impatiently for Ethan's eyes to acknowledge her.

Yet it was another who claimed him next. Margaret Peyton, following Susan's example, also bestowed on Ethan a congratulatory kiss, this one full on the mouth. In a reflexive motion, his hands caught the blond beauty's waist. A few in the press of people turned sympathetic eyes on Jane, but she refused to show the pain that whipped clutching tentacles about her heart. Some of the people ducked their heads or shuffled away. At last, Ethan lifted his head, his eyes meeting her flashing ones. Sidestepping Margaret, he approached Jane and sheepishly made a leg. "Madam."

"Sir, you have powder on your shirt," she said with precisely articulated speech, and whirled away. She did not know where she was heading. Only far away from the embarrassing scene.

Ethan caught up with her along the thickly foliaged path that paralleled the bank of the James. His hands caught her shoulders and spun her to face him. She would not look at the dark eyes that beseeched her but rather turned her gaze on the tangled undergrowth on either side of the path. "Jane, the kiss was not of my doing."

"You did not seem to repel it. It would seem that I cannot trust you."

"And can I trust thee?"

Her gaze darted up to lock with his steady one. "I know not what you mean," she stuttered. Just how much did he suspect about her covert activities?

A tirade, denunciation, disgust—any of those reactions she expected, except the mouth that ground down on hers in an angry kiss. Stunned, she stood passive for a moment beneath the lips that bruised hers and the tongue that demanded entry. But the hand that squeezed her breast possessively set off some primitive response in her. She leaned into him, making a soft little mewing moan when his finger and thumb extracted their punishing caress on the nipple that thrust against the soft lawn material.

Words were superfluous. He pressed her down upon the mossy black earth. Her fingers feverishly found his breeches' buttons; his hands hastily hiked her skirts about her waist. Someone could chance upon them. She cared not, only desiring that he quench the yearning that boiled in her blood.

Without a word between them, she spread her legs to enfold his massive body and accepted the plunging thrust with an arching of her hips. His hands pinned her shoulders against the spongy ground. Time and again he slammed into her, as if to rid himself of his desire for her once and for all.

Her legs entwined about his buttocks, seeking the leverage to meet and hold him within her.

All the while his eyes burned into hers. She would not turn from that scalding gaze, would not let him dominate her in that wild ride of passion. Yet at that last moment, when she was afraid he would halt the furious pounding, her lids closed and a great climactic shuddering claimed her body. At the same time he cried out in a hoarse rasp.

Silently they lay side by side, panting, neither wanting to acknowledge the devastating effect their lovemaking had on one another. With great dignity she sat up and smoothed down her skirts. She could only feel a fury at herself for giving herself so wantonly to him. It was done. She was satiated. She would no longer have that damnable aching need for him.

"Tell me about him."

Her shoulders stiffened, but she did not turn around. "Who?"

"The man you are seeking—this Terence."

"What do you want to know?" she hedged.

"What he means to you."

"I don't know if I can convey what he means to me," she said in a dry, flat voice. "My first memory of him is the sight of him riding up to Wychwood like some knight on a white steed. He bowed to me and plucked a rose from our arbor, placing it behind my ear. 'You shall grow into a beautiful young woman,' he told me."

She looked over her shoulder at Ethan, who lay now with his arms crossed behind his head. His instrument of pleasure was flaccid now, yet still enormous in size.

She dragged her gaze away, saying, "At that time I was ungainly, tall, thin . . . and very ugly. At least I felt so. But he saw beauty in me, Ethan. I think he was half in love with my mother. But he always took time with me. After she died, he became my companion, my friend . . . my very heart. He talked to me of things I hadn't seen and didn't know, he listened to my prattle—I was so desperate for attention then with my mother dead and my father off in London."

She paused. Overhead the fireworks display was already beginning. "And?" Ethan prompted.

"Then when Terence went off to serve in India, my whole world seemed to—"

Ethan's eyes flared. "You said India?"

"Yes. Why?"

"Nothing, Jane. Only tell me what it is that binds you to him still."

"There is some bond between us I can't explain. A bond as tenuous and yet as strong as a cobweb. When we would sit in the garden or read to each other from my father's books, I often found him watching me. And I caught a glimpse in his eyes of a wretchedness that was—it would catch my breath, it was so powerful, as if some tormented secret writhed in his soul. Whatever the bond, Terence MacKenzie has beguiled me."

"But I have bought thee—and I have married thee. I shall not relinquish thee."

He said the words with such a calm assurance that no power on earth could alter the fact; but then, she thought sadly, he did not know Terence, who was as obstinate and determined as he was. She knew the day would come when Terence would find her and take her away with him.

Chapter 38

Ethan Gordon was irresistible to the ladies, and it surprised Jane that he was unconscious of his raw masculine appeal, that he was innocent of all conceit or self-importance.

She sat beside him in Williamsburg's theater, the first theater in English America, but gave little heed to Shakespeare's *The Merchant of Venice*, invariably the opening play for the Assembly's session.

During intermission, while French horns and trumpets played, she could see the flirtatious glances cast from behind the swaying fans of ladies seated both on the pewlike benches below and in the boxes opposite her. Yet she behaved like some silly ninny, shyly looking at her husband when he spoke, blushing when he gently teased her before the others. What had happened to her? And how ridiculous was her assumption that that one act of passion the day of the Tidewater Race would quench for all time her desire for her husband.

God help her, was she falling in love with him?

She moved through the days of Assembly performing the proper tasks—running the rented Paradise house with consummate skill, gracing the dinners they attended with intrinsic polish and charm. But at night—at night in Ethan's arms all dignity and decorum were abandoned. His tenderness, his total attention to her intimate responses, awoke a wild strain in her she had not suspected.

When the play resumed, the theater darkened but for the candles at the foot of the stage. The third act began, yet still she was aware only of her husband, who sat mere inches away. She heard the rustle of his program as he leaned toward her, then felt his hand cup her thigh, exerting gentle pressure on the inside, despite the welter of skirts. Recalling the kiss *à la cannible* that he had planted high inside her thigh only that afternoon, she felt the treacherous desire welling in her again.

Her innate shyness collapsed beneath the excitement he stirred in her. In the darkness her fingers reached out to rest lightly on that coiled bulge at the fork of his powerful thighs. She was rewarded by his husky intake of breath, and her fingers gathered courage to initiate a gentle manipulation. His hand captured hers. "Madam," he whispered at her ear, "does thee realize the havoc thy lovely fingers are inflicting?"

"I can't help myself," she murmured wickedly. "You make me lose all sense of restraint."

"Please . . . don't restrain yourself now."

She gratified his request by cupping the heavy orbs and gently rolling them in her palm. His smothered groan and the recapture of her hand ended her foreplay. "Later tonight, madam, I shall teach you the various acts of pleasure which the tongue is capable of bestowing."

A quiver of anticipation raced up her spine as the theater's candles flickered to life. Whatever strict ideas Ethan Gordon entertained about religion, he certainly did not let them inhibit his sexual prowess.

Afterward a dinner party was to be held at the home of George Wythe, in whose office Thomas Jefferson first practiced law. Ethan was detained near the foyer by Governor Henry, who spoke of the first invasion of the Southern colonies, in Charleston. "Britain's Sir Peter Parker was defeated, but it was a close scare, my friend."

Jane wandered off on her own. She would rather have returned to the sensual sanctuary of the Paradise house— especially when she spotted the Widow Grundy. What information would the old woman ask of her this time?

"There you are, dear," cried the wall-eyed Lucy Knowles, laying a plump, beringed hand on Jane's gloved arm. Jane never knew which eye to watch. "Do come with me. I've someone I want you to meet, a gentleman who seems to know you. I believe he said you two were neighbors in the same shire in England."

Gratefully Jane escaped the proximity of the Widow Grundy. "Here he is," said Lucy, indicating a man whose crimson-clad back was to them. Even with the powdered wig concealing his hair, Jane sensed something familiar about the man—perhaps in his stance. "Dear, let me present Richard Carter, our new dancing master. Mr. Carter, Mrs. Ethan Gordon."

The man turned, and Jane froze. She looked into the pale blue eyes that had obsessed her all her life. "Terence," she breathed.

He bowed low, his lips lingering on her suddenly cold fingertips. Before she could withdraw her hand, he turned it over and planted a light kiss on her palm.

Lucy Knowles caught the romantic gesture, and sighed. If only she herself were so young, so slender. "Well, I'll leave you two to renew your friendship."

Jane thought her knees would buckle, but Terence's hand was at her elbow, lending support as he led her to the French doors, open to the night's coolness. Out on the terrace, she clutched the cool stone balustrade for support. Lanterns lit a symmetrical pleasure garden and a pleached arbor of hornbeam that afforded a secluded place for young lovers to wander. Yet she was as immobile as the tree-box topiary.

Terence's fingers caught her arms and forced her to face him. "You did not wait for me."

"You didn't come for me," she cried. Why? Why now, when it was too late?

His hand cupped her chin. His face drew near to hers. "Are you still loyal to England?"

"Yes . . . yes, of course," she stuttered, distracted, confused.

"And to me?"

"Oh, Terence, what has happened to us?"

"Nothing. And nothing can keep you from me, Jane."

"But I'm married to another!" she cried piteously.

"And if you remember the old Hindu's words, I wait for you at the end of the long road."

"But how—"

His lips silenced hers. For a moment she forgot all else and clung to him with the desperate need for his love—the seed that he had planted in her childhood. When he at last released her, she was breathless. Her head spun as if she had consumed too much champagne. He pulled her head into the hollow beneath his jaw and stroked the delicate arch of her neck. She could smell the light scent of lilac water about him. She had forgotten how devilishly handsome he was.

"I have been staying at the Knowles', instructing the

children from nearby families in the art of dancing," he said at her ear. "I fear I won't be seeing you again before I leave."

She lifted her head. "Before you leave?"

"I have a task to do, my Jane, before I can make you mine. But when it is carried out, no one shall keep us from one another."

"I shall."

Terence turned slowly, still holding Jane. Ethan stood in the doorway, the bright light of the candelabra silhouetting his enormous build. His smoky eyes bore into hers as he held out his hand. "Come, Jane."

She stood between the two men, feeling the tearing of her soul into two parts. The clasp of Terence's hand at her elbow thrilled her; yet some compunction of integrity prompted her to put her hand in Ethan's.

Terence bowed low, his sun-darkened face mocking. "Keep Jane well, for I shall make my claim of her at the proper moment."

The hired phaeton's team clipclopped along the hard-packed dirt avenue that marked the Palace Green and turned off onto the Duke of Gloucester. The tension within the coach was claustrophobic. Jane let the glass down to the hot wind. A harbinger of a Southern summer night's thunderstorm, the wind tossed the live oak leaves wildly, while shreds of clouds scuttled across dawn's waning moon.

Inside the carriage the silence grew deafening. How much of the reunion between her and Terence had Ethan witnessed? In the face of Ethan's controlled calm, Jane tried to contain her growing anxiety.

When they arrived at the Paradise house, she hurried ahead of him to the door, wanting only to escape his silent anger. She glanced over her shoulder. He was making no effort to lengthen his stride, yet she sensed she was his quarry. Lifting her skirts, she scurried up the stairs. He overtook her just before she gained the landing and spun her around. The melting candle in the wall sconce cast a pale glow on her alabaster skin where his fingers dug into her bare shoulders.

"What do you want?" she asked with a haughty tone that did not hide her skittishness.

"I want my wife."

She saw the brutal set of his face. "No. Not in anger."

"Yes. Anytime. I ask only that which you would so willingly bestow on other men."

She pulled from his grasp, but his hand streaked out to grab her hair, painfully halting her escape. Her pins tumbled loose, and the powder on her curls dusted the air as her hair tumbled about her shoulders. He pressed his lips into hers, and she sensed he did not care if he hurt her. Fear coiled inside her. She tried to push him away, but his hands pinioned her arms to her sides with ease while his tongue sabered every corner of her mouth. Tasting the brandy on his lips, her own tongue parried the thrust of his.

Her resistance, she knew, angered him. Better to submit. But some primitive force goaded her into provoking him further, even as his mouth continued to subjugate hers. When his hand slid inside the lace ruffle of her décolletage to cup the swell of one breast, she bit him.

"Damn you!" he said lowly. Gone was the mild Quaker. He thrust her from him, and she saw in the candlelight the blood that crimsoned his lower lip.

Her hand flew to her mouth, and she fled the rest of the way up the stairs and along the corridor to her room. Behind her she could hear him loping easily. Gaining her room, she slammed the door with a force that sputtered candles in their wall sconces. She leaned against one of the bedposts, her breasts heaving in breathless fright.

He kicked the door open. She tried to conceal her fear

with the arrogant tilt of chin. "Take me then, Ethan, and get it over with."

She saw the deep self-disgust that tightened his lips.

"'Tis all right, Jane, I shall not hurt thee." He wiped the back of his hand across his brow and muttered almost to himself, "I must be out of my mind."

"No . . . no, Ethan. I think I am." She lowered her face so she did not have to see the tortured look in his eyes. "Oh, Ethan, I feel like—like I belong in Williamsburg's Public Mental Hospital. I don't know what I want. I don't understand myself."

"Jane, I'm staying at Raleigh Tavern tonight. Then I'm going back to Mood Hill." He put his hand on the doorknob, adding, "Paradise house is at thy disposal until thee can sail for England."

He was leaving her! Only her lacerated pride saved her from crying out foolishly. "And if I choose not to return to England?" she asked in a cool tone.

He shrugged. "'Tis thy choice." Then the door closed behind him.

Chapter 39

Polly curtseyed. "Mistress? Yew have a visitor."

Jane sighed. She was to get no work done that morning. All morning Bruton Parish's church bells had rung out, making concentration difficult, until at last she had gone out to see what all the hue and cry was about.

Every soul in town seemed to have turned out to read the proclamation on the courthouse door. She shouldered her way through the crowd's outskirts and from her great height was able to read a portion of the proclamation.

> *. . . that these United Colonies are free and independent states and the connection between them and the State of Great Britain be dissolved.*

The young man next to her said in an uneasy voice, "There's no going back. The ties are severed irrevocably."

At first Jane felt numb. The idea would take some getting used to. But then, if she stayed in the colonies, it might be exciting to be part of a new adventure, part of history in the making. The idea had distracted her from her work the rest of the morning. And now she had a visitor, who probably wanted to gloat about the event.

"Who is it' Polly?"

"The Widow Grundy is 'ere to see ye, missus."

Jane bit her lip in vexation. The widow would want to know what she learned about the mysterious Leper at Wythe's party last night.

"Thank you, Polly," she said with a small smile. She knew the young woman, drawn away from her Peter, was as miserable as she. Jane knew now she loved Ethan. Wildly. He was a man among men. But how to deny that loyalty she felt to Terence?

Putting aside her market list, she rose and went into the parlor. Seated on the couch, the widow was tapping her pipe impatiently against the palm of her hand. "Good afternoon, Mrs. Grundy." Jane sat opposite her in the armless Queen Anne chair and arranged her farthingale.

"Are we alone, child?"

Nonplussed, Jane looked around her. "Well . . . yes."

"Good. Your Terence is here, in Williamsburg, isn't he?"

Jane nodded. "How did you know?"

"I'm not the only one who knows. The Leper's Colony knows also."

Jane's hand went to her throat, and the old woman said, "The Colony knows that the British Army's top spy is in Virginia. They don't know it's Terence MacKenzie. But with the Leper's wide network of informants, he'll know soon. If you care about England, girl—if you care about your Terence, then you must help us expose the Leper."

Jane rose to pace the room. "I have watched and listened but seen nothing out of the ordinary—nothing to indicate that the Leper operates out of Williamsburg."

The widow took the pipe from her seamed lips and pulled on the pipe's tubular end. Like the quill pen, the pipe's end separated. From its hollow she extracted a narrow strip of rolled paper and passed it to Jane, saying, "Governor Henry carelessly left this in his wastebasket, and his underservant, one of us, was able to retrieve it."

Jane read the strip. *Have information for the Leper about Ahmad. Tonight at 11:00 at the middle chamber.*

"A ball celebrating the colonies' Declaration of Independence, doomed as it is, will be given tonight, and the Leper will be there. So must you—at eleven in the middle chamber upstairs, child."

Food was carried to the palace's formal dining room in great covered containers from the service area west of the building. The independence celebration was an elaborate affair, with the Binn Cellar beneath the Georgian executive mansion providing hundreds of gallons of imported wines. Governor Henry was at his wittiest, his sharp ripostes keeping the guests amused.

After the meal, a violin, harpsichord, and cello, played by students from William and Mary, furnished the entertainment for the evening.

A glorious evening for everyone but Jane. Now she could understand why people were said to die from heartbreak. She could actually feel the throbbing pain in her chest. Lest anyone guess her distress, she danced merrily with partner after partner, waiting for that fateful hour of eleven. To those who asked about Ethan's absence she lightly explained that mercantile business called him out of town.

How, anyway, did she ever expect to compete with a woman such as Susan? Having never made love to Susan or grown uncontrollably angry with her or laughed with her until tears came, Ethan could never know that she might not be suited for him—though he might have realized it had he ever gotten close enough to hold her in his arms.

She wanted only to go to Terence, to seek solace in those arms that always held comfort. She wanted to leave this little rural college town and all its memories; to leave the colonies and return to the civilization that was England. However, Terence was in danger, and she would see the party through. Yet just thinking of the contempt she glimpsed in Ethan's eyes the night before gave her an unbearable headache. She knew she was not the woman he deserved. But the thought of another woman lying beneath him shafted the backs of her eyes with streaks of searing red.

By ten, she could no longer hide behind the façade of the witty and brilliant lady. Claiming fatigue, she withdrew from the rigors of the dance. She sought out the dowagers along the wall and, listlessly fanning herself, watched the dancing couples move in the stately grace of the gavotte. She could find no joy in the evening. Only an anxious waiting. Above the din of the laughter and music, she was sure she heard the slow, monotonous tick of the clock above the great marble mantel. Her gaze followed the slow progress of the clock's hands. Fifteen before eleven.

Another ten minutes and she would desert her wallflower's post to climb the red-carpeted stairs to the middle chamber, which was in effect a much-used council room.

Her gaze passed over the guests. Who among them was also waiting for the hour of eleven? In an ironical way, she almost dreaded discovering the identity of the Leper. She knew that he was brave, that he risked his life for ideals. She knew that once she gave the information to the Widow Grundy, the Leper's days were numbered. Yet if she withheld his identity, Terence's life was in jeopardy.

At five before eleven, she saw Daniel Franks desert his dancing partner, the beauteous Margaret, and head for the stairs. Was Daniel a member of the Leper's Colony—or the Leper himself? She thought not. He did not have the resourcefulness to mastermind such an organization. The Leper must be in the middle chamber, waiting. With a laden heart, she rose, made her excuses to the matrons, and followed Daniel up the stairs at a discreet distance.

By the time she reached the landing, the door to the chamber was closed. Was she too soon? She stepped inside one of the boudoirs, waiting in the shadows for some seconds. But no one else proceeded down the hall.

She stepped out into the hall again, crossed to the chamber door, and listened. Nothing. No sound. From below came the faint strains of the music. Barely half a minute had passed since Daniel had entered the chamber. Gathering her courage, she opened the door. Her gaze swept over the room with its crimson damask wall hangings and green Chinese Chippendale furniture until she spied Daniel in the far corner next to an enormous silver candelabra. Not another soul was in the room. Was Daniel indeed the Leper? His back was three quarters to her, a scrap of paper in his hand.

She moved stealthily forward, but the rustling of her many petticoats gave her away. Daniel jerked around. "Mrs. Gordon!"

She had to read the note. "I—I felt so hot down there." The back of her hand went to her forehead. "Smelling salts . . ." she murmured, and swayed.

As he rushed to catch her about the waist, the candlestand lurched violently, the light shimmering eerily across the walls and ceiling. He grabbed to set it right, and the sheet of paper fluttered to the floor near the green settee. Weaving slightly, she stepped back from him, her full skirts lapping over the folded missive, and braced herself against the couch's arm. "Smelling salts . . ." she murmured again in a faint voice. "Will you get me a bottle somewhere . . . please, Daniel."

He looked at her with worried eyes, before his gaze swept the carpet with confusion. His hands searched his pockets. In his eyes she saw the realization dawn that the note must be beneath her voluminous skirts. Embarrassment at his predicament flooded his pale face.

"The smelling salts . . ." she reminded him with a gasp that heaved her snow-white breasts.

"Of course . . . of course. I'll be right back, Mrs. Gordon."

No sooner had the door closed than she lifted her skirts and bent to retrieve the note. It read: *The dancing master, Terence MacKenzie, is Ahmad. He must be prevented from carrying out his mission—immediately.*

Chapter 40

~❦~

B ut for Polly, who admitted him, the Paradise house was empty. "The missus didn't come 'ome, sir," the woman told him sleepily.

Ethan was not surprised. Before daybreak that morning Daniel sought him out at the Raleigh Tavern and relayed the story of Jane and the message—as well as the fact that Jane had pleaded a headache and left the party early. Ethan shouldered past Polly and took the stairs two at a time. For a long moment he stood looking at Jane's empty bed. The puzzle of Ahmad was completed. And now she was on her way to join MacKenzie.

He had already guessed the fact that Ahmad and Mac-Kenzie were one and the same. The afternoon Jane mentioned MacKenzie had served in India, the correlation between Ahmad and MacKenzie had wormed its way into Ethan's mind. But he had forestalled action, beguiled by the woman he loved. She had played him for a fool. Ethan's Folly.

Chapter 41

Rather than occupy a guest room, the spy Ahmad was given his own guest house to the rear of the Knowles' large, two-story brick mansion that was set off the Post Road that stretched between Williamsburg and Alexandria. With dawn breaking, the lamps in the mansion had long since been extinguished. But the candle in the guest house still burned.

By the light of daybreak Terence's eyes stared at the house plan laid out on the table before him, trying to memorize the location of Mount Vernon's various rooms. The ground floor contained six rooms, and a massive staircase in the spacious passage led to the chambers above. But it was the narrow staircase on the mansion's south side, ascending from Washington's breakfast room to his private study on the second floor, that most interested the spy.

Already he knew the names of all the servants and the details of their habits, cunningly gleaned from friends and relatives of the Washingtons in both New Kent and Williamsburg. There was Breechy the butler and Mulatto Jack, his assistant; Moll the cook; Martha's personal maid, Sally; and a score of others—including the most important, old Bishop, Washington's orderly, whom he had inherited along with a saddle from the dying Braddock in the French and Indian Wars.

The old man would be the most serious problem, for he shadowed Washington's footsteps whenever the general was about. But Bishop could be dealt with in a quick, silent, and most effective manner.

Ahmad picked up the letter he had received only days before from Martha Washington. In the neatly penned note the general's lady graciously acknowledged receipt of the letters of recommendation from her friend, Lucy Knowles, and her sister Nancy.

> *I am of the opinion that Alexandria would be most appreciative of a dancing master of your accomplishments, sir, and forthwith extend an invitation to present yourself at Mount Vernon.*

He permitted himself the slightest smile. After all his years of striving, of patient waiting, of humiliation and deprivation, his goal was near.

All but for Jane.

His smile faded in a thin hard line. He would have her, all right. In the early stages of his planning he had never considered the possibility that she might belong to anyone but him. He had believed—nay, he had known of his hold over her. A hold he had carefully nurtured, so that none existed for her but him. Yet still the Quaker had managed to snare her.

Ahmad rose, rubbing his tired eyes with his fingers. Before he would leave for England, there was the Quaker to settle with. There could be nothing to stand in the way of his marrying Jane once he possessed Wychwood Estates and Manor House. There could be nothing to stand in the way of his complete and devastating revenge on Robert Lennox.

The spy went to the press and began taking out the few articles of clothing he traveled with. Quickly he packed them into the small portmanteau. Mount Vernon was two days of hard riding from Williamsburg. And he meant to be at Mount Vernon on the heels of Martha Washington's arrival. There could be no slipup. No leeway for the general to come to or leave Mount Vernon prior to his own arrival.

Meticulously he collected all the sheets of scrawled notes and shoved them into the embers that slumbered in the fireplace. Within the hour the evidence of his mission would be only ashes. Within the year the general's body would be little more than ashes.

Chapter 42

The hood fell away from Jane's head, and her cape flapped behind her as she used the quirt to spur the horse she had rented to a greater speed. The sleepy black custodian at the livery had looked at her as if she were daft for wanting to rent a horse in the small hours of the morning. Perhaps she was.

In the clearing the Knowles' guest house stood white against the gray-green of the surrounding cypresses and spiraling pines, with morning's eerie mist writhing low about the trees' herniated trunks. Was she too late? Could a fanatic like Uriah Wainwright —or a phantom like the Leper—have reached Terence ahead of her? Her heart pounded against her ribs as she slid from the horse and ran the short distance to the small house. Without waiting to knock, she shoved open the door. Her gaze took in the room before her. Empty.

She stepped inside, moving slowly about the room. Had Terence been kidnaped and taken elsewhere?

Her fingers trailed over the low post of the bed; the bed linens were smooth—the bed had not been slept in. She scrutinized the room. Nothing was out of place. No over-turned chairs to indicate a struggle. No signs of clothing—books—shaving utensils—to evidence that Terence had ever been there. Had he learned that he had been exposed as a spy and fled already? And where to?

Her glance picked up the cinders in the fireplace. She knelt to touch the peripheral ash, testing the lingering warmth between her thumb and forefinger. The fire had only recently burned low. He couldn't have been gone long. As she began to rise her gaze fell upon the thatch of papers. Their edges were charred, but the writing could be made out. Instinctively she knew what the papers were—information Terence had gathered about the rebel colonies. Apparently he had counted on the hot coals destroying the incriminating evidence. And they would—if someone didn't arrive immediately on her heels. Someone like Uriah Wainwright.

She knelt to tug the papers from the weight of ashes and shove them toward the center of the pile of glowing embers. But a curious drawing caught her eyes. She laid aside her quirt and held the papers up to the pale light sifting through the chintz curtains. Cinder flecked off the pages to drift over her skirts as she read.

The top sheet was a floor plan of—her gaze dropped to the words scribbled at the bottom of the sheet—Mount Vernon. Quickly she thumbed through the rest of the sheets. Names of servants, their personal habits, some of them intimate habits—breakfast and dinner hours—descriptions of various rooms—and always the recurring notation *G. Washington.*

Then that last sheet, a rougher sketch of the house with further notes: . . . *should take no more than two minutes from library to river bank. Must arrange for rowboat. Eng. frigate to be waiting a mile beyond.*

But it was the abbreviated notation beneath the area marked *Library* that riveted her eyes: *Assas. here.*

The sheets fluttered about her knees as a dawning horror crept over her. Terence's intentions—the mission of which he had spoken. Assassination!

Her fingers massaged her suddenly throbbing temples as she tried to make herself think clearly. Logic told her that a war was going on; that agents—spies—had to do unpleasant things if the war was to be won.

Assassination was more than merely unpleasant, her mind screamed. But people killed on both sides in a war. Killing was part of war. And it wasn't her duty to stop Terence. Let people like the Leper's Colony worry about stopping—

She rose and ran to the door. But her heart was leaden as she spurred her mount away from the cottage's clearing. She was betraying England . . . forfeiting all the childhood dreams of the happiness that was to have been hers. Yet what Terence was about to do was abominable. Her growing kinship with the American colonies that was changing her viewpoint about the revolution, the realization of her love for Ethan—these overrode her past feelings for England and Terence. She knew she had to stop him.

She took the only road north she knew—the lengthy Post Road that stretched through more than half the colonies. The Post Road, walled by towering sycamores and beeches and oaks, led toward Alexandria and Mount Vernon—and Terence. And with a sudden clarity she heard again the old Hindu's prophecy: *Terence awaited her at the end of a long road.*

No one was out on the road at that early hour. In the still silence of dawn her heart thudded in furious tempo with her mount's galloping hooves. The mammoth trees arched above her, shadowing the road into a tunnel of leaves. How far ahead was Terence—thirty minutes? an hour? She spurred the horse faster.

Suddenly she was flung from the horse by the man who dropped from the tree limb overhead. Her breath whooshed from her lungs as she hit the hard-packed earth. Her vision grayed for a lost moment.

"Jane!" Terence growled as he half straddled her. "It was you who was following me! Why?"

"Terence . . . you can't do it."

Her words were little more than a gasp, but she felt his body stiffen against hers. "I can't do what?"

"I saw your . . . plans . . . your notations." She inhaled deeply. "Terence, you can't kill General Washington!"

He grasped her elbows and drew her upright. She clutched at his sides for support, feeling the hard pistol lodged in the inside pocket of his frockcoat. "You don't know what you're talking about, Jane."

"I'm not stupid!"

He smoothed the hair back from her face. "Have you no loyalty to England, Jane?"

"Have you no principles or ethics or morals? What you're doing isn't patriotism. It's cold-blooded murder!"

She saw in his cold blue eyes a relentlessness of purpose that brooked no intervention. And she knew she had no alternative. Swiftly her hand drew out his pistol and she backed off, leveling the barrel at his red brocade waistcoat.

"What do you think you're doing?" he growled.

Trying to control the trembling of the barrel, she

moved toward her mount, which had wandered off to join Terence's piebald, placidly cropping the turf at the road's far edge. "I'm taking both horses. By the time I reach Mount Vernon, you will have had long enough to escape." Her eyes misted over. "Go back to England, Terence."

A gentle smile softened his lean features. "I won't, Jane." Slowly he walked toward her, hand outstretched. "I won't leave the colonies without you."

She grasped the barrel with both hands. "Don't! Don't move!"

"You won't shoot, Jane, because you love me."

She retreated another step. "I love Ethan," she sobbed and brought the gun up to eye level.

His pace never altered as he continued to stalk her. "But you still won't shoot me."

"I will—I will!" Her voice sounded shrill to her ears.

"No," he said calmly. "With your naive belief in morals and ethics, you would not kill your own brother."

"My own brother?"

"Aye, Jane. Why do you think your father was so against our marriage? I am his bastard by the Lady Mac-Kenzie. But his damnable pride would not acknowledge me. Now his pride will cost him dearly."

"You knew?" The pistol's barrel wavered and dropped an inch. "You knew all the time we were brother and sister—and still feigned love for me?"

A vicar could not have smiled more benevolently. "I loved you all the more, my sweet Jane."

Oh, God, her brother. The bond of blood! Her stomach roiled.

His hand cupped the back of her neck and drew her unresistingly against him to plant a brotherly kiss on her forehead. "Ah, Jane, the old Hindu was right after all."

The brother she had so desperately wanted when she was a child. Oh, Terence!

"We can return to England together, Jane." He stroked her back as he made the plans. "Soon Manor House shall be mine again, and we can—"

His hand, stroking her, hit her elbow, loosening the pistol from her grip. At once she was on her knees, grappling for the pistol, as was Terence. Then the explosion shattered her ears—and shattered her heart.

Chapter 43

"H it's all right, missus," Polly cooed, as she unbuttoned the myriad buttons of her mistress's blood-splattered dress. A frown puckered her rounded face. What dreadful thing had happened? The missus would say nothing. She moved, instead, almost like a sleepwalker.

Polly slipped the pink morning dress over the woman's shoulders. "Just ye sit there before the looking glass, and I'll brush those tangles from yer 'air." She tried to restore some semblance of propriety to the young woman's wild appearance, all the while wondering where she could find the master. The missus needed him in a bad way.

Numb, Jane sat before her reflection. Terence was dead, and she would never know now if she would have had the courage to pull the trigger.

A thundering noise erupted from below, like the battering of a drawgate. With a small cry, Polly dropped the brush. Jane whirled around, eyes wide. Nerve-rending shouts rumbled up the stairway, followed by the pounding of feet on the wooden stairs. "Hang the bloody bitch!" came a woman's shrill cry.

A score of men and women—young and old—burst through the doorway to overflow the room. But Jane saw only the victorious lear of Uriah Wainwright—and the object his left hand held. Her quirt.

"You recognize it, do you now, Lady Jane? Found it at the Tory's place—along with these." He tossed sheets of charred paper upon the bed. "They brand you as a Tory spy, my lady. As we shall brand you."

"No!" she whispered in a raw voice. "You're wrong!" Panic filled her lungs, so that even breathing was an effort, to say nothing of the words she might utter in her defense.

They gave her no chance. Her arms were twisted behind her, and the rabid mob hauled her down the stairs. Behind her she could hear Polly screeching the invective of a dockside whore, only to be suddenly silenced.

The size of the mob increased as Jane was dragged along the Duke of Gloucester, with Uriah proclaiming her treachery for all to hear. "Plotting to kill Washington, she was!" he answered to the curious who questioned the commotion. Whereupon near riots would break out. Angry jeers were hurled down upon her. A tomato, thrown by a boy who could not have been more than twelve, splattered against her stomach.

In the blinding summer sunlight the grim and forbidding public jail loomed on the knoll ahead of her. Here almost sixty years earlier thirteen of Blackbeard's henchmen were imprisoned and later hanged. Now the jail was badly overcrowded with British redcoats, Tory sympathizers, deserters, and spies. Yet she welcomed the refuge from the abusive hands that mauled her and the sight of the violent, blood-lusting faces.

But such was not to be her good fortune. Instead she was thrust roughly upon the pillory, her hands and head shoved into the apertures. Her loose hair was caught painfully in the padlock's closure, smarting her eyes with fresh tears.

"Is it ready, gents?" came Uriah's brittle voice.

She strained to see what was happening behind the cascade of her hair. The crowd of outraged citizens parted for someone, then Uriah came into her line of vision. His hand wielded—not her quirt this time but a branding iron, glowing red-hot. As he drew near her, she could hear the sizzle of its tip, formed in the letter *T*.

For once his slitted eyes were on a level with her own. Grasping a handful of her hair, he jerked her face upright and held the branding iron immediately before her. Its heat alone singed her flesh. Great silent sobs racked her body. "Please . . . oh God, no!" she gasped. She didn't want to scream, to give the horde the satisfaction of seeing her cringe. She was a lady, wasn't she? Her lids closed out the horror awaiting her, and her teeth sank into her lower lip to contain her cowardly outcry. Shudder after shudder passed over her.

The pleasure that awaited the task glowed as hot as the branding iron in his fox's eyes. "The letter *T* for traitoress, milady."

Chapter 44

"Milady is no traitoress."

All heads swiveled in the direction of the baritone voice. As they had for Uriah, the crowd once more parted—this time for Ethan Gordon. His gaze swept over the mob, hungry for blood. But it would not be Jane's. He permitted himself only the briefest glance at her to assure himself she was unharmed. His guts wrenched at the sight of her bound. Yet there was still that haughty glare in her eyes. A lady to the death, unless he could sway the mob's intention otherwise.

He recalled the powder-smeared remains of Terence MacKenzie. Incredible that this meticulous, highborn lady was capable of such bravery. But then he should not find it incredible at all—had she not surprised him at every turn, this tempestuous madcap who was also capable of great warmth and giving?

Jane, resolute and faithful, dauntless and dear.

He turned his attention on the bastard before him. "Release her."

The calm assurance in his voice visibly disconcerted Uriah. "We have proof she was in league with the plot to assassinate Washington!" he gloated. Behind him the agitated citizens muttered their agreement.

Ethan planted his fists on his hips and lazily surveyed the crowd. "Milady is a counterspy, good people."

The milling crowd entirely missed his sarcasm. They were being cheated of their entertainment. Their vengefulness would not be appeased. "Prove it," Uriah snarled.

Ethan swept a deep mocking bow. "The Leper, at thy service."

"The Leper!" The exclamation leaped from person to person.

Derangement played across Uriah's narrow face, but he kept the crowd in his grasp as he snapped, "That is equally impossible to credit!"

"Nevertheless, 'tis the truth," Ethan drawled. The idea was so preposterous that he could see a few of the people entertaining the possibility of the statement. He strolled toward the pillory, throwing over his shoulder, "Check with Governor Henry, if thee doubts me."

How long the surprising admission could hold sway over the people was uncertain. His large fingers worked deftly at the padlock. He saw the relief in Jane's eyes—and that other quality he had been looking for these agonizing last few months. He quickly swept her up into the cradle of his arms before she could collapse.

As if he were the proverbial leper, the stunned citizens parted for him. Unmolested, he carried Jane along the oak-shaded avenue toward the Paradise house. He knew he would not release her even when they reached his bedroom.

She murmured into the hollow of his shoulder, "Your heart is thudding like a drum, Ethan."

"'Tis because thee is so heavy."

She threw back her head, spilling her disheveled hair over his arm, and grinned up into his face. "I don't know why I ever agreed to marry such a big lout as you." Then, her lips—sensuously formed lips, he observed for not the first time—her lips lost their impish curve, as she said, "It's true, isn't it? You are the Leper."

"No longer, mistress."

"Jane."

He grunted. "'Od's blood, Jane, but thee is heavy!"

She nibbled at his earlobe, which made it difficult to concentrate on where he was going. "You exposed your cover—for me!" she marveled, low. "You must love me, Ethan Gordon."

"Aye," he panted. "I suppose I must."

She tilted her head back again. "But what will happen now? The Leper is exposed. You can no longer serve the colonies."

Polly opened the door with an enormous grin. "Saved the missus, yew did, did yew, sir!"

He winked and climbed the stairs—slowly, laboriously. The spurs of his riding boots clinked in triumph. "My work for the . . . colonies . . . isn't finished, Jane. I have been . . . asked by the general . . . to move to Paris to serve as . . . as Mr. Franklin's diplomatic aide on . . . behalf of the American Colonies."

"You—are going alone?" she asked in a small voice.

He kicked open the door and fell with her across the bed. "I didn't think I was going to make it," he gasped.

She wriggled from beneath his heavy thigh and leaned

over him. Her unbound hair tickled his nose. "Ethan Gordon, I'm going with you!"

He caught her oval face between his great paws. "Did thee think otherwise? I have bought thee—I have married thee—and I am certainly not going to relinquish thee now, Jane Gordon."

And then he whispered those words that for so long his pride had made him afraid to speak. "Thee I love."

About the Author

A favorite of romance readers everywhere, Parris Afton Bonds is the author of twelve books and the mother of five sons, in addition to being a teacher of creative writing at a local community college. She is co-founder and board member of Romance Writers of America and was the recipient of the Best Novel of 1981 Award given by the Texas Press Women for DUST DEVIL. Her previous Fawcett trade paperbacks, DEEP PURPLE and LAVENDER BLUE, were bestsellers and STARDUST had an enthusiastic response as well from her many ardent fans.